Fateful Reunion

Neive Denis

Book nine in the Sonoma Whittington series

Copyright

First published in 2021
Copyright © Neive Denis 2021
All rights reserved.

Cataloguing-in-publication data
Creator: Denis, Neive, author

Cataloguing-in-Publication details are available from the National Library of Australia
www.trove.nla.gov.au

ISBN: 978-0-6489423-3-7 (paperback)
ISBN: 978-0-6489423-4-4 (digital)

Cover design: T A Marshall, Mackay, Australia

Disclaimer

This novel is a work of fiction. All characters and events are the product of the imagination of the author. While some of the characters might remind you of people you know, they are fictitious and any resemblance to anyone living or dead is purely coincidental. Although some locations also may seem real and familiar, most places referred to in this work constitute a collage of places the author has known. But they are fictitious, and any resemblance to an existing location is coincidental.

Contents

Chapter 1

"Aha, I knew I wouldn't be disappointed! I am surprised your bloody phone waited this long before it rang," our frustrated hostess exclaimed as Ben Richards checked the caller ID on his phone before hurrying outside to take the call. A minute or two later he resumed his place at the table, and Emily continued berating him. "No doubt you will have to dash off now. Would you like a doggie bag to take the rest of your dinner with you?" Emily's sarcasm wasn't lost on Ben, but his only response was to cock an eyebrow at her and continue eating. As soon as he cleaned his plate, the situation changed.

"I'm afraid I do have to leave," he announced as he pushed his chair back from the table. "Duty calls. What do you want to do, Sonny? You can leave with me, or you could walk back to your office later. Emily's already had two glasses of wine, so she won't be able to drive you back to collect your car."

Emily answered on my behalf. "She could call a cab, or she could spend the night in my spare room. Anyway, Sonny, how come you arrived with Ben tonight instead of in your own car?" Emily remained prickly, and I was aware Ben was in a hurry to leave.

"It's a long story. I'll tell you about it later. Right now, I need to go with Ben." I rushed after him and dived into the passenger's seat as he fastened his seatbelt. "Okay, Ben, what have the good citizens of Millhaven been up to tonight to ruin your evening?"

"I'm not so sure about the 'good citizens' bit, but someone has left a body in an alleyway to give my officers something to do tonight. If you don't mind waiting for a few minutes, I'll have a quick look at the crime scene before dropping you back at your office – or I could drop you off first. Which would you prefer?"

What a silly question. I'm not nosey by nature for nothing. "I'm in no hurry. Perhaps you should check the crime scene before the various people who need to work it make too many changes."

Relief was in his voice as he laid out the ground rules for how the next part of the evening would play out. "Good; but you are to stay in the car while I inspect the scene. We don't want any extra people crammed into the alley and getting in the way, and we don't need any extraneous forensics to deal with."

The cheek of the man! As if I don't know how to behave at a crime scene. And, as for *extraneous forensics...* the crime scene is in an alleyway in the city heart! How many 'extraneous' people use the alley every day? Nevertheless, I kept my opinions to myself, and feigned enthusiasm as I agreed to his conditions.

If Ben believed for one moment I would sit placidly in the car while he inspected the crime scene, he hasn't bothered to get to know me during all the years we've been friends. Anyone who knows me would be aware it wasn't going to happen. Although I did try to comply – really, I did. In fact, I think I gave it a pretty good shot – for at least five minutes or so after Ben disappeared into the alley. To keep myself amused after he left, I let my mind reflect on how this evening began and why I was travelling with Ben.

We hadn't long sat down to eat when Ben's phone call came. It is ages since we last ate at Emily Ibbotson's place. The logistics of gathering the three of us together for an uninterrupted dinner party sometimes seem impossible. No matter how well timed and planned the event, before the meal is over, invariably Emily or Ben has to rush off to attend to an urgent work matter. This week, Emily was on leave and took advantage of it to invite us to dinner, not the usual casual affair like those at my place, but a proper three-course dinner party.

Most nights, those of us who aren't working congregate at my place. Ben Richards, as the top cop for the Millhaven region can't always make it, and Emily Ibbotson, as head of the district's forensic laboratory, often finds herself working late to push through analyses for a police investigation. Then, there are nights when I'm working. They always check during the day whether I'm working or at home. And, they don't arrive empty-handed, usually bringing food and/or wine with them. On some nights though, the cooking happens at my house – by me or others – and either in the kitchen or on the barbeque out on the deck.

Tonight was different. It was a sit-down occasion at a beautifully laid table, resplendent with starched tablecloth and napkins, and with candlelight glinting off fine glassware. The whole wonderfully stage-managed event had me feeling … inappropriate. I worked late and lost track of time. My intention was to go home, freshen up and slip into something more 'evening' for the occasion.

None of it happened. If Ben hadn't rescued me, I probably would have embarrassed myself further by continuing in my office until our hostess rang to find out where I was. Driving along my street on his way to dinner, Ben saw my office lights were still on and came up to drag me off to Emily's. So, here I am, still in today's jeans and tee shirt, sitting in Ben's vehicle parked across the front of an alleyway in the city heart.

After about five minutes, I ran out of whatever it takes to amuse myself. I succumbed to the lure of the alleyway. After all, whatever was happening in there had to be more interesting than sitting in Ben's car with nothing better to do than stare along a darkened street. I eased myself out of the car, closing the door as quietly as possible. Then, for the benefit of anyone who happened to be watching, it was a nonchalant saunter across the footpath to the alley's entrance.

After just a couple of steps into the alley, I paused for a few moments to listen and let my eyes adjust to the darker shade of night occupying the space. I needed to acquaint myself as much as possible with what was happening further along in the intriguing tunnel of darkness. As I stood still and silent, in the distance, a bright light came on. It illuminated an area I judged to be about three-quarters of the way along towards the exit of the alley. Judging by the level of activity occurring in that patch of light, I knew it was Ben's crime scene. Not much to see from here, I told myself and, staying close to the wall, I started picking my way towards the light.

"Where the hell do you think you're going?" a harsh voice, in not much above a whisper, demanded. "I thought I told you to wait in the car."

"Uhmm… well, yes, you did, but … er … I thought you might want to stay at the scene a while … and I didn't want you to feel you needed to hurry away because of me. So… uhmm … I thought I would come and tell you … not to worry about me … It's only a block or so to my office from here. I'll walk back to collect my car."

"Not a bad attempt at quick thinking on your feet but, if you think I'm going to believe…" Footsteps racing through the darkness towards us cut short Ben's admonishment of me. Then a voice was shouting above the clatter of boots on concrete. The outline of a man emerged from the darkness and the noise coming from further along the alley.

"Sir, Sir; wait up, please." I assumed it was one of Ben's officers. The voice was male, young, a bit breathless, and the next words suggested he was a newish constable. "Sir, Sarge said to let you know the paramedics have arrived … and they say the body is not dead."

"What? He seemed pretty dead to me. Are they sure?"

"They say he is alive, and they are trying to stabilise him before transporting him to hospital. Sarge thought you might want to know before you left the scene."

"This I have to see. I checked him for signs of life myself. I was sure he was dead... and I don't think his name is Lazarus." Ben hurried towards the crime scene. As he seemed to have forgotten about me, I trailed along – quietly – a short distance behind him. "Who is in charge here?" Ben demanded as he strode into the light.

"I am," a female paramedic, with a long blonde plait snaking down her back almost to her waist, responded as she eased herself upright. "And, who might you be, Sir, and what's your business here? … Oh… sorry Superintendent Richards; I couldn't see who you were."

"What's all this nonsense about the victim still being alive? I checked him myself. He seemed well and truly dead to me. Are you sure about…?"

"He is in a bad way, but we picked up weak vital signs. His injuries aren't confined to his head. Whoever attacked him gave him a good going-over. There are a few broken ribs." As she spoke, the paramedic flicked back the victim's shirt to reveal a torso covered in welts and bruises of various hues.

An officer I recognised as Sergeant McIntosh oozed out of the darkness and strode over to stand beside Ben. The two men stood in silence for a few heartbeats watching the paras at work before Ben spoke. "I suppose it's too much to hope you found any ID on the bloke."

"No, Sir; picked clean. They did a thorough job on him. …Another mugging gone wrong by the look of it. I don't understand why people keep using this alley after dark when it has been the scene of so many muggings in the past."

"Thanks, Jock, but I don't think this was a mugging. He might have been robbed, but it wasn't the motivation for the attack. Look at the victim. He's not exactly a strapping specimen, is he? An office worker of some sort I suspect. I'm sure I've seen him around in the city heart on a few occasions. It only would take a couple of belts around the ears for him to be laid out cold and offering no resistance to any would-be robber. No, the workout this bloke received suggests there was more at stake here than a watch and the contents of a wallet."

"Oh aye, I see what you mean. I'll ask the dispatcher to send the detectives. If you're right, this is more their case than mine."

"True. This is something for the detectives to handle. How come it took the paramedics so long to arrive?"

"There's been a major pileup out on the main highway. Traffic has been banked up in both directions for a couple of hours. As I understand it, this was a bad one; several dead. All the paramedic units from within the immediate city area were called to attend the scene. The only one available to us was a team from way out of town. It took them something of a Cook's tour of the district to come in without being held-up by the situation out on the highway."

As the two men stood chatting, I inched my way closer behind them until I was standing about a step back from the gap between them. This was the only vantage point from which I could see the crime scene. The two big lumps of coppers in front of me blocked any other chance of seeing what was happening. Jock pulled out his phone and started walking back to where all the activity was occurring. I assumed he was calling for the detectives. It was then Ben noticed my presence.

"I thought you were going to walk back to your office to collect your car and go home. Why are you still here?"

"I'm out and about in the city heart all the time. After all, it is where my office is located. Perhaps I can help you identify the bloke."

"His face is pretty badly knocked about. I doubt you'll be able to recognise him."

"There is only one way to find out. Shall we take a look?"

We sidestepped around a couple of paramedics to find a good place to view the victim. "Step away from the victim for a few moments please, so we can have a clear view of the man," Ben asked, and the paramedic blocking our view scrambled up off his haunches and moved away a couple of steps. "Right, Sonny, there's our victim. Is there anything familiar about him?" Ben demanded.

"Ye-es, I know who he is."

"What? Are you sure? His face is badly knocked about. Who do you think he is?"

The rising bile burnt the back of my throat. I swallowed hard a couple of times before managing to croak, *"He's my client!* At least, since lunchtime today, he has been my client."

"Okay … That's interesting. I assume you have started a new case file." Not capable of speaking again, I simply nodded. "Good; let's go to your office for look at your file." He grabbed me by the shoulders and spun me around to face back towards the car. "Come on, hurry up. We need some details for this bloke. He probably has family who need to know what's happened."

Ben pulled up beside my car in the parking lot behind my building. "I think it's time you went home. Grab your case file and then go home." It wasn't a suggestion. It was a directive. Still too stunned to argue, I let myself into the building and galloped up the stairs to my office.

A couple of minutes later, I scrambled into my car, and eased out from behind the building and onto the street. It came as no surprise when Ben followed me home.

Chapter 2

"We need to talk," Ben announced as he followed me into my lounge room. "Let's take our coffees through to your office and get stuck in."

"I assume you would like me to make us coffees before we begin work in my office?"

"…And something to go with them would be nice, since we missed out on dessert at Emily's place – and I don't mean dry biscuits. What do you have stashed away?"

"Not much at all; have a look in the fridge. There might be a couple of TimTams left."

A few minutes later, armed with our coffees and half a packet of TimTams firmly in Ben's grasp, we settled on opposite sides of the desk in my home office. I pulled the new case file from my tote bag and placed it on the desk in front of me without opening it. When I looked up, Ben had his notebook open and was sitting, pen in hand at the ready to make notes.

"Ben, I don't know how much use any of this will be to you. As I told you earlier, I only spoke to the man at lunchtime. In reality, I haven't actually taken him on as a client yet. At the end of our meeting, I still wasn't sure what the case was about. In the end, I offered to do a preliminary investigation to determine whether I would accept it as a case."

"Right; but your case file will have the details I need. So, come on, give me the information you know I need to contact his family and other relevant people: name, address, where he works, anything else you know about the man."

"And that's about all I can give you. His name is Trent Martin. He is married to Stella, and he is employed as the assistant accountant – or something similar – at the big office supplies firm in the next street from my office building." When Ben stopped scribbling those details, I gave him the man's Wentworth Drive address on the north side of the city.

"Good; got it. Now what else can you tell me about him?"

"Nothing … That's all I know. And it looks like it might be all I'll know for a while. Maybe it will be the end of the story if he doesn't pull through."

"What about the case? What did he want you to investigate?"

"It's what I was trying to tell you. I don't know what the case is about, or even if there is a case to investigate. He was so agitated, I couldn't make sense of what he was telling me. My thinking behind telling him I'd have a preliminary poke about was in the hope something would crop up to help clarify the situation."

"I'm sure you gained something from the interview, but I'll leave it for now. I need to go and break the bad news to Mrs Martin."

"Shouldn't one of your officers involved in the case talk to her?"

"Under normal circumstances, yes. But, as I'm the only one so far who knows his identity, and to save time, I'll talk to her."

I heaved a sigh of relief as I watched him drive off. I wasn't being deliberately obtuse when Ben asked about the case. Truth is, I don't know what the case is going to be about until I do some digging. All I know is I am to observe where Stella Martin goes and what she does when she is there. My gut insists my first reaction was correct, and Trent Martin should take his concerns to the police. It's not unusual for Private Investigators to get strange cases. In view of tonight's events, I wished I understood what my latest 'strange case' was about.

After I rinsed the coffee mugs and added them to the dishwasher, I sat in the lounge to think about Trent Martin and his visit today – and finished the last TimTam while I was about it. Why did he have such a firm belief his wife wasn't playing away from home? Had he seen or heard more than he shared with me? If so, I definitely won't take the case. If he wasn't prepared to share all the facts with me – wasn't prepared to be completely honest – then I'm not interested in the case.

It was then my phone, still in my bag in my office, chirped loudly for attention. It was Ben. "I've been to the Martins' house on the north side. Nobody is home. While I waited outside her house, the old couple from next door came home from walking their dog. The conversation with them proved interesting. Apart from anything else, they told me Mrs Martin goes out quite a bit at night. Some nights she comes home quite late, but they didn't think tonight was one of those. It seems the woman is a creature of habit when it comes to her night time outings and she doesn't go out on Saturday nights. Anyway, I decided hanging around out front of her house was a lost cause. I'm on my way home. If no one else has spoken to her in the meantime, I'll see if I can catch her in the morning."

For some reason, I found Ben's call unsettling. While I couldn't work out why, I knew it was going to keep me awake for most of the night. If I was going to be awake for a while, it occurred to me I might as well do something productive with the time. After splashing water on my face to freshen up, and adding a bottle of water and a couple of muesli bars to my bag, I was in my car and heading down the driveway.

On my way across to the north side of town, it did occur to me Stella Martin might already be home from her night's outing. I tried convincing myself not too much time had elapsed between when Ben gave up waiting for her and when I left home. It didn't matter how hard I tried, I didn't believe she wouldn't be home. After all, Ben might have passed her somewhere after he left. She might have arrived home a minute or two afterwards. Did it matter if she were home or not when I arrived? What would it prove?

My concerns and mental gymnastics about whether the woman would or would not be home proved a waste of time and energy. When I located the address and parked on the opposite side of the street a little way along from the house, the place was in darkness. The question then was: had she arrived home in the interim, or was she still to come home? There was no way of knowing. I had set myself up for a stakeout, so I might as well stay and observe for a while.

Just as I was beginning to question the wisdom of such a move, headlights turned into the street. It was only half an hour after I'd arrived, so it wasn't such a late night – if this were Stella Martin coming home. And, if it were Mrs Martin, what would her return home prove? Regardless, I told myself being there tonight was worthwhile. I had located the address, and soon would have details of Mrs Martin's vehicle. As I watched, the headlights turned onto the driveway of the address in question. She didn't go into the garage, but parked on the concrete in front of its closed roller door.

With one eye on the house while waiting for Stella to get out of the car, I recorded the details in my notebook. Just as I finished, the lady scrambled out of her car. Thank goodness for a clear night and a bright moon. If this were Stella Martin, she was a tall slim woman with a shock of long, darkish coloured-hair, and she appeared loaded-up as she strode towards the front door.

She had a handbag over her left shoulder and another bag with a long strap hanging from the other shoulder. A pile of parcels or books – it was too hard to tell from where I was – was clutched to her chest. Something of a juggling act happened at the door as she attempted to find her keys and unlock the door without dropping anything. It appeared as though she had no concern about making a noise or waking anyone who might be asleep inside. After a few moments of fumbling and juggling, the door opened and she disappeared inside. Lights came on in the house, reinforcing her lack of concern for anyone who might be asleep in there.

So ended the show; time to go home. I spent the journey home weighing up the outcome of tonight's stakeout. In reality, I hadn't gained much. But then, it hadn't taken up much of my night to do it. The one thing to come out of it was, with my client likely to be incommunicado for some time, I was going to become a familiar visitor to Wentworth Drive. Now, with no other way of knowing when Stella was going out at night, I would need to stake out the place every night until she did, and then follow her to find out what she was up to.

Home again, I decided to type up my notes from tonight – including Trent Martin's unhappy encounter in the alley – before turning in for the night. It proved just enough activity to ensure I was sound asleep soon after I went to bed.

*****

Dawdling over breakfast helped fill in time until I felt compelled to leave home and go into my city office for the day. With no pending cases to attend to, other than those of Trent Martin and his wife, there didn't seem to be any need to rush this morning. In view of my lazy start to the day, I decided I might skim the newspaper while indulging in my second coffee. Having reached the end of the paper, I started again and went through it slowly this time. No, I wasn't mistaken. There was no mention of a bloke being beaten up in an alley last night. While it seemed odd, I put it down to the attack having occurred after the deadline for today's paper.

Since all good things must come to an end, I finally made my way into town, and collected a couple of slices of cheesecake on my way up to my office. Wracked with indecision, I struggled to choose between having another coffee and one of those slices of cheesecake as soon as I was in my office, or exercising some self-restraint and waiting an hour or so before indulging. It was in the midst of such weighty decision-making that Ben called.

"Are you in your city office this morning?" After establishing I was, he continued, "Good; I'll be straight over to see you."

Damn! Now I'll have to share my cheesecakes with Ben. I suppose it's a good thing. It will be a few calories I won't add to my waistline. As promised, about five minutes later I heard him pounding up the stairs. And, yes thanks, he would have coffee and cheesecake before we started.

"If you can eat and talk, perhaps you should tell me what brings you to my door so early this morning?"

"I want to go over your meeting with Trent Martin again. I don't mean what's in his case file, I want to know what was said when he came to see you. Every nuance or anything else you picked up at the time might prove important."

"It wasn't a long meeting. I'm not sure anything of use to you was said." Ben can be quite persuasive and continued pressing for details. "Okay. Okay, I'll tell you how it went. It won't be verbatim, but I'll tell you all I remember about the meeting."

"Thank you. You said Trent Martin came to see you around lunchtime yesterday. How was he?"

"He was hesitant about talking to me. At first I thought he was having difficulty working out how to explain things, but I soon realised it was something else. 'Explaining' wasn't his problem. It was more like embarrassment at having to tell me about his situation. As the interview progressed, I realised there was more involved; something more sinister. The man was frightened; really scared. No, don't ask me about the cause. I still haven't worked it out for myself."

"… But you did get the gist of what he wanted you to do?"

"Ye-es; quite early in the conversation, I worked out his problem had something to do with his wife, and he wanted me to find out what she was up to. I jumped to the immediate conclusion he suspected she was playing away. He spoke about her going out at night – a lot – and not telling him why, or where she was going. When I suggested maybe she was meeting another man, he was quite definite that was not the case. I tried suggesting the same thing in slightly different ways a couple more times during the early stages of the meeting. His response remained the same. He was adamant there was nothing of that nature happening."

"So, what did he think was going on … Or, maybe the question should be: what was his problem? Why didn't he just ask his wife about her nocturnal outings?"

"Exactly…! But, I don't think he was game to ask her about it. If I sensed anything from the meeting, I thought he was afraid of his wife – more than afraid, if such a situation is possible. At some point, I came to the conclusion, regardless of whatever else might be happening, domestic violence was at the root of his troubles. I said as much and told him he should go to the police or, if reluctant to talk to the police, to seek the assistance of one of the domestic violence counselling services."

"What was his response?

"He strenuously denied domestic violence of any sort had ever occurred. Apart from refuting everything I came up with, he seemed to become more agitated with every suggestion I made. We were getting nowhere with the question-and-answer approach, so I asked him just to detail for me everything causing him concern, starting from when he first felt something was not right."

"If he feared physical abuse or injury, he should have gone to the police. Maybe if he had, he now might not be fighting for his life."

"As I said, he seemed almost terrified of his wife. Every time I mentioned the police, his fear became obvious. It didn't matter how hard I tried to assure him it wouldn't happen, he was quite convinced his wife would find out he'd been to the police and things would turn bad for him."

"Did you get the impression he was suggesting his wife was capable of dishing out what happened to him last night? She was out somewhere, so could have been responsible for it."

"No-o, not really. He indicated she could be violent, but I don't think he was suggesting anything so violent. Anyway, from what I saw of the bloke lying in the alley, it didn't look like a woman's handiwork to me. It was the sort of beating dished out by a burly bloke – or possibly two blokes working in tandem."

"So, you don't think the wife was responsible … not even if she found out he'd talked to you?"

"Nah, I don't put it down to the wife at all. I think there's a bigger picture to investigate; something else going on behind the scenes. He talked about his wife seeming to undergo a complete personality change over the last couple of months or so. Most of the time she was sullen and withdrawn, and he was reluctant to interact with her in any way. Also, there were violent outbursts of temper and aggression. He likened her to a constantly brooding volcano about to erupt at any moment. No, I don't see what happened to him being down to a woman. Think about it. If it were the wife who was responsible for his injuries, why not wait until he came home to belt him up?"

"Well, it's better not to have it on your own doorstep if you want to claim no knowledge of it after the event. What about his work? You said he worked for the office supplies firm. It seems unlikely, but is there any chance his attack might be connected to his work in some way?"

"I doubt it. He's an assistant accountant in a fairly ordinary commercial enterprise selling stationery, and office supplies and equipment. From the point of view of his work, you would be hard-pressed to find a more unlikely victim."

"Sonny, I'm more than a little confused about why you even considered taking this bloke on as a client, and I'm intrigued about what he wanted you to do for him – more importantly, what you agreed to do for him."

"The simple – and obtuse – answer might be, *he was persistent.* Although I couldn't extract from him the exact nature of what he wanted me to investigate, I felt as though there might be a need to follow his wife for a week or so to see where she went, who she met, and what she did. After I outlined my approach, he elected to give me the 'schedule' – for want of a better word – of her nocturnal outings. He claimed she went out on the same night every second week and was gone for at least a couple of hours; probably longer. On the alternate week, she went out at least one night and sometimes on a second night as well. Her outings on the alternate week were much shorter. She usually returned about an hour later. On the alternate week, the nights can vary, so it's impossible to predict when she will go out."

"So, when were you supposed to start work on this case?

With the random element involved in her activities, how are you supposed to know which nights to follow her?"

"It's complicated. Today is Saturday of the alternate week, so we can expect her to go out at least once sometime this week. He assured me there isn't any warning about which night it's going to be. The usual process is, straight after dinner, she announces she is going out for a while, walks out and drives off. There is a clue he's picked up on: if dinner is ready a bit earlier than usual, he knows she is going out. Because there is no warning, sometimes, he flukes working late on the night she goes out. It doesn't create a problem at home. She still goes out as intended. He always rings to tell her he will be working late. She tells him she is going out and, if he is not home before 6:30, he should make his own arrangements for dinner."

"Okay, but how does that help you?"

"To avoid using his normal mobile phone, Trent bought a cheap phone to use to call me when there is any sign she might be going out on a particular night during the alternate week. In the second week, it's not a problem. She always goes out on Thursday night. About three weeks ago, he joined a local chess club which meets on Thursday nights. He always wanted to join the club to learn to play better and now, being out of the way on Thursday nights, seemed like a good idea."

"I'm still amazed you took the job. It's not as though you aren't busy, or you need the money. By the way, did Mr Martin call you last night?"

"Last night…? No, I didn't hear from him after our lunchtime meeting. Yesterday being Saturday, I didn't expect to hear from him. Why do you ask?"

"As you say, it was Saturday. But, your client appears to have been working late yesterday. And, we know Stella Martin went out last night. Why didn't her husband let you know? … And, should we consider Saturday night a part of last week, or the beginning of this week?"

A quick check of my phone showed no missed calls from my client. "What? Oh, I don't know. Maybe it wasn't one of her scheduled outings but, seeing as how he was working late, she took advantage of it to go out anyway. As for why I took the job, I can't explain it. Put it down to something akin to gut instinct. Whatever my reason, Trent Martin must have been confident I would take his case to go to the trouble and expense of acquiring a 'burn' phone before he came to see me."

"So what happens now? At the moment, there's a fair chance he won't be around much longer. If you proceed with the case, you are unlikely to be paid."

"He was so confident, he brought a cheque with him. So, I have been paid. And, having accepted his cheque – reluctantly, I might add – I now feel obligated to follow through with the case."

"How did he know how much to put on the cheque? And how much investigation will his cheque cover?"

"I told him $5,000 was too much for a retainer. The whole job was unlikely to cost so much. He insisted I take it. At the end of the job, if it proved too much, I could refund him the excess."

"Christ…$5,000! I think I'm in the wrong game. By the way, I still haven't been able to catch up with Mrs Martin. I went to the Wentworth Drive address early enough to catch her in case she planned to go out, but no one was home. I half expected her not to go out today after her husband didn't come home last night. I checked with the station before I called you, but nobody reported or enquired after a missing husband. Maybe we do have to keep her on the top of our list of potential suspects. You don't happen to know where she works do you?"

"Hang about while I make a call." Debbie, a friend of a friend, works in the HR section of the office supplies firm and often worked on Sundays. A quick check of their personnel records and she could tell me Stella Martin's place of employment as listed on her husband's file. "Ben, I don't know if the information is still current, but she was working as a secretary at Grenville Construction Company."

"Thanks. Wish me luck when I journey into the industrial area of town." After snapping his notebook closed, he stood up to leave.

As he walked to the door, I called after him, "Let me know how it goes when you do catch up with her. It might help me determine how to proceed – or not to proceed – with my case." I took his wave as confirmation.

For the rest of the afternoon, I couldn't help but wonder if he would bother to let me know how he went with tracking down Stella Martin to inform her about her husband.

Sunday proved a frustrating day for both of us. Ben reported an unsuccessful day trying to catch up with Stella Martin. I had cleared my desk of all current work and was keen to start on the Martin case … But start where and with what?

Chapter 3

Monday morning saw me out of bed early and eager to be in my city office to start work on the Martin case. That was the only positive thing to say about a day spent dealing with minor administrative tasks, mailing out reports and emailing brochures in response to enquiries. When that was done, I resorted to reading today's newspaper and catching up on reading the bits of the weekend papers I hadn't found too exciting at the time. The fact I hadn't heard a murmur from Ben all day didn't help, and only added to my frustration.

It was just after five o'clock when Ben called. "Trying to talk to Stella Martin is like trying to catch smoke. When I first went to where she works, she was out on a site visit – or something like that – with the managing director. I waited until after lunch when they thought she should be back in her office before I went there again. Then, she was in a board meeting and couldn't be disturbed. They thought the meeting would finish around four o'clock. To be safe, I waited until a few minutes after four o'clock before trying my luck again. This time I couldn't see her because she went home early with a headache."

"So, there's a possibility she still doesn't know what happened to her husband?"

"Well, no. She does know now. When they told me she left early, I went to her home address. There didn't seem much evidence of the headache that forced her to leave work early."

"Okay, but how did she take the news … or, did she already know about her husband?"

"It's what struck me as interesting. Her reaction was not what I expected. She claimed not to know about her husband. …Hadn't noticed he was missing!"

"How could she not notice he hadn't come home last night, and wasn't at breakfast this morning?"

"I don't think it's the sort of household where people share the same bed, or breakfast together. It seems Mr Martin has his own bedroom and tends to go to bed early, whereas his wife claims to be a night owl and likes to read until at least midnight. As a result, he wakes early and is off to work by seven o'clock, while she rarely gets out of bed until almost eight o'clock."

"Not exactly a happy family situation then… But it tends to fit with the assumption I made after I spoke with him. Everything aside though, what was her reaction to the news about her husband?"

"There was no indication she wanted to dash to the hospital to be with him. If I had to define her reaction, I'd say it was 'acceptance' … almost as though it wasn't unexpected. I asked if either of them had prior indication something like this might happen. She was adamant there hadn't been."

"Her reaction isn't what I would expect from a concerned wife. Still, maybe she is 'wife' in name only. Their separate living arrangements suggest there wasn't much happening between them. Would that be consistent with her behaviour?"

"My assessment of the situation was the news I gave her was inevitable; not unexpected. I tried pressing her to be more forthcoming, but it was a waste of time. The hospital will keep me updated on Mr Martin's condition. They will let me know if his wife visits and how she reacts. I know there is more to this story, but that's all I have for now. By the way, it's almost time to think about dinner. Are you at home tonight?"

"Uhmm … no … I have a surveillance job to do. Although, tonight might prove a fizzer and I could still end up with an early night."

"Okay; it fits with my night as well. Having wasted so much time today trying to talk to Stella Martin, I might stay late to catch up a bit. While I think of it, what did your client think his wife was up to, if she wasn't seeing someone else? I imagine it is the first thing a bloke would suspect, if his wife kept disappearing off somewhere at night."

"I'm not sure. No reason was given, but he was quite adamant she wasn't having an affair. Although, a couple of times, he alluded to 'something bad; something illegal'. How is my client holding-up? I assume you've checked with the hospital."

"Not good; they don't like his chances, and say the next twenty-four hours are critical."

I had hoped, if Ben spoke to Stella Martin, I might gain some idea how to progress with my case. I was wrong. If anything, her reaction made it more difficult. Oh well, I had planned to stakeout the Wentworth Drive address tonight, and nothing has happened to change the plan.

With no real information on when Stella Martin might leave home if she were going out tonight, I needed to be in place sometime between six and seven o'clock. Her husband mentioned having to be home by 6:30, or he would have to fix his own dinner. Perhaps it might be a good time to be in position to observe the house. As it was almost six o'clock, I checked the contents of my tote bag, and added a fresh bottle of water. Then, I was out of my office and along the street to buy a couple of muesli bars to help keep hunger at bay while on surveillance.

Wentworth Drive is not the best place for a stakeout. There is nowhere to park unobtrusively. Regardless of where I pulled up, it would look as though I was visiting someone's house. I kept expecting the owner to come out and demand to know what I was up to. To make it look a little more reassuring to householders in the vicinity, I often pulled out my phone and mimed making a long and heated phone call, waving my arms around and generally behaving like someone slightly demented.

It was 6:35 when I turned onto Wentworth Drive. Although nightfall came early on these winter nights, it couldn't become dark soon enough tonight for my liking. The lights were on in the Martin house when I drove by on my way in. If Stella Martin were at home, she was spending her time in the back part of the house, as no movement was visible through the front windows.

By seven o'clock, I was beginning to doubt myself. I still hadn't detected any movement in the house in spite of quite a few lights being on inside. Had she left them on to cover the fact she was out? This will be the waste of a long night if I can't satisfy myself whether she is home or has gone out. I noted yet again how slowly time passes when you're sitting in the dark in a cold car with nothing better to do than stare at a house further along the street.

My first moment of excitement came at a little after 7:30. Some lights in the house went off, and someone inside cast shadows across the front windows. Through a gap in the drapes, I saw the bright screen of the TV come to life. It appears Stella Martin is going nowhere tonight. After waiting a few minutes in case she changed her mind, I went with my instinct and called off tonight's stakeout. As I started the car, my stomach rumbled loudly. The muesli bars purchased earlier remained unmolested in the bottom of my tote bag, and I was hungry – but not for muesli bars.

My watch told me it wasn't yet eight o'clock. I decided it was worth a phone call to see what Ben Richards was doing and whether he'd eaten yet this evening. He answered almost straight away. "I thought you were working this evening."

"I was. It was a waste of time, and I've called it off. And, now I'm starving. Have you eaten yet?"

"No. I'm on my way out to my car, and was debating what to get for dinner. Shall we eat at my place or yours tonight?"

Why break with a long established tradition? While I drove home, Ben picked-up something for our dinner before joining me at my place. I barely had time to splash water on my face to freshen up a bit before he arrived. It was obvious we were both starving. Wasting no time on conversation or anything else, we began dispatching the pasta dishes Ben brought. Conversation was on hold until we were settled in the lounge room with our coffees.

"Any update on Trent Martin's condition?" I asked as I passed him a new packet of TimTams to open.

"No improvement. The best they can say at the moment is he is holding his own, and his condition remains unchanged. I gained the distinct impression they weren't hopeful. What about your case, any further developments?"

Now, what is my answer to be? Do I tell him about tonight's surveillance? I decided a white lie was safer. "No, nothing new here either." I don't like being less than honest with Ben but, if he becomes aware of my surveillance plans, he will invite himself along, whether I want him there or not. Best he goes on thinking nothing is happening with the case for the moment. "Nevertheless, what happened to Trent Martin has me feeling obliged to push on with the case he hired me for."

"The question remains the same. Now he is not around to let you know what is happening, how are you going to know when Stella Martin goes out?"

"Yeah, it's frustrating. I will just have to wait until Thursday night next week when her next long night out should occur." Don't tell him too much, I counselled myself. Ben will want to get involved and will ruin it for me.

Ben was gone by ten o'clock, and I was ready for bed and the restless night I knew lay ahead. With no other active cases at the moment, the frustration of no progress on the one case I did have, the Trent Martin case, did not sit well.

*****

Tuesday morning saw me lacking enthusiasm for the day ahead. Having made no progress, and with nothing to go on with, I was in for a long day in the office. By the time I arrived at my city office, I had a vague idea about how to fill in at least some of the morning.

After dealing with the usual first-thing-each-morning administrative chores, I decided to go out again. While not sure what I thought it might achieve, I decided to take a look at the Wentworth Drive address in daylight. As I turned onto the street, I checked the time. If Stella Martin was going to work today, she should have left home some time ago.

As expected, no activity was obvious at the house … and the same seemed the case for the whole street. I drove past slowly and on to the end of the street, before turning and heading back towards the house. While the place looked clean and tidy, judging by the lack of shrubs and garden beds in the front yard, the Martins were not keen gardeners. The tour of the street proved worthwhile. I identified a couple of potential parking places for future nights.

Back in my office – and probably going to be stuck there for the rest of the day – I had to think about how to achieve traction on the Martin case. 'Research' seemed to be the answer. It would fill in time, and who knows what I might uncover. While I didn't hold much hope of finding anything useful, I threw myself into digging around in my client's background.

Having spent an hour or so for no result, I needed to change tack. There was little to find on Trent Martin, and none of it was any use to my case. In desperation, I decided to have a look at what I might find on his wife, Stella. Again, it appeared to be just another exercise in frustration. The commonest problem with research is: all sorts of interesting articles, with not even a remote connection to your focus, catch your eye and waylay you. It happened while researching Stella Martin.

A passing glance at a picture on a page as I was about to flick past it caught my eye. There was nothing special about the small image of a number of women standing in a group. The article carried the headline *Welcome Back*. A skim of the story told me the group of women were attending a High School reunion in a south-western corner of the state. Intrigued about why it warranted mention in the Millhaven newspaper, I elected to read it properly… And there it was. The only –albeit minor – connection with Millhaven: *Among those attending the reunion was Millhaven resident, Stella Martin (the former Stella Gillespie),who said she enjoyed being back in her home town and catching up again with people she hadn't seen in twenty years.*

Not a monumental breakthrough, it was the only information of any note to come from my research. As I entered Stella's maiden name to my notes, a stray thought crashed in. How does her former name help my case in any way? There was only one honest answer: it's of no help whatsoever. I was consoling my bruised ego when Emily arrived. "It's my last day of leave. I thought we might at least go for lunch together. Just say if you're busy and can't spare the time."

"Let's make it a l-o-n-g lunch shall we? How about we indulge ourselves at one of the marina's eateries?"

"Oh…So, your case is going well, is it? You're right. Perhaps a long lunch is exactly what you need."

It appears Tuesdays are not bust at the marina. As it was a glorious day, and the sun on the surrounding concrete warmed the environment, we sat undercover outside. It took only a few moments for the ambience of the place to impose its calming effect. The warmth of the sun, the smell of the sea, which seemed bluer than usual today, all combined to create a magical effect. We sat in silence for a few moments just soaking up the atmosphere until Emily broke the spell.

"So, tell me about why this case is causing you some amount of indigestion at the moment. Is it a new one, or one that's been dragging on for a while?"

"It's a new one; since Saturday."

"How did you get a new client on Saturday? You don't work on Saturdays. Well, you do work on weekends, but you're not in your office. If you're working on a Saturday you're usually out in the field investigating a case."

"I forgot to take a file home, and I wanted to complete the paperwork for a case I wrapped up on Friday. Rather than wait until Monday, I decided to come into my city office on Saturday instead. A bloke rang, and said he wanted to see me, and it was urgent. He was at work and could come during his lunch break. I suspect, from down on the street, he noticed the lights on in my office and decided to try his luck. I didn't have a case to go on with, so talking to him seemed like it might be a good idea."

"He might have been some nutter just out to make a nuisance of himself. Seeing him was a bit of a risk, wasn't it?"

"Maybe… He did give me his name, and I sort of knew who he was. So, I decided to take the risk. Besides, the urgency he mentioned intrigued me."

"Okay, so you took the case, and now it's not going well. Why not?"

"Long story short, I'm not sure my client is still alive." I watched Emily's eyebrows head towards her hairline. As she shuffled to the edge of her chair, excitement was plastered across her face.

"Well, I am available for the remainder of today – and I could take the rest of the week off. Between us, we might be able to move this case along. Perhaps you should tell me what it's all about."

My friendship with Emily Ibbotson began during a case I was called to investigate some years ago. In those days, she was a chemical engineer working in the mining industry, but harbouring an interest in forensic science. She increased her qualifications to achieve her dream, and has gone on from there to head up the region's forensic laboratory. There is nothing she enjoys more than working with me on my cases. I have utilised her services on a number of occasions, and in many capacities, since then.

"Although it's a tempting offer, Emily, at the moment, I still don't know what I'm supposed to be investigating. Who knows … if I finally gain some traction on this one, you might have some 'outside' jobs to do in your lab."

"Saturday, you said … does this have anything to do with the call Ben received during dinner on Saturday night?" I shrugged and nodded. "Well, come on, tell me about it."

I gave her an executive summary of everything since our hurried departure from her table last Saturday night. "It's as much as I can tell you so far. Come to think of it, you probably know more than I do about the case. I imagine you received plenty from the crime scene to analyse."

"I didn't, because I've been on leave… but the lab probably has been involved. I might have to drop in to my workplace after lunch to see what they have been doing in my absence. I could report back tonight."

"Nice thought, but there will be no one at my place this evening. I'll be working. Anyway, I don't think Ben should hear you reporting to me."

"Good point; I'll give you a call late this afternoon to share whatever I discover."

Thanks to Emily's enthusiasm for my case, lunch didn't last as long as I thought it might. Nevertheless, it was almost three o'clock by the time I was back in my office. Soon after, Ben called to see if I would be home tonight. "No, working again tonight. What about you, anything more on the Trent Martin case?"

"Nothing new to report from here yet, but the hospital's news at lunchtime was not encouraging. They assessed a slight deterioration in his condition since last night. While it was too slight and too soon to form any conclusions from it, they intimated it was in line with their expectations. I asked for a prognosis, but was told it was too soon to know."

With nothing better to do until it was time to stake out the Wentworth Drive address again, I returned to researching Trent and Stella Martin. When Emily rang at about 5:30, nothing new had been added to my file. Her call didn't add anything more to it either. As expected, quite a few samples from the alleyway were sent for analysis, but none was likely to prove useful at this stage.

In spite of a big lunch, by six o'clock, I was beginning to feel peckish again. Rather than rely on a couple of second-hand muesli bars tonight, I decided to look for something more substantial to take with me. Late in the day, there is little left to be had, but I did capture the last tired looking corned beef and pickles sandwich from the deli along the street. Thanks to my food gathering expedition, it was 6:40 by the time I was parked in Wentworth Drive.

Lights on in the Martins' house were a reasonable indication I wasn't too late. Until I saw someone moving about inside, I didn't feel confident my target was still at home. A few minutes before seven o'clock, lights started being turned off throughout the house. Moments later, the same tall, slim woman emerged and went to the garage. I waited about a minute before following her car out of Wentworth Drive and onto the road into the city.

Murphy's Law came into play. Stella Martin seemed to catch nothing but green lights all the way into the city, whereas I caught nothing but red ones. I was cursing to the universe about the situation. As I approached the city heart, her car seemed to disappear. Then, up ahead, I saw her pull into the left-hand turning lane. My luck changed. The lights turned green and I followed her away from the city heart and towards the boat ramp end of town.

"Damn! Why did she have to go there?" I asked the universe. It provided no answer. Just before the boat ramp end of the street, Stella Martin turned off onto a side road. I knew where the road led, and it was not somewhere I wanted to go. The area of town she was driving into had become a slum. It consisted of many derelict and abandoned buildings, and a few citizens still living in shanties and other makeshift accommodation.

It was not a salubrious part of town, and was one where the residents didn't appreciate uninvited visitors. Memories flashed back of previous cases which took me into this part of town. The memories of those nights were not comfortable, and were not something I wanted to relive tonight. If I thought having to revisit the slum area was bad news, it got worse.

The very nature of the place made it difficult to tail someone into the area without their becoming aware of the tail. In my efforts to avoid becoming obvious, I managed to lose the target. There wasn't much I could do. Stella Martin's car seemed to evaporate into thin air. I crawled along the street, almost screwing my head off as I swivelled it from side to side searching for any sign of her car. The street originally came to a dead end. Some time ago, the enterprising locals involved in not-quite-legal activities saw fit to alter the existing situation. They created a track from the end of their street back around the block to the previous parallel street.

I discovered the rough connecting track and used it to escape while working a case a couple of years ago. Having accepted I had lost Stella Martin tonight, I continued through the area to the end of the street and onto the rough track. If anything, I think the track was rougher than the last time I used it. Nevertheless, it brought me onto the previous street. This street marked the end of a light industrial area which had enjoyed better times many years ago. I continued out onto the High Street and headed towards the city heart. About a block further along was a little diner in the true tradition of a 'greasy spoon'. I pulled into a bay in the minuscule parking lot along one side of the building.

There was no way I was going inside to eat anything, but it's parking lot provided an excellent vantage point from which to watch passing traffic. I was beginning to lose interest in the exercise when, about half an hour later, Stella Martin's car flew past heading towards the city. Moments later, I eased out of the parking lot and followed her towards the north side of town. I drove past the entrance to Wentworth Drive and continued on to enter the street from the other end. By the time I was cruising along Wentworth Drive, lights were being turned on in the Martins' house.

It was clear there was nothing more to achieve tonight, other than to go home and toast my now dried and curling corned beef and pickles sandwich.

Chapter 4

Today looked like being a repeat of Yesterday. It might be more productive to stay home and tackle domestic chores than go into my city office and sit there wondering what to do all day. Domestic chores not being a favoured way of filling in time, I managed only the laundry and a couple of other minor jobs before chucking it in and heading into the city.

"Right … now I'm here, what am I supposed to do until 6:30 this evening?" I asked my empty office. As it was not forthcoming with anything inspirational, I settled for flopping down at my desk and booting up my computer. My email inbox kept me occupied for a few minutes responding to enquiries and sending off brochures.

If all else fails, 'have another coffee' seemed a sound move … but something highly calorific might help the grey cells function better. A quick trip to the bakery soon had me sitting in one of my ancient lounge chairs with an enormous slice of black forest gateau and a freshly brewed coffee on the low table in front of me. I had dispatched the cake and was lingering over the last of the coffee when Ben arrived.

"So, this is how some people earn a living? Yes, thanks, I will have a coffee."

Of course he would. Somehow, I refrained from making myself another one as well. "What brings you here this morning?" I asked as I set his coffee down in front of him. "I hope you have something exciting or inspirational to tell me."

"Neither I'm afraid. I've just come from checking on Trent Martin. The news is not good. The doctor in charge of his case was doing his rounds when I arrived, so I had the opportunity to quiz him. In spite of their best efforts, your client continues to slowly deteriorate. They doubt he will last another twenty-four hours. I asked about Mrs Martin as, in view of her husband's worsening condition, I expected her to be sitting by his bedside. The 'special' nurses appointed to care for him around the clock were both there at the time, so we were able to ask them."

"Those nurses would be working twelve-hour shifts I imagine, and would know exactly who came to enquire after him."

"It seems Stella Martin's concern for her husband doesn't extend beyond the one hasty visit to the hospital immediately after I broke the news of his attack. She hasn't been back since, or phoned to enquire after his condition. The doctor admitted, if things kept going as they were, it was likely they would call her in tonight to be with him and say her goodbyes."

"Christ… it is not what I wanted to hear. Common sense says I should refund the money and just walk away from the case."

"But…?"

"Yes, all right … but I now feel even more obligated to him to sort out what is going on in his wife's life. It might be too late for him to know about it, but I owe it to him to find out."

"That's my girl. There for a moment, I thought you might be losing your touch … might have lost the lure of the chase. So, what's your next move?"

"As soon as I get rid of you, I intend taking a few minutes to think about it … and to reorganise some things so I can focus on just this case."

He wasn't too impressed – and it wasn't quite the truth. I didn't have any other active cases to 'reorganise'. If Ben knew, he would want to know what I was working on every night if it wasn't the Martin case. Nevertheless, he took the hint and left in a bit of a huff. Sometime in the near future, a special effort will be required to square off, but I will deal with it when circumstances permit.

So, now I was alone and it was not yet lunchtime, what was I going to do? Back at my desk, I read through my meagre case notes. My note about my client's joining a chess club so as to be out of the house every Thursday night caught my attention. Which chess club, and where do they meet?

A quick check discovered three chess clubs in Millhaven. I could rule one out straight away. It presented itself as upmarket, elitist, and welcoming only top class players as members. I had two left to look into. Social media told me members of one met at the local library on Tuesday nights and Saturday afternoons. The remaining club used a room in the local community centre. It appeared the club's activities occurred at various times on various days throughout the week. As the latter appeared the only one to fit the criteria, I decided to try confirming Trent Martin's membership.

A young woman manned a reception window in the admin area of the community centre. I passed two men playing chess as I made my way through to her. In response to my enquiry, the young woman pointed me in the direction of the two chess players, one of whom was packing up the set ready to leave as I made my way over to them. The remaining player also seemed to be preparing to leave as I approached his table.

With nothing planned, I had to improvise. "Hi, I'm Sandi. Could you spare me a few moments please?" He nodded and gestured for me to take the chair so recently vacated by his mate. "I was hoping to obtain some information about the chess club which meets here."

"You've come to the right person. I'm John, and I'm the president of the club. What did you want to know?"

"An acquaintance and I were discussing chess recently. I mentioned I would like to learn to play better. I don't mean I want to enter major competitions or anything so extreme. I just want to play well."

"A good chess club will help you."

"My friend said the same thing. He recommended this club and said he recently became a member."

"It was good of him to recommend us. He was right. Playing with other members of clubs like ours helps people improve. By the way, who is your friend?"

"I don't think he has been a member for more than a few weeks – and I don't know how good a player he is, but his name is Trent Martin."

"Martin… Trent Martin…? Oh yes, he is one of our newest members. He is an okay player, but is still a long way from being up to competition standard; more at the good-for-a-game-with-a-mate standard. So, how can I help? Do you want to join our club?"

"I'm still thinking about it. My friend said he played on Thursday nights. If I joined, it would mean giving up something else I have on Thursday nights."

He brought up a small case from beside his chair and scrabbled around in it for a moment or two before handing me a pamphlet. "Look, I'm sorry but I do have to go. I have an appointment in about five minutes. Here, take this with you. It lists all the times we play chess during the week. Maybe there is a time to suit you without your having to give up something else."

Back in my office, I went straight to the coffee machine. Okay, I've looked into the chess club, and it appears the chess club part of Trent Martin's story rings true. So, how does it help me? It took me about a second to admit to myself it didn't progress my case one iota. What else could I do to fill in the rest of my day? And, at the end of my day in the office, what would I do? Should I watch the Wentworth Drive address again tonight?

My gut was telling me, after going out to do whatever last night, Stella Martin was unlikely to go out again tonight. It made sense, but I didn't want to believe it. Maybe my ego was still stinging from having botched tailing her. What if I didn't go tonight, and I wasted another perfectly good opportunity to find out what she is up to? As I walked back to my desk with my fresh coffee, I was shaking my head. Who was I kidding? Of course I'm going to stakeout Stella Martin again tonight – and every night for the rest of the week. There is no question about it. So, if I have nothing else to be getting on with, I may as well go and buy a newspaper to read for the rest of the afternoon.

After draining my coffee mug, I fished my purse out of my tote bag and was on my way to the door when Ben Richards strode in. "I thought I'd drop by on the off chance you weren't busy. Were you going somewhere important, or can we talk?"

"Nowhere important; I was on the way to buy a newspaper, but it can wait. I suppose you'd like a coffee now you're here."

"Yeah, coffee would be great – and something to go with it if you've got anything." His enthusiasm evaporated when I assured him 'Mother Hubbard's cupboard was bare today'.

We settled on opposite sides of my desk and I opened the conversation. "So, what brings you here at this hour of the day … And, more importantly, what did you want to talk about?"

"I'm on my way back into town from a crime scene. I decided to check on Trent Martin's condition. I don't think there's any real change, but they are still quite negative about his chances of making it through the night. Anyway, seeing as how I was out and about, I decided to call into the office supplies firm and ask about their employee. They were concerned about Martin as he hadn't come into work this week and hadn't notified them he was ill. They confirmed the last time Trent Martin came into work was last Saturday. He and another person worked late after the place closed for the day in order to complete some sort of major software update on their system. The person I was speaking to didn't know what time they left, but confirmed the time with the other person who had worked with Martin. He said he left the building at about 6:40. Martin was still there when he left, but was packing up ready to leave. He assumed Trent Martin left the building no more than a few minutes after he did."

"Okay, so we've confirmed he did work on Saturday and the approximate time he left the office supplies building. Why was he in the alleyway? Why didn't he go home when he finished work?"

"Ah well, Sherlock, I asked the other employee if Martin had any plans for after they finished work. It appears Martin planned to eat at the bistro a block or so from here. The one where you often eat. So, before I came here, I checked whether he ate there on Saturday night. His credit card slip showed he did, and paid his bill on his way out at 7:15."

"What time did you get that phone call about a body in the alley? It wasn't much later was it?"

"I got the call at 7:55."

"Think about that timeline. They must have been waiting for Martin when he left the bistro. It wouldn't take too much to work out he probably would go back, via the alley, to the office supplies place to collect his car to go home. So, we now know they ambushed him on his way back to the office, not on his way to the bistro. Still, the timing is tight. There was little time after Trent Martin left the bistro for them to work over the bloke, and for the police to find and check what they thought was a body before they called you. How did the uniforms happen to find the body?"

"The same question occurred to me. So, on my way from the bistro to here, I called to find out. Surprise, surprise – an anonymous call reported a fracas occurring in the alley. The uniforms on patrol were sent to investigate."

"No way of tracing that call, I suppose…?"

"I'll know the answer to that when I'm back in my office."

Although consumed in great detail, the newspaper I bought after Ben's departure didn't make much of a dent in the rest of my day. In spite of its not bringing any good news, Emily's phone call came as a welcome relief from the boredom. "Am I interrupting anything, or are you able to talk?"

"Please talk to me. I was just about to go home to look for something to amuse myself with for a couple of hours. What would you like to talk about?"

"I checked all the analyses of the samples from Ben's alleyway crime scene. There were plenty of them, but none are likely to be of any use. The bloke's attackers probably left some trace evidence behind, but you wouldn't know which was theirs amongst all the other stuff that came in. I think they must have rolled him around on the ground a bit before they left him."

"It's not exactly what I was hoping to hear, and I imagine Ben and his merry men are disappointed too."

"Yeah, I knew he would be. It's why I checked all the results again. Are you working tonight?"

"Probably… no, that's not true. Yes, I will be working, but I'm not sure whether it will be an early or late finish. It will depend on what my target decides to do." Another incoming call for Emily ended our conversation. Well, it seems I've made a decision about tonight.

I spent the next little while updating my case file with information from the chess club and Ben's comments about Trent Martin's movements on the night of his attack. While it confirmed what we knew and helped build a picture of the crime, there was nothing so far to help with my case.

Six o'clock rolled around. I packed up and headed for my car. In the quest for something better than a stale corned beef sandwich, I took advantage of a drive-through facility to obtain an evening meal of fried chicken and chips. Then it was over to the north side of town and the search for somewhere to park.

In spite of my earlier thoughts, Wentworth Drive really didn't offer any suitable parking places. A strange car parking in much the same place every night in a quiet suburban street was bound to attract unwanted attention. I needed to find somewhere else which still allowed me to see if Stella went out. A couple of lay-by areas along the side of the main road into the city heart might be worth a look. I drove past two such locations as I travelled about three kilometres past the turnoff to Wentworth Drive, then doubled back to test those two locations.

The first lay-by was the further of the two beyond the Wentworth Drive entrance. It wasn't too bad, but a bit too far away for my liking. I pulled out and drove to the other lay-by area. People were driving home from work at the end of the day. I watched a handful of cars coming from the city turn onto Wentworth Drive. My vantage point offered a good clear view, and the street lighting at the intersection made it easy to identify the make and colour of the cars. This was where I would eat my chicken and chips while I waited to see if Stella Martin went out tonight.

It was a few minutes after seven o'clock when I saw her car emerge from Wentworth Drive and head towards the city. Keeping another vehicle between us, I followed her into town. There was no surprise when she turned left at the traffic lights and headed towards the boat ramp. It was even less of a surprise when she turned off onto the side street into the slum area. This was going to be tricky. How to tail her through the slum area without her becoming aware of it, and without losing her again?

While not my preferred mode of operation, the only logical way I could think of was to abandon my car and proceed on foot. In any other area, it wouldn't bother me, but this was not the safest of places for a woman to be at night, alone and on foot. Unhappy memories of another case on another similar night in this area came rushing back to remind me of the risk. 'Too late,' I told those memories. 'I've parked now. Wish me luck.' I slid out of the car and locked it behind me.

I had watched Stella Martin drive about two hundred metres along the street before turning off abruptly at a two-storey derelict building. The gods were smiling on me tonight. The building in question stood out above a cluster of equally derelict single storey houses. Keeping to the shadows, I made my way as quickly and silently as I could towards the two-story building.

My gut kept reminding me everything was going too well. No other cars entered the street. No lights were on in any of the buildings along this stretch of it. No one was out taking an evening constitutional, and no dogs barked. Perhaps my gut was right on the money: everything definitely was going too well. It was while I silently acknowledged my luck, Stella Martin's car shot out from behind the building.

She hadn't turned on her headlights, but had her foot planted down hard as she fishtailed out onto the street and roared off away from me. I was only about fifty metres from the house, and thought it wise to pause and wait to see what else might happen. After a couple of minutes of standing motionless in the shadows and still nothing else had happened, I began inching my way towards the building again, all the while expecting another vehicle to come rocketing out from the house at any moment.

Pressed hard against the front corner of the building, I strained my ears to pick up any sounds coming from inside the building or its surrounds. Nothing. Absolute silence assaulted my ears on a night when even the slightest sound would carry on the crisp air. Caution was the keyword as I eased my way across the front of the building, carefully stepping over and around piles of rubbish. At the opposite corner, I took a couple of deep breaths before risking a quick look along the side of the house.

A once gravelled driveway, now sprouting a healthy crop of grass and weeds, ran along the side and around to the back of the building. If I wanted to know what was happening behind this place, I had to follow the driveway. My preferred option would be to approach the rear from along the other side of the building, but the narrow access along there was blocked by a jumble of empty drums and a discarded car body. I plastered myself to the wall and set off 'crab-wise' towards the rear. By avoiding the gravel as much as possible in the dark, I hoped not to alert anyone to my presence.

No vehicles were parked in the small cleared space out back. Still no lights were visible anywhere. I knew the building wouldn't have power, but anyone moving about inside would need at least a torch to avoid injuring themselves in the darkness. The back door hung off its hinges at a crazy angle and stood about half open. Time spent standing beside the open door listening for sounds produced nothing. This cautious approach was getting me nowhere. I delved into my pocket for my small LED torch … and, for a brief moment, I wished my Glock was in there too.

The top door hinge had rusted away, allowing the door to drop down and its bottom corner to wedge itself firmly against the concrete floor. Through the open door, I played my torch across the area of floor immediately inside. Unlike the rest of the building, this part of the floor had seen activity in recent times. As my torch appeared not to attract the attention of any inhabitants of the building, I peered around the door, all the while continuing to play my torch across the area in front of me.

Although it shouldn't have come as a surprise, what I saw in my torchlight made me pause and question the wisdom of what I was about to do. Unlike the appearance of the exterior of the building, the area immediately inside the back door had been cleared of rubbish. Only a few strategically placed bits and pieces occupied the space: a couple of dodgy looking wooden kitchen chairs, a large wooden packing case, a small scarred table, and what might once have been a bedside cabinet. It was obvious this was 'home base' for some form of covert operation. What had Stella Martin become involved in?

Having come this far without encountering any opposition, I ventured in to explore the small room. I stood in the centre and followed my torchlight as I played it in a circle around the room. Then I saw it. It was on the floor, partially hidden by the table and small cabinet.

Indecision and caution were no longer my companions as I bolted out the door and sprinted all the way back to my car. I was right. This is no place for a woman alone to be. Once safely locked in my car, I flicked through my contacts to Ben Richards' name.

Chapter 5

Minutes after my call, I saw headlights turn onto the street. Ben's car pulled up beside mine. He left it idling while he scrambled out and rushed over to my window. Another set of headlights turned onto the street as he barked at me, "Where is it?"

"The two-storey place along there on the left... around the back... the backdoor is open."

During our short exchange, the second set of headlights arrived and we were now parked three abreast. "Stay in your car," Ben ordered, before rushing over to the patrol car now waiting on the other side of Ben's vehicle. After a few quick words from Ben, it drove off and parked across the entrance to the driveway along the side of the double-storey building. Then Ben was back at my window again. "Are you armed tonight?"

Although he probably couldn't see it in the dark, I shook my head. "No. I didn't expect to need a weapon on surveillance." I'm sure he said something under his breath, but I didn't catch what it was ... but I did hear what came next.

"Right; get out, lock your car and get into mine. You can give me the details on our way to the house."

Obviously, he didn't think there was much to tell. It doesn't take long to travel a couple of hundred metres. Still, I did my best in the time available. "On foot, I followed the driveway around to the back of the building. The backdoor was open, and looked like it had been for years. In the small room immediately inside the door, against the right-hand wall, and partially hidden by a table and small cupboard, I saw a woman's body on the floor." He grunted as he pulled on the handbrake at the same time as I finished speaking.

"So, could you identify the body?"

"No ... well, I don't know if I could or not. I didn't look."

"You said you found a *woman's* body. How do you know it was a woman, if you didn't look?" He was making no effort to hide his rising exasperation.

"Poking out past the table was a pair of female's legs, with its feet sporting strappy sandals tied around the ankles. And, the toenails of those feet were painted bright pink. I thought assuming it to be a female's body was a safe bet."

While we exchanged 'pleasantries' in Ben's car, the two uniformed officers from the patrol vehicle rolled out crime scene tape and donned bullet-proof vests. I expected Ben to dive out of the car and rush to inspect the scene, but he wasn't done with me yet. "Why were you here in the first place? I thought you learned your lesson about this area the last time you were here."

Here we go. I knew the hard question would come sooner or later. "Okay, after I tailed a target into this area last night and lost it in here somewhere, I decided to see if it came back here again tonight. It did, and this time I saw where the car went – and worked out why I lost it last night. While I was watching the place, the car I saw go around to the rear of the building, shot out of there like the Hounds of Hell were after it. I went on foot to investigate – and found the body. That's it."

"And… Come on. Then what happened?"

"Nothing… Well, nothing worth reporting. I saw the legs and scarpered. After sprinting back to my car and locking myself in, I called you. Then I sat there until you arrived. There has been no activity in the area since I called you. No sign even of anyone moving about."

"Am I to understand, the car you followed tonight was the same car as you followed and lost here last night?"

"Yes. I now know I lost it last night because it disappeared around the back of the building before I turned onto the street, and I couldn't see it anywhere when I drove through the area."

"You've omitted one important fact from your statement: the identity of the driver of the car, and if that driver was the person you were tailing?"

"I'm fairly sure there was only one person in the car; the driver. And, yes, if the driver was the owner of the car, it's who I was tailing."

"And their identity is…?"

"Uhmm … It probably was Stella Martin."

"So, you think the body in there is that of Stella Martin?"

"Well, no. I don't know what to think. I'm fairly sure it was Stella Martin I followed in her car. There was no one else around out here when she went around to the back of the house, or when I went to see what was going on. So, my immediate thought was the body was Stella Martin. The only thing wrong with the assumption is, if the body was Stella Martin, who drove off in her car? And, yeah, I know the short answer is, whoever murdered her." I shrugged and left it at that.

"I can't believe this. You were already in there poking around in the crime scene, but didn't bother to confirm it was Stella Martin lying on the floor in there?"

"It's not that I didn't think about it. There was no point in my doing so. I only know what Stella Martin looks like from a distance in the dark. So, I wouldn't have been able to identify if the body was Stella."

"And, you didn't think it important enough to mention any of this to me before now?"

Oh, I knew this would happen the moment he asked the first hard question. Now I have an unhappy copper to contend with.

"Right, here's what's going to happen: you will lock yourself in, and remain in my car while I have a quick look at the crime scene. You will not get out of the car until I return, regardless of what bright ideas you might have in the meantime. When I return from inspecting the crime scene, I will drive you back to your vehicle … *And you will go home and stay there for the rest of the night."*

Yep, not a happy chap at the moment is Ben Richards. While there is nothing else happening in the vicinity, I'm just as happy to sit here in his car as sit in my own. But later, when I'm back in my own car, I doubt I'll be going straight home. My gut is suggesting I should stakeout Stella Martin's house for a while.

Ben wasn't gone more than five minutes before striding back and scrambling in behind the wheel. "We both owe the gods one tonight. It is not Stella Martin on the floor in there. It is some other unfortunate – very dead – female." As he finished speaking, Ben started his car. "I'll take you back to your vehicle now, and then you are to go home and stay there."

"Are you planning to stay and work the scene? I wouldn't expect to find the top cop in the region investigating a murder. Where are your detectives?"

"Yes well, you ask a very good question. At the moment I have one detective at my disposal, and he has just finished a twelve-hour day. We are supposed to have four stationed here in Millhaven. I'm told they are recruiting two more for here, but God knows when they might arrive."

"What happened to the other three detectives you had?"

"Let's see… One resigned to go home and work in the family business; one transferred on promotion to another precinct; one was on a skiing holiday in Switzerland and is now laid up in hospital there with multiple serious injuries. The only one I have left has been pulling twelve-hour days for the last week. He's probably sound asleep by now. At least, I hope he is. He is in for another big day tomorrow."

It was obvious Ben was anxious to get back to the crime scene. "Okay, I'll leave you to it. If you manage to confirm her identity, I'd be interested to know who she is. You never know, it might have some bearing on Stella Martin's recent behaviour." He didn't respond. I took it as a sign it was time to go.

I slid out of Ben's vehicle and scrambled into mine. My hope was, if I made as though I was about to leave, Ben would return his focus to the crime scene and drive back there to begin his investigation. He knows me too well, and sat there idling until I was on my way out of the area. I consoled myself with the thought there probably was nothing more to be gained from hanging around in the slum area anyway. At the main intersection on the High Street, I turned right and headed for the northern suburbs.

After driving past the first entrance, I continued on to the other end of the street before turning onto Wentworth Drive. My crawl along the street paused just short of the Martins' house. A number of lights were on, making the interior of the house well lit. During the brief time I watched the place, I saw the tall, slim woman I'd seen before come out and throw a bag into the wheelie bin parked beside the garage.

Okay, so Stella Martin came home after her shocking discovery in the derelict building. Now I want to know what is in the bag of rubbish she threw in the bin. My 'itch' is not going to be easy to scratch. There is unlikely to be any chance to inspect the contents of her bin until after she leaves for work tomorrow. To add to my frustration, the little voice in my head kept asking me if I was sure Stella Martin wasn't responsible for the body Ben now was investigating.

All the way home, that question dominated my thinking. I was halfway through a nightcap single malt scotch before I finally accepted there just wasn't sufficient time for Stella to have murdered the woman before she fled the house. In spite of my resolve, a weak doubt lingered in the back of my mind. It resulted in my kicking myself for not having checked the body before following Stella's example and fleeing.

How was the woman killed? A skilled stabbing wouldn't require much time to achieve its intended outcome, but that is not a method preferred by women. They are more likely to shoot their victim … if they have access to a gun. I would have heard a gunshot – and I didn't. While still not completely convinced about anything, when I slid into bed, I was accompanied by a reasonably strong belief Stella Martin did not murder the woman.

*****

This morning had me suffering the onset of mental exhaustion before I finished breakfast. So many questions about last night occupied my thinking. The frustrating thing about it was I had no ideas on how to go about finding answers to any of them. My big hope was for Ben to contact me early this morning to share information gathered in the course of his efforts last night. I also knew my need-to-know would not be high on Ben's list of priorities today. Still, with no real purpose in mind, I dragged myself into my city office.

A blinking red light on my phone welcomed me. The message had arrived about five minutes before I did. Ben demanded to know where I was, and would I be in my office in about half an hour's time? Via a text to his mobile, I told him I was in my office and whenever he arrived would be convenient. My approach to the day brightened no end at the prospect of a meeting with Ben. It was my only chance so far to maybe gain some answers – or even clues – as to what my case might be about.

To fill in time until Ben's arrival, I had two tasks to complete: updating my case file with notes from last night, and dashing to the bakery nextdoor for something to have with our coffees. I had just refilled the coffee machine and set out two mugs on the benchtop in readiness when Ben marched in. "I hope you have at least a biscuit to go with the coffee," he said, gesturing towards the coffee mugs. Yes, he was suffering the after effects of a late night – very late, I guessed.

He wasted no time launching into the reason for his visit. "Suppose you tell me again – and in detail this time – why you were in the slum area and how you came to discover the body last night."

"There isn't anything more to add to everything I told you last night. I followed Stella Martin's car into the area the previous night and lost her. On the off chance she might go out again last night, a bit after 6:30, I was in position to tail her if she left home. She did, and I followed her. This time, I saw where she went and knew why I lost her the previous evening."

I paused my commentary to allow Ben to catch-up with the notes he scribbled as I spoke. The pause was longer than I intended. Having caught up, Ben realised his coffee was getting cold and he hadn't taken more than a bite out of his lemon meringue tart. When we began again, I expected to continue reiterating last night's information. Ben had other ideas.

"Why did you stake out her place on two consecutive nights? Didn't it strike you as being a waste of time?"

"Yeah, it did seem a bit of a longshot, but it was part of my surveillance plan."

"You had better explain your plan to me before we go any further."

"Now Trent Martin is in no position to alert me when his wife goes out at night, I decided to watch her place every night this week to see what happened. Next week, if she sticks with past practice, she will go out only on Thursday night, and is likely to be busy doing whatever she does for a couple of hours. I might restrict my surveillance to just the one night next week."

"I know the answer to this question before I ask but, did you go straight home after leaving the slum area last night?"

"Not exactly…"

"So, *exactly* what did you do, and where did you go?"

The question wasn't unexpected, but I preferred it hadn't been asked. "I took a quick trip along Wentworth Drive before heading home. Lights were on in the house, and Stella Martin was home." I saw Ben prepare to ask another question, but I cut him off. Having answered enough of his questions for the moment, I had a few of my own I wanted answered. "By the way, Ben, I meant to ask as soon as you arrived, have you identified the body?"

"Not a definite identification yet, but it seems she is a local. One of the uniforms thinks he has seen her around town on occasion. I've got uniforms out today showing her photo around to see if anyone recognises her."

"How was she killed? And, have you established a timeframe for the crime?"

"She was strangled. It appears she hadn't been dead too long when you found her; possibly no more than an hour or two."

"That's good news. It leaves Stella Martin out of the picture. Oh, and I meant to ask as well, have you checked on Trent Martin's condition today?"

"In spite of the hospital's expectations, it seems he made it through the night. Nevertheless, they say his condition is still precarious, and hasn't improved any since yesterday. As for Stella Martin being out of the picture for the murder, it's not a sound assumption on your part. We don't know what she was doing before you saw her leave home and go into the slum area. She might have gone out earlier, done the deed, and returned home, before going out again."

"What? Are you suggesting she went back again to check on her handiwork? I think it highly unlikely."

"No, it's not what I was suggesting. Perhaps it happened in a fit of rage or something and, after she calmed down at home, she had trouble believing what she might have done and went back to check. It wouldn't take her more than a few moments to check on the horror she found in the house, and it would explain why she left in such a hurry."

"As I told you last night, I don't know what Stella Martin looks like. I've only seen her silhouetted in the dark, but she doesn't appear built like a weightlifter or anything of that ilk. Strangulation is not one of women's favoured methods of murder, and Stella Martin doesn't appear built for it anyway. Judging by what I saw of the legs in that back room, the victim was of sturdy construction, and might have proved difficult for a man to strangle, let alone Stella Martin."

"All valid points, I have to concede, but it doesn't get us any closer to finding out what was going on."

"It's just a random thought at the moment, but might both women somehow be involved in the same thing? I grant you, I have no idea what it might be, but I doubt they were both on the game. The derelict house would be the last place they'd be peddling their wares."

"Hmm … I agree, no self-respecting prostitute would operate out of such a place. But, if they were being run by someone – a pimp of sorts – it might be a meeting place where they handed over their takings. While I can't say there was any indication they were involved in something of that nature, at the moment, anything and everything is on the table."

"Apart from being strangled, was the victim knocked about at all?"

"Nothing obvious, but some bruising does take a while to show up."

"The other question bothering me at the moment is, how did she get to the house in the first place? There was no vehicle parked at, or near, the house. Did someone take her to the house and then do her in, or was there more than one person involved? If the victim went there under her own steam, how did she get there? Where is her vehicle?"

"Sonny, I came here this morning to ask you questions … to find answers to my questions. I didn't come here to end up leaving with more questions than when I arrived, but it seems to be what's happening. Do you have any other interesting questions you might like to ask at this point in time?"

"Not really… Except, have you checked on Stella Martin this morning?"

"No. Why would I want to check on her?"

"I'm wondering whether she went in to work today. Her discovery last night must've unnerved her to the point where she might not feel up to going to work today."

"Possibly; but does it matter whether she's gone into work today or not?"

"Uhmm … well, it is of interest to me." I saw him raise his eyebrows and roll his eyes in exasperation. Fully expecting a tirade to follow, I jumped in before it could happen. "While it's not important I suppose, I do want to have a look in her wheelie bin. I'm a bit interested in the contents of the bag she threw in the bin after she returned home last night."

"You were really planning to go there in broad daylight, were you?"

"Dunno … Hadn't given it any real thought at this stage, beyond wondering what was in the bag she threw out."

"Of course, it could be just kitchen scraps. Nevertheless, you have my interest. I don't think I'm ready to request a search warrant on the basis of your observation, but I might give some thought to how to engineer obtaining a look in her bin. I assume, if I put something in place, you would expect to be involved?"

"Why do you think I mentioned it, if I didn't want to be involved? I saw her put the bag in the bin, and I want to know what was in the bag. That's how simple it is. If I can't be a part of your operation, I'll have to devise my own way of accessing what's in the bin."

It seems I had made my point. Before he left, Ben agreed he would let me know what he came up with and when he was likely to implement it. In the meantime, as soon as he was back in his office, he was going to check with the council's rubbish contractor about when rubbish is collected from Wentworth Drive.

Chapter 6

After two nights of tailing Stella Martin and finding out nothing more about what was going on in her life, I didn't feel inclined to repeat the performance again tonight. Ben rang late in the afternoon to say he would bring something for dinner – unless I planned to cook. Of course, I wasn't planning to cook. I hadn't yet moved on to thinking about dinner. In fact, I only decided not to work tonight just before he called. Come to think of it, it might have been the purpose behind his call: to make sure I didn't go out again tonight.

It was almost six o'clock when I locked my office and bounced down the stairs to my car. From just before lunch, I was kept busy dealing with a number of phone enquiries, sending out information, and interviewing two potential clients. If they all came good, I could be in for an interesting time juggling cases in the near future. At home, I went straight through to my office, dumped my bag, and extracted the Martin case file I grabbed as an afterthought before I left. I placed it squarely in the centre of my desk. At some point tonight, there was no doubt we would be discussing the Martin case.

A few minutes after seven o'clock, Ben arrived laden with a selection of pasta dishes and a bottle of wine. In the interest of eating the food while it was still hot, little time was wasted on conversation or anything else before we sat down to eat. The good food and wine seemed to mellow both of us. We lingered at the table sipping our wine long after we dispatched the food, before adjourning to the lounge room with coffees and leftover sweet treats from the bakery in hand. Then tonight's conversation began in earnest.

Ben chose the predicted topic and was straight down to business. "Any new developments in the Martin case at your end?"

I shook my head. "The way the rest of my day panned out, I barely had time to think about it anyway. What about your investigation; has there been any progress at all?"

"Nothing to get excited about so far. Forensics have analysed the body's DNA. Now all we have to do is find a match for it. No one has come forward to report a missing person. I suppose it would be accurate to say my investigation has stalled. There was one thing to come out of today. As I mentioned this morning, I contacted the council's rubbish contractor regarding Wentworth Drive rubbish collection days. Their truck services Wentworth Drive tomorrow morning, usually between six and seven o'clock. The residents put out their bins the night before to avoid an early morning scramble, or missing the truck altogether."

"Tomorrow morning…! That's not what I want to hear. Whatever Stella Martin put in her bin last night will disappear forever early tomorrow morning. No, it doesn't suit me at all."

"What makes you think it wasn't just a bag of household rubbish she threw in the bin? Maybe you're becoming desperate enough to pin your hopes on anything. Tell me why you think it is more than a bag of rubbish she threw out."

"I would if I could. It's a bit hard to explain. All I can say is, the way she went about it suggested something more than rubbish was disposed of… And yes, I know some people put their kitchen rubbish out last thing before they go to bed. Judging by her demeanour, there seemed more involved than just putting out the kitchen rubbish."

"If you say so, but I'm having trouble working out how walking out to the bin, lifting the lid, and throwing in a bag of rubbish can look anything but a normal, routine activity."

"As I said, I can't explain it, but it was different. Anyway, this discussion isn't solving my problem. I want to know what's in that bin – and I only have a few hours in which to find out before it disappears to the tip. I don't suppose we could go and inspect her bin's contents now, could we?"

"Not a hope, and not even later tonight after all the good citizens of Wentworth Drive have gone to bed. If you stop carrying on about it and give me a chance to explain, I'll tell you why it isn't important to do anything about it tonight." He stopped me in my tracks, and I'm sure I looked as stunned as I felt. I gestured for him to continue. "I've arranged for the contents of Stella's bin to be set aside when it's collected tomorrow. Apparently, it's not a simple process, but the boss has worked out how they can do it without drawing too much attention to themselves while they're about it."

With the bin issue seeming to be under control, my mind went off in another direction. "If no one has come forward to report a missing person, does it suggest the woman might not have been a local or, if she were local, she lived alone?"

"Either of those explanations could apply in this case. As no handbag, or phone, or anything else to help identify her, was found at the scene, we've nothing to work with. Uniformed officers spent some time showing her photo around the city heart today in the hope someone recognised her. No one did. Our best hope remains for someone to come forward with concerns about her apparent absence."

"Okay, back to the bin…"

"Christ, Sonny, do we have to?"

"Yeah … You haven't told me how and when you're going to go through the contents they isolate for you. And, before you ask, yes, I do want to be there when it happens."

"Why doesn't it come as a surprise? The contractor will let me know when the truck returns to base and the contents are available for inspection. It will happen on site so, when we are done with it, the contents can join other rubbish on its way to the tip. I will call you when we are right to go."

Having explored all there was to discuss regarding the Martin case, the night came to an early end. Ben was on his way down my driveway before ten o'clock and, after a quick shower, I wasn't out of bed for long afterwards. Nothing delayed the onset of an untroubled sleep.

*****

This morning saw a return to normal routine. Out of bed at my usual hour, no time was wasted lingering over breakfast before the peak hour traffic was carrying me along to my city office. Unlocking my office was about the end of my good intentions. Once I attended to the morning's basic admin tasks, I was reluctant to find something else to go on with.

While I didn't know what time the relevant garbage truck would return to its depot, I knew, as soon as I received a call from Ben, I would be out of my office in a flash and on my way to the depot to go through the contents of Stella's bin. I reminded myself I could never have imagined being so interested in going through someone else's garbage. Then it occurred to me: how would I identify the bag I saw Stella Martin throw in the bin two nights ago?

Unaware of anything distinctive about the bag itself, a sobering reality came home to me. With no way of identifying the bag in question, there was nothing for it but to go through each and every bag from the bin. It gave pause for thought for a few moments. How badly did I want to know what was in that bag? I could imagine Ben's reaction if, after organising for the segregation of the bin's contents and having gone through each bag, we came up with nothing of use to either of our investigations.

A couple of phone calls helped fill in time until ten o'clock, when I decided I needed something sweet to go with my mid-morning coffee. I found myself waiting in a queue for longer than I wanted when a whole herd of other people seemed to share my idea of something nice for morning tea. My phone was ringing as I let myself back into my office. I grabbed it on what must have been almost its last ring before reverting to answering machine.

"It took you long enough to answer. I was beginning to think I was wasting my time." Ben was not in one of his better moods today. I hoped it wasn't a sign something went wrong with his garbage segregation plan. "I am about to head out to the garbage contractor's depot. If you're too busy doing whatever you're doing to come along…"

"No. No, I'm not too busy. I just was out of the office for a few minutes. I'm ready to go. Should I take my car?" No, he would pick me up, and was on his way to my office as we spoke. I grabbed my bag, locked the door behind me, galloped down the stairs, and out the back door in time to see Ben nose into the tenants' car park behind the building.

The drive to the garbage contractor's depot on the outskirts of town was notable for its complete lack of conversation. As much as I wanted to know what had gone wrong for him today, I wasn't game to ask. When Ben is in one of his 'silent' moods, it is best to follow his example. He uttered his first words as we pulled into a parking bay out front of the depot's main office building. "I hope you are prepared for this. I don't know how messy it's going to be; probably won't smell too good either."

"It's not the first rubbish bin's contents I've rummaged through. I've come prepared." I pulled a pair of overalls part way out of my oversized tote bag so he could see them. "And, I have long gloves in here too." My preparedness received nothing more than a grunt of approval.

As we stepped into the reception area, the boss – or the bloke in charge, whatever his title – rushed to meet us, and promptly set about trying to ingratiate himself to Ben. I couldn't help but think, 'don't waste your time, mate'. To my surprise, Ben seemed to respond well to the treatment. So far, the depot had been one surprise after another. Not only did the exchange between the bloke and Ben intrigue me, but the bloke himself was not what I expected.

While not sure what I had expected, I think it was something along the lines of the boss of the operation kitted out in workman's attire, including a high-visibility shirt and hard hat. But that was not for this chap. He wore a long-sleeved pale blue pinstriped shirt, well-cut grey slacks, and a vivid blue and pink patterned tie. The hand he extended to Ben sported an impressive gold and opal dress ring. Seems there's money in rubbish these days.

We were escorted to another large shed-like building, in which two garbage trucks were parked. In a small crib room with a large glass window occupying a rear corner of the building, the truck drivers appeared to be on a meal break. Our escort led us to the other rear corner of the building where a blue tarpaulin was spread out on the concrete floor. "Your requested bin's contents are in the purple bin over there. I'll leave you to get on with whatever you need to do. Try to keep everything on the tarpaulin, and leave it there when you are finished. I'll be in my office if you need to see me before you leave."

The bloke's offhand departure seemed to wrong-foot Ben for a moment. I couldn't work out why. Ben, wearing jeans and a work shirt, had come dressed to trawl through the rubbish. While surveying the expanse of blue on the floor and the purple rubbish bin, he seemed to remember I was there too. "I see there are toilets over there if you want to change," he said, pointing to the 'toilets' sign.

"Thanks, but I'm fine. I'll slip into my overalls here." I saw a startled look flit across his face. "Don't get your hopes up. They'll go on over everything I'm wearing. They are big enough to accommodate both of us at the same time." As I spoke, I wrestled the overalls out of my bag and started climbing into them. "As it's not going to be the spectacle you hoped for, you could make yourself useful by tipping out the contents of the bin while I get kitted out for the task ahead."

He shot me a look before marching over and upending the bin onto the centre of the tarpaulin. There wasn't as much rubbish as I expected. "Now, where the hell in amongst all this lot is this bag you're so fixated on?" he demanded as he stood hands on hips peering down at the pile of bags in front of him.

How does he expect me to know? All the bags appear the same colour, size and brand. A few loose items were amongst the bags. The Martins don't appear to be into recycling. I strode over to the pile and, while trying to work out how best and easiest to tackle our task, I removed a couple of newspapers, small cartons of various sizes, and a wine bottle from amongst the bags. Then, it was down to business.

I separated out the bigger bags and stacked them off to one side, leaving me with four smaller bags to consider. Those I set out in a line ranging from the largest to the smallest. So far, the exercise hadn't required much time or energy, but I had noticed Ben's contribution was that of an interested bystander. I couldn't complain, not really. After all, I was the only one of us who knew what I was looking for – *sort of knew* what I was looking for.

As none of the bags actually jumped up and down shouting 'pick me, pick me', I had to choose some other method of working out where to begin. Somehow, the smallest of the bags kept drawing my eyes to it. Was it about the right size for the one I saw Stella Martin put in the bin? It could be, but the next one along in the line also looked about the right size. "Standing here wondering about it won't get you anywhere," I muttered to myself, and strode over to the smallest bag.

The knotted top of the bag was not about to be undone. That left only one other approach. "Do you happen to have a knife in your pocket?" I asked a bit tartly. "If you have one, it might amount to your contribution to the operation." Ben gave me a somewhat nonplussed look before shaking his head. "Fine … Then it's just as well there is a Swiss army knife in my bag. Do you think you might fetch it for me?"

Ben looked over at my bag, and then hesitated. "Er … I think it might not be appropriate for me to be scrabbling around in your bag. I could bring the bag to you, and you could fish out the knife." After a couple of caustic comments from me, Ben brought my tote and thrust it into my outstretched hand. Moments later, the contents of the suspect rubbish bag were strewn on the tarpaulin.

"I don't see anything of interest in that lot," he commented.

"No; but I don't know how you can tell from way over there." Nevertheless, he was right. This stuff looked like the contents of a bathroom's rubbish bin: tissues, empty tube of toothpaste, a soap wrapper, and a couple of cotton wool balls smeared with make-up. There was nothing for it but to move on to the next bag in the line. It underwent the same surgery as the first.

Only a solitary item fell out of the bag. A woman's blouse in a delicate shade of apricot lay in a crumpled heap at my feet. It looked fine and delicate, and I wondered how hard it must've been to dispose of it. I slipped off a glove to feel the fabric: silk, or maybe a silk blend of some sort. After putting my glove back on, I spread out the blouse on the tarpaulin for a better look at it.

"Oh, now that is interesting. Well done … But, what does it tell us?" Ben asked.

From where he was standing, he couldn't see the jagged rip in one of the three-quarter length sleeves. My perverse mind instantly asked the question: why throw it out when she could simply cut off the sleeves to make it a short-sleeved blouse? I didn't share the thought with Ben, settling for a truce instead. "At this stage, I'm not sure. I am inclined to think this is what I saw Stella Martin dispose of after finding the woman's body. You didn't happen to find any apricot- coloured threads at the crime scene, did you?" I held up the blouse so Ben could see its torn sleeve.

"Can't say I did; but I'll be going back for another look – with better lighting this time."

"Well, I've satisfied my curiosity. You're welcome to carry on with the rest of this lot, if you wish." He didn't 'wish'. What he wished to do was go back to the crime scene to search for threads from the blouse. I wanted to have a look too. And, as he hadn't mentioned anything about dropping me back at my office, I was careful to say and do nothing which might remind him I was still with him. I stuffed the blouse in an evidence bag, and followed him to his vehicle.

Not drawing attention to myself paid off. After calling at the police precinct to collect a couple of battery-powered work lights, we headed for the slum area of town and our crime scene. He pulled up in front of the derelict two-storey house and told me to get out and remove the crime scene tape from across the entrance to the driveway. Then, as he drove around to the rear of the building, I trudged after him on foot.

As I hoofed it along the driveway and helped him carry in and set up the lights, I let my mind replay my visit here that fateful night. It recalled the sagging door, the table, the small cupboard, the legs, the latest style of bright coloured sandals, and the vivid pink toenails. What was missing was an image of anything likely to snag a sleeve. In spite of my doubts about the actual site where the body was found, I followed Ben over to it.

Both the table and cupboard had been moved to allow access to the body. It took only one swift glance to confirm my doubts. There was nothing on the other side of the table or the back of the cupboard likely to snag a sleeve. Having satisfied myself, I moved to stand in the middle of the room and directly in front of the doorway. In my mind's eye, I tried to picture Stella Martin's visit to this room. Almost convinced I had it right, I tried a re-enactment of how I thought it happened.

Standing outside on the doorstep, for realism, I took out the small torch I had slipped into my pocket, but didn't bother switching it on. Then, I went through the motions of someone, torch in hand, cautiously entering the dark room. The way the door was jammed less than half open forced anyone entering to step around the edge of the door ... a manoeuvre which had the visitor facing the far wall – where the body lay.

If the visitor carried a torch, the act of stepping around the door would swing their torch's beam towards the far wall and illuminate the woman's legs. The natural inclination would be to move closer to investigate. Assuming the sight she found there shocked Stella to the core, she would rush back to her car and flee the scene. Back, standing in the middle of the room, I scanned Stella's likely path from the body to her car.

The only obstacle she would encounter in her hasty exit was the door itself. "Hmm ... looks nasty enough to warrant closer inspection," I murmured to myself as I moved to a position between the location of the body and the door as someone rushing from the scene might occupy. A couple of steps, and

I reached the door. While entering the room required nothing more than a smooth pivot around the edge of the door, exiting the place was a little trickier.

It required the person to veer off from their direct line to the door for at least a couple of steps to the right. Then, it required a pivot to give them a straight path out of the place. The door had to be the culprit. Perhaps in her rush to escape, Stella's arm connected with some part of it. My pulse was racing as I stood close to the rear of the door. I turned on my torch and played it over the splintered timber.

"There it is," I yelped. It caused Ben to bang his shoulder on the table as he sprang up from down on his haunches.

"There what is? What have you found – or think you've found?"

"Come and see for yourself. I'll put my money on the threads snagged on this door as coming from Stella Martin's blouse. I think this is how the left sleeve of her blouse was ripped as she raced out of the building."

A few minutes later, with the threads safely sealed in an evidence bag, and the crime scene tape back in position across the entrance to the driveway, Ben was dropping me off at my office before taking the evidence collected today to Emily for analysis.

Accompanied by a salad roll from the deli, I went back to my office for a coffee and to spend some time contemplating the morning's events.

Chapter 7

With my feet up on the desk, I munched my salad roll and sipped my coffee until my phone interrupted proceedings: Emily.

"I analysed those threads from the crime scene, and thought you might want to know the results before I talk to Ben." Of course I wanted to know. "Okay, it was a no brainer. The threads are from the blouse with the torn sleeve. It's pure silk and would have been expensive. It probably broke her heart to throw it away. I'm amazed she disposed of it, instead of cutting off the sleeves so she still could wear it."

"Perhaps the memories attaching to the blouse sealed its fate."

"The other good news about the blouse is, we managed to isolate a possible DNA sample. I'm assuming the shirt's owner had long, dark hair. We found a couple of hairs caught in the makers tag at the back of the blouse. The tag was one of those that scratch you all the time. In spite of how lovely the fabric was, that tag must have made it uncomfortable to wear. Anyway, both the hairs we retrieved have their roots attached, so we're hopeful of recovering sufficient sample for a DNA analysis."

"Well, it's one tiny part of the equation confirmed and ticked off, but it still doesn't give us a suspect."

My next big decision to wrestle with for the rest of the afternoon was whether to stake out Stella Martin again tonight or not. Logic said, don't bother. She already was out twice this week. Perhaps, as things hadn't gone to plan, she might go out again tonight. If I knew more about what was going on, and what she did when she went out at night, a decision would be easier. By the time I left the office, I had decided I wasn't working tonight, but still hadn't decided about the rest of the nights between now and next Thursday.

Ben arrived at about seven o'clock with a selection of Chinese takeaway dishes for dinner. Neither of us was particularly talkative. The day hadn't produced much of use to either of our investigations. I wouldn't bother asking Ben about the threads. Instead, I asked what has become my routine question these days. "Any news on my client, Trent Martin; any change in his condition at all?"

"Nothing to report; the hospital staff is amazed at his resilience. They had written him off days ago, but he is hanging in there. I think they're being cautious when I talk to them, to avoid creating any unreal expectations. Under pressure, one of the doctors admitted they kept picking up tiny encouraging signs of a possible improvement."

"That seems to be in keeping with the rest of the investigation: no change, no improvement, and very little happening."

"Yeah, I know how you feel. What are your plans for your investigation?"

"I wish I knew. I've almost decided not to worry about Stella Martin until next Thursday night, which is the next time she should go out for a couple of hours. The other thing I thought of doing was to hang around where she works at lunchtime and possibly after work to see what she does, who she meets, or where she goes. The way this investigation is going, I'll probably find she has lunch in the staff lunchroom, and goes straight home after work." Ben agreed keeping an eye on her at those times might prove beneficial, but there was no other helpful comment.

Although I waited for him to mention the blouse and the threads we collected as evidence today, nothing was forthcoming. I tried convincing myself his lack of comment was due to how insignificant to the overall investigation those items were. Our lack of enthusiasm about everything resulted in the inevitable early night for both of us. Ben left around nine o'clock, and I was in bed by ten o'clock.

*****

After a frustrating weekend of no progress on the Martin case, Monday morning brought an overwhelming lack of enthusiasm. It dogged my day from the moment I woke. Still in need of inspiration on how to progress my case, I dawdled over breakfast, and then decided to take care of the laundry before leaving for work. All it achieved was I didn't have to contend with the morning's peak hour traffic on my way into the city.

With a folded newspaper under my arm and a large chunk of chocolate cake in a takeaway box in my hand, I dragged myself up the stairs to my office. A few moments of idle thought accompanied me: how long have I had an office in this building, and has the lift ever worked properly since I've been here? I couldn't remember how long I'd had my office here in the city heart, but I was sure the lift had never worked properly from the day I arrived. Only thrill seekers or the unaware ever risked the lift. It moved at the rate of about a floor-a- fortnight. You were never sure it would reach somewhere the doors could open to let you out – never mind if was your intended destination.

It was while engrossed in thinking about the vagaries of the building's lift's operation, someone calling my name brought me back to reality. A woman waited by my office door. Smartly dressed, she looked nervous – and was someone I'd never met before. Acutely aware of my newspaper and chocolate cake, I tried hiding my embarrassment as I rushed to open the door and usher her to one of my ancient lounge chairs.

After dumping everything on my desk, I took over the other lounge chair. "I apologise for being out of the office when you arrived. How can I help you?"

"There's the problem. I'm not sure if you can help me. I'm not sure if it's what you do, but I didn't want to go to the police." She had my undivided attention. I encouraged her to explain. "Well, it's a chap I work with you see, and I'm not sure I even should be doing anything about it."

"Perhaps, if you tell me what is concerning you about your colleague, I'll be able to judge whether I'm the right person to help you or not."

"Okay … but it's a bit delicate. He has a wife." She paused and fidgeted uncomfortably in her chair. I groaned inwardly. Please don't let it be one of *those* situations … but she continued before I had time to become too uptight. "My concern is, he hasn't been at work all this week. It's not like him, not like him at all. He's never sick. If he ever is going to be late – like the time the road was blocked for a couple of hours by a terrible accident – he always calls to let us know."

"So, he hasn't come to work at all this week and there hasn't been any explanation for it. Am I correct so far?" she shrugged and nodded. "Are you the only person in your workplace who has noticed his absence?"

"No. Everyone's been commenting on it, but they don't know him as well as I do. They don't work as closely with him. I think they believe they shouldn't pry into someone's private affairs, and therefore don't want to know what's going on."

"Is it possible your colleague did contact someone, perhaps someone in the personnel department? Maybe management knows what's going on, but don't see the need to share it with everyone else. His reason might be something private and personal and he wouldn't want everyone knowing about."

"If he wanted anyone to know, he would tell me. We were close… We are close. Anyway, I'm sure something funny is happening. I've tried ringing his wife a few times to ask her, but she doesn't answer. I called the house number a few times before I remembered she worked somewhere during the day. Then I found her mobile number in a list he had scribbled in the diary he keeps on his desk. I tried her mobile number a few times – at different times during the day. She didn't answer her mobile either. So I followed up with a text message. I've now left four messages, but she doesn't respond."

"Have you considered she sees your interest in her husband as something more than a work colleague's concern?"

"I don't know what she thinks, or why she would think it, if she does. He is a very honourable man and respects his marriage vows. I'm only here talking to you because I'm concerned something bad has happened to him ... Or, perhaps his marriage became too much for him and he cleared out. Don't get me wrong, for him to clear out, he must've had some sort of breakdown. He would never just leave without telling anyone."

The interview was going nowhere in a rush. Still unconvinced there wasn't an ulterior motive behind her concern for her workmate, I decided to collect the man's details and bring the meeting to an end. "Before we go further, I have to admit you have me at a disadvantage. While you know who I am, I haven't asked for your name. I feel silly not knowing what to call you."

"Oh, I'm sorry. I should have introduced myself. I'm Colleen; Colleen Jenkins."

"Thank you, Colleen. It's much better being able to address you by your first name. Now, maybe you could give me a few details about the man you're worried about. Often in such cases, there is a simple explanation and it turns out there was nothing to worry about at all. I'm not suggesting it's true in this case, but let's hope so, shall we? First of all, I believe looking for your missing colleague falls within the work I do. So, I'd like to..."

"I hope you're right – and there is nothing seriously wrong, I mean. I know the people I work for are not so sure about it. They are thinking the worst of him."

"Why do you say that?" Colleen might be a good-looking, well-dressed young woman but, if I could hear, but not see her, I'd guess her age to be about fourteen. She's not lacking intelligence. It's more like there is an overwhelming childlike quality – a naivety – about her and her way of speaking.

"The bosses at work think he's done the wrong thing; made off with the firm's money or something. They've asked old Brannigan to look into everything from the last few months."

God, this is going nowhere, but becoming more confusing by the moment. "Colleen, who is old Brannigan? No, before you answer, I want to explain how the next part of our meeting works. I will ask you simple, straightforward questions, and you will give me straightforward answers to those questions. Okay?"

She bit her lip and nodded, before apologising for rambling on. "Right… so who is old Brannigan?"

"He's the firm's accountant, but he doesn't do what most accountants do. I mean he doesn't look after the accounts. He looks after purchasing and organising special deals with suppliers." I held up my hand to stop her before she launched into Mr Brannigan's history.

"I see. And what is your position in the firm?"

"Me…? Oh, I'm nothing really; nothing important. I'm just the accounts clerk."

"Right… and the man you work with, the man you are concerned about, what is his position in the business?"

"He has a much more important job than I do. He's the assistant accountant." Alarm bells started clanging as she waffled on. "It's his job to do all the accounts; to do all the bookkeeping and manage the firm's money … what comes in and what's spent, if you know what I mean."

I'm thinking I do know what you mean, My Lovely, and, more importantly, I think I know WHO you mean. "What's the name of the business where you work, Colleen?"

"You won't contact them, will you? You won't tell them I've talked to you about this?"

"Of course not. Any conversation I have with a client – or potential client – is confidential. So, where do you work?"

She gave me the company's name, and those alarm bells became deafening. We could be discussing none other than my client, Trent Martin, but I needed her to confirm it. "Right … Good … now Colleen, this man you work with and whom you are concerned about, what is his name?"

"Mr Martin – Mr Trent Martin, and he is the loveliest man to work for. In fact, I think he is the loveliest man I've ever met."

More alarm bells joined the cacophony, but different sounding ones this time. Perhaps Stella Martin has good reason for not answering Colleen's calls. Maybe she already suspected what was going on at work was more than a sound working relationship between colleagues. After taking down a few more

– probably irrelevant – details from Colleen, I brought the interview to an end.

"I understand why you feel concerned. There is nothing more we can do here this morning, but I will see if I can find out anything, and then I'll give you a call in the next day or so. How does that suit you?"

"That would be wonderful. But, there is one small problem. I don't know how much you charge for this kind of work. You see, I'm not paid much, so I don't have much money to pay you."

"Don't you worry about paying me. It's more important we look into your Mr Martin's disappearance than worry about money."

The words *your Mr Martin* made her fidget in embarrassment, and I saw a pink tinge rise up her neck to spread across her cheeks. Oh yes, perhaps Stella Martin was aware. The question is: was Mr Martin aware? It occurred to me Colleen should be at work. I didn't want her getting into trouble there for having spent so much time with me.

"Colleen, won't you be missed at work this morning? We don't want to upset your employer, do we?"

"It's okay. I swapped my day off with another girl who is getting married next Saturday. It suited her better to have my Friday off rather than today."

After 'soothing her troubled brow' as much as possible, I saw her out and on her way to enjoy the rest of her day off. Then, it was time for an overdue coffee and the chocolate cake, which had been teasing me with its siren call ever since I dumped it on my desk. With sustenance to hand and my feet up on the desk, I took time to ponder what to do about Colleen Jenkins' visit and her information. One question I didn't ask, and Colleen couldn't have answered anyway, now nagged me.

Had Trent Martin's employers attempted to contact him about his absence from work? It begs a second question. As I knew they had Stella Martin's work contact details, had they tried to contact her about her husband's absence? One thing I was certain about: I wasn't going to find answers sitting here drinking coffee and eating cake. I called Ben Richards. He might know the answers already. If not, he could find out easier than I could.

He sounded distracted when he answered and let me know he was busy. "Is this call urgent, or can it wait a while?"

"I gathered some interesting information from a visitor this morning. It can wait until you're free to discuss it."

"Organise some lunch. I'll see you around twelve o'clock."

If Ben is coming here to talk to me, the police investigation must be going nowhere as fast as mine. I occupied myself typing up my notes from Colleen Jenkins' visit, and updating my Martin case file until it was time to go in search of something for lunch. About twenty minutes later, I was back in my office with two fish and salad lunchboxes and half a dozen cupcakes. As I refilled the coffee machine, Ben arrived.

"Yes please; coffee would go down well right now," he quipped as he strode into my office. I set our coffees and lunchboxes on the low table in front of my two ancient lounge chairs. Ben lifted the lid on his lunch and looked pleased with my choice – for a moment. "Hang on…! Where are the fries? It's not normal to have fish without chips." I forgot about the pack of fries I'd put in my microwave to keep warm until Ben arrived. I fetched it and plonked it down in front of him… and received a grunt in lieu of thanks.

I didn't need to be a genius to work out Ben's day was not going well. His mood had me questioning the wisdom of bringing him here on the strength of information unlikely to result in a breakthrough in his investigation. After dispatching a couple of mouthfuls of lunch, he demanded, "So, why am I here?"

"Oh… you expected more than a free lunch?" The look he gave me curbed any further sarcasm. "This morning, a young, attractive –perhaps not too bright – woman came to hire my services to find her missing work colleague. In spite of her denial, it is obvious she carries a torch for the missing man.

Nevertheless, her concern for his welfare is genuine, and her efforts to find out what's going on have produced some interesting outcomes." I had Ben's attention.

Over the next few minutes, I acquainted him with everything Colleen told me. When I finished, I handed him a copy of my notes from this morning's meeting. "I know you confirmed with his employers Trent Martin was at work all day last Saturday, but did they say anything about his being absent from work since then?"

"No, but I don't think the person I spoke to was a member of the management team. Once the woman claimed she also spent the day at work and confirmed Martin was there, although she didn't work directly with him, I didn't see the need to check it with any higher authority."

"There isn't any question about whether he was at work. I'm interested in why Stella Martin is not responding to phone calls. The other thing I find interesting is the speed at which the business has instigated an audit of the accounts, and of Trent Martin's work in general. Did they have pre-existing concerns about something 'fishy' happening in the money department … like embezzlement, maybe?"

"Ye-es, I agree. Something smells a bit off about both the way Stella Martin is behaving and the firm's actions. What have you done about following up on any of this?"

"Nothing; there isn't any way I can go about finding answers to my questions."

"What questions do you want answered?"

"Well, in the first instance, I'm curious about Stella Martin's behaviour. She knows about her husband's situation. So, has she advised his employers about what's happened? I realise it is possible she spoke to senior management about it, but doesn't want to talk to the young woman. So, the answer might depend on whether she is aware of Colleen's feelings towards Trent Martin."

"Good point; what else nags you?"

"Does the employer know about the attack on Trent Martin,

and his current condition? Martin has been absent from work all week. Has anyone from management attempted to find out why? To extrapolate that, if management is aware of what happened to their employee, are they assuming it is as a result of some rort Martin was running at work?"

"Another good point – and it appears our thinking is along the same lines. So, you haven't followed up on any of this yet…?"

"No. Well, I can't, can I? I don't have the authority to barge in there and ask management what they know, any more than I have the right to ask Stella Martin why she isn't answering her calls."

"How do you feel about being pressed into service as a detective?"

"No, thanks. I take it your detective squad remains depleted."

"The two replacements I selected also said 'no thanks'."

"Could it be your deodorant…? At least you still have one bloke to do some legwork for you."

"If only… He only made detective six weeks ago, and doesn't have much idea about being one yet. Argh, he'll be all right with time, but he is not intuitive. So, for the foreseeable future, I'm either going to be extra busy … or I'll have to ask Pete Messell to lend me one of his Ralston detectives."

"I can imagine how the latter option would be received. According to the newspapers, Ralston is in the grip of a crime wave at the moment."

"Bugger! I haven't had time to read the paper, so I wasn't aware. Regardless, I still might ask an old friend to help out. Anyway, thanks for lunch, but I better get going if I'm going to find answers to any of your questions."

After Ben left, I enjoyed a lighter moment picturing Ben's request for a loan of one of Pete Messell's detectives. He might just pull it off. Ben, Pete and I go back a long way as close friends. Back to when the guys were young coppers stationed in Millhaven, and I was just beginning my journey to becoming a private investigator. At one stage, Ben and I looked like becoming more than good friends. Then life got in the way. I lost touch with the men for a few years after they began climbing the rankings ladder and moved around all over the state. They often competed for the same positions, but Ben always seemed to have a slight edge over Pete.

Our trio renewed its connection a few years ago when I was working a case in Ralston. That case also introduced me to Emily Ibbotson. Ben was the top cop at Ralston precinct and Pete was his understudy. When Ben became top cop in Millhaven soon after, Pete slipped into the top cop position at Ralston. At different times over the years, we've helped each other solve cases. On more than one occasion, Ben has borrowed officers from Pete, but there have been 'special' circumstances surrounding each of those occasions. While this case also merits the 'special circumstances' tag, I'm not sure the friendship runs deep enough for Pete to lend Ben one of his detectives right now.

Chapter 8

Ben had warned he might be late tonight, and arrived not much before eight o'clock. As dinner would be later than usual, leaving the office a little early allowed plenty of time to prepare a baked leg of lamb with all the trimmings. Everything was just about done when I heard his car coming up the driveway.

He announced he was starving, so no time was wasted before we sat down to eat. Although looking tired and tense when he arrived, by the end of dinner, he seemed more relaxed. Not feeling inclined to make dessert, I brought home two large wedges of a strawberries and cream filled sponge cake instead. We took them through to the lounge room with our coffees. Looking as tired as he did earlier made me reluctant to press him about what he discovered after leaving my office. My best approach was to remain silent and allow Ben to dictate how the night played out. I didn't have long to wait.

"This afternoon, I spent some time following up on information your young woman gave you this morning. I went to the office supplies place and asked to see the manager. He wasn't available, so they palmed me off to the personnel manager. She knew Trent Martin had been absent all week, but didn't know why. While I was with her, a secretary came to fetch me. The manager was available now and wanted to see me."

"How odd... Having fobbed you off, I would expect him to leave the personnel manager to deal with the matter."

"When I was fobbed off, my thinking ran along much the same lines. I had decided, if I didn't see the manager today, I would be back tomorrow, and would happily interrupt whatever he was doing. So, then I thought I wouldn't have to. Nevertheless, my meeting with him was brief and to the point."

"Because he answered your questions without hesitation, or because he was uncooperative?"

"He went through the motions of being cooperative and appearing to answer all my questions without hesitation. But, I wasn't getting the whole story, and I was running short on patience. I elected to leave and come back tomorrow with a warrant to interview management and employees. When halfway to the door, I threw in one last question to test the response."

"Don't stop there. What was the question, and what happened?"

"I asked if they had noticed anything suspicious about the way Mr Martin carried out his duties, or if he gave any indication he might be ill, or something might be troubling him?"

"Oh, that was a litmus test, given we already know they initiated an audit of his work."

"Funny thing… There was point-blank denial there were any concerns or suspicions about Mr Martin or his work. Before you ask, I *will* be back there with a warrant tomorrow."

"Did the manager confirm the personnel manager's statement about not having received any word regarding Mr Martin's absence?"

"Not to my satisfaction; I believe his answer amounted to 'no', but the way he delivered it, left it open to speculation. He claimed he was 'sure there is a very good reason Mr Martin was absent'. He was a long-time employee who never took a day off, and this led them to assume he must be ill. I asked if they had contacted Mrs Martin to confirm he was ill. His reply was: *he was sure someone had contacted her and had confirmed that to be the case.*"

"Do we believe it?"

"Not a chance; it was a boldfaced lie … And, I intend to ensure it comes back to bite him." I nodded and gave him a thumbs-up to signify my approval.

"Did you have a chance to talk to Mrs Martin this afternoon?"

"The receptionist at Mrs Martin's workplace told me Stella Martin was 'tied up' for most of the afternoon. I suppose, of itself, there was nothing wrong with that. It's quite possible she was unavailable. Nevertheless, the receptionist's apparent discomfort as she fed me the line made me think it might be a bit shy of the truth. I again flashed my badge, and asked where I might find the woman in question. When I told the woman I intended to speak to Mrs Martin regardless of what she was doing, and demanded to know where to find Mrs Martin, she was only too happy to point me in the direction of a small office where Stella Martin was drinking coffee and reading something on her computer screen."

"Oh, I do like it when you flash your badge and throw your weight around. On this occasion, did it get you anywhere?" His raucous laughter answered the question, but he did tell me about it.

"She insisted her husband's employer hadn't contacted her. She didn't think it odd, as 'she expected the police would have notified them as part of their investigation'."

"Am I to assume you might be having more words with Stella Martin in the near future?"

"While I am in the warrant-requesting frame of mind, I shall be asking for one to access her phone and her emails. Stay tuned tomorrow for the next instalment of this saga. Speaking of Stella Martin, what are your next moves to progress your investigation?"

"Frustrating though it is, I don't have anything planned until Thursday night. If she maintains her usual routine, she will go out only one night this week, and the 'outing' should take about two hours."

We had nothing else to discuss, and Ben was looking worn out again. I suggested he have an early night. He grabbed at the idea and, about ten minutes later, he was on his way home.

*****

Wednesday saw me facing another long boring day with nothing to do. It changed about mid-morning when a couple of potential clients I spoke with and sent information to last week requested appointments to see me. One kept me busy until almost lunch time. The second one took up a fair slab of my afternoon. By the end of the day I had two new clients for neither of whom I could do any work until next week at the earliest. Sometimes things work out well when you least expect it.

Ben called at about four o'clock to say he was working tonight and wouldn't see me for dinner. Damn! I was hoping to hear what the warrants he executed today produced. He did tell me there wasn't an opportunity to speak again to the manager of the office supplies firm today. It seems the man was at work, but left suddenly after telling his secretary something had come up and he wasn't sure when he would return.

At a bit after six o'clock, with my eyes glued to the Wentworth Drive intersection, I sat parked in the layby beside the road into the city. When eight o'clock rolled by, and Stella still hadn't ventured out, I opted for a quick drive along Wentworth Drive before heading home.

As usual, all the residents appeared to be indoors watching TV. Lights were on in the Martin house. I caught a glimpse of her TV through a gap in the drapes as I drove past. Good; there is nothing to suggest anything is wrong. A car was parked a little further along and on the opposite side of the street from the Martin residence. I was almost certain my headlights picked up someone sitting in the car. I slowed as I drove past and risked a long look at the car. Nobody was in it but, in a dark distant corner of my mind, a little bell was ringing.

Something about the car unnerved me. Was it the car itself, or the fact I was confident I saw someone in it when there wasn't? By the time I reached the end of Wentworth Drive, all my senses were on high alert. Instinct told me I was being followed – but no sign of headlights behind me. I switched the view on my dashboard screen to my car's rear camera. Yep, there it was. A couple of car lengths back, a vehicle with its lights off was following me. The 'no lights' was a dead give-away. Someone was up to no good – and it seemed I was the target.

I hit Ben's number and hoped he would answer. My stomach

was beginning to tighten into a squirming mass when it took several rings before he picked up. "Where are you?" I bellowed.

"In the police compound. I've just climbed into my car to go home. Sonny, what's happening? You sound like you're in trouble. Where are you?"

"I've just come out of Wentworth Drive and am heading into the city. I picked up a tail near the Martin's house in Wentworth. He' following close behind with no headlights at the moment." I heard Ben's gutsy V8 roar into life.

"Don't rush; stick with your normal speed. Swing left at the major intersection, and then turn into Green Street which runs behind the police precinct. Keep talking to me as you drive." Although we remained connected, I heard him call someone on his radio.

Almost hyperventilating, I drove to the major intersection on the High Street at the city heart. Expecting to lose the tail as I closed in on the centre of town, I kept checking the rear camera feed. The vehicle remained glued to my tail, but had closed-up to be I estimated only a car's length behind me. The gods were in my corner. I caught a green light at the major intersection and swung left onto the eastern end of the High Street. I called it to Ben as I went.

"Through the major intersection … coming up to Green Street intersection now … tail still with me … turning onto Green Street…"

"Keep driving past the police compound. Don't change speed until I tell you, and then plant your foot. Right... I have eyes on you; keep coming."

As I drew level with the exit from the police car compound, Ben yelled, "Now! Go!"

I planted the accelerator to the floor. My turbo-charged SUV bucked and skidded in response to the sudden surge of power. Out of the corner of my eye, I thought I saw an image from my rear camera flash across the screen. So busy muscling my brute of a wagon along the street, I didn't dare focus on anything else. After about a hundred metres, I slowed and eased into the kerb. The rear camera's image on the screen was of Ben's SUV parked across the road to form an effective roadblock. I tried to work out what happened.

Green Street is quite a narrow carriageway. After yelling at me, He must have shot straight out of the police compound onto the street to park across it as he was now. At the time it all happened, there wasn't much distance between me and the following vehicle. Ben must have missed hitting my car by not much, and he probably went close to slamming into the nose of the car tailing me. There appeared to be some activity happening back along the street, but Ben's car blocked my view.

Curiosity had the better of me. I slipped out of my car and ran on tiptoes to Ben's car to peer across its bonnet. The scene on the other side of the car was amazing. What I couldn't see before was, behind my tail's vehicle, a patrol car had parked across the street parallel to Ben's. Parked up close behind the tail's vehicle, the patrol car left no room for the tail to reverse and duck around Ben's car … or try anything else creative. More people than I expected were involved in the action, most of them uniformed officers.

Two officers stood, weapons drawn, on the pavement on the passenger's side of the tail's car. The second officer in the patrol vehicle jumped out and sprinted up to the driver door of the tail's vehicle and reefed open the door. His radio remained turned on and tuned into the one in Ben's vehicle. I heard the officer ask my tail, "Would you care to step out of the car please, Sir?"

The man's response, being further away from the microphone, was not as loud as the officer's voice, but loud enough to be heard clearly. His string of language was not fit for sensitive ears. In essence, he rejected the invitation with a 'no thank you', and remained in the car. Bad move … By then, the driver of the patrol car had joined the party. My tail suddenly found himself hauled out of his vehicle and kissing the bitumen.

Ben sauntered up to the man and began explaining a few things. "Sir, was there a reason you were driving without headlights tonight?" The man tried spitting at Ben but, being pinned down, couldn't get his head around far enough to do any damage. Ben continued.

"I'll take that as a 'no comment'. Right, here's what's going to happen. For starters you will be charged with dangerous operation of a motor vehicle and refusing to comply with a police directive. Your vehicle will be impounded and thoroughly searched. Is there anything you would like to tell us beforehand which later might prove to be to your advantage?"

The man's response sounded similar to his earlier one, and again amounted to a rejection of the invitation. Ben's tone became steely. "Lock him up. I'll be over to talk to him soon." Handcuffed and being uncooperative, the man was dragged to the patrol car and bundled into the back, before being driven into the police compound, and frogmarched inside – presumably to the cells.

While the scenario was playing out on the driver's side of the vehicle, on the other side of the car, the other two uniformed officers had both doors open and were searching its interior. One suddenly stood up and called across the top of the car to Ben. "Sir… Sir, take a look at this." He ducked down again and Ben leaned in to see what was of interest. "In here, Sir; in the door pocket … a weapon, Sir."

"Well done, Constable. Bag it. Our friend's list of charges just became longer. Okay, Lads, that will do for now. Stay with the vehicle until the truck comes to collect it. Then, follow it back to the forensic team's lock-up and make sure it is logged and secured properly."

I heard Ben murmur to himself as he walked around to get into his car, "Right, now for a little chat with our friend."

Then he noticed me standing there. "What the hell are you still doing here? I thought you would go home. Silly of me, I know. Have you eaten this evening?" I shook my head. "Neither have I. Do you think your kitchen might run to even as much as a toasted cheese sandwich at this hour of the night?"

"Of course I could manage something along those lines."

"Good; I'll see you at your place in about half an hour. Now, go home."

With no wriggle room available, I did as I was told. After dumping my bag, I returned to the kitchen. I had two nice steaks in the fridge. I took them out and put them on the bench to come to room temperature. While at the fridge, I remembered I had a bag of new potatoes. A few of those went on to cook while I went to freshen up. Feeling half human again, I started on a salad. Ben arrived as I finished making the salad.

"Nice looking steaks," as he stood at the kitchen bench. "Do you want me to throw those on the barbeque?"

"No, I'll do them in here. There's salad and jacket potatoes to go with them. Okay…?" The menu met with his approval. We were both starving by the time we sat down to eat. Unfortunately, dessert amounted to nothing more again than TimTams with our coffee.

Settled in the lounge room with our coffees and biscuits, there was no surprise when conversation focused on tonight's events. As usual, Ben opened our 'conversation' with an interrogation. "When you called, you said you picked up the tail on Wentworth Drive. Why were you there? You said you weren't going to do anything until tomorrow night."

"Since I didn't have to rush home for dinner, I thought I would check Stella Martin didn't break her usual routine by going out tonight as well." I outlined my movements from when I set up for surveillance soon after 6:30, through until I picked up my tail.

"Did you get the impression the car was waiting in Wentworth Drive for you to come by?

"No-o, I don't think so. I can't be sure why he was there, but he was quick to decide to follow me after I drove past. As I came along the street, I'm sure my headlights picked up the outline of someone in the driver's seat. Then, when I was closer, and as I drove past, the vehicle appeared empty."

"So, what are you saying? He was waiting for you or he wasn't?"

"As I said, I can't be sure. When I first noticed someone sitting in the car, I thought they might be watching the Martin house. Maybe he was keeping an eye on Stella Martin. What did the bloke have to say about his activities tonight?"

"Not a thing; the only thing of any consequence was to tell me I could do what I liked, but he was saying nothing; 'other people scared him more than I did'."

"Hmm … it suggests Stella Martin has become involved in some way with an unsavoury bunch. Did you learn anything else at all?"

"Yep… The vehicle he was driving was reported stolen from northern New South Wales about two weeks ago. So, your 'unsavoury bunch' appears to have long tentacles stretching interstate. Now, if we could just work out what their game is, we might be able to start closing them down."

"If their operation crosses state borders, might your brother, Neil, receive a phone call in the near future?"

"There's a real possibility. I was thinking I'd call him tomorrow morning to see if the Federal Police have anything on their books with possible links to whatever's going on here at the moment. I was hoping to have a bit more information on the operation here before calling him, but it seems I won't have."

"When will the forensic gang go through the vehicle? Maybe they will find clues about what this mob is into."

"I requested forensics start work on it tonight, but I doubt they'll have anything for me by morning. Anyway, it's been a long day. I might call it a night. Before I leave, perhaps you should forewarn me about whatever your plans are for tomorrow night."

"Tomorrow night is the alternate Thursday. If reports are correct, Stella Martin should leave home at her usual time and be gone for about a couple of hours. I'll be working surveillance again tomorrow night. Somehow, I doubt she'll go back to the derelict building in the slum area after what happened there, so it will be interesting to see where she does go and what she does there. Who she meets might be interesting too."

Our night ended on a slightly sour note. Ben was not happy about my plans for tomorrow night, but stopped just short of ordering me not to follow Stella Martin. I guess he knew he wouldn't have stopped me anyway.

After he left, I poured myself a single malt nightcap and spent some time analysing tonight's events and planning tomorrow night's.

*****

A rugged night troubled by bad dreams had me out of bed late this morning. Once I finally levered myself upright, I felt a distinct lack of urgency about anything, including going into my city office. Devoting more than two hours to domestic chores is an indication of the depth of my blue funk. Over yet another cup of coffee at about ten o'clock, I tried to work out what was wrong with me. Was this some form of delayed reaction to last night's events, or was it something else about the case? Was it down to my inability to progress it? With no answers, credible or otherwise, presenting, I headed into the city and was in my office by midday.

After writing up my notes on last night's events, I set up case files for yesterday's two new clients, and entered a reminder in my diary to contact them next week to confirm the investigations' start dates. The rest of the afternoon comprised a few hours of boredom, except for a visit from Emily. Having worked much of the night and all morning, she clocked off for the day at about 2:30. Bearing a box of cream doughnuts, she came for coffee and spent about an hour with me.

It wasn't just a social visit. She had overseen the stripping down of my tail's impounded vehicle, and thought I might be interested in what they found. While, in some ways, it amounted to very little, it was interesting. Her lab was still analysing some of the material taken from the vehicle, so there might be more information to come. Patience is not my strong suit, but I had no option except to exercise some, at least until tomorrow anyway.

I had just about read every word off every page of the local newspaper by the time six o'clock rolled around. After again visiting the drive-through for chicken and chips, I headed to the north side of town. As I pulled into my now familiar layby beside the road into the city, I considered whether it was foolhardy to continue to use the same location for my surveillance. A quick drive further along the road and back again provided me with no better option, so I pulled into my layby and began sampling the chicken and chips.

With the takeaway boxes emptied some time ago, I was becoming fidgety. Seven o'clock ticked by ten minutes ago with still no sign of Stella Martin exiting Wentworth Drive. Was my information incorrect? Had I missed seeing her? Was there a change of plans as a result of recent events? Was the threat too great for her to leave home? Questions were queueing up to flash through my mind, but there wasn't an answer in sight. I was debating whether a cruise along Wentworth Drive might be useful, when I saw her car turn out onto the road into the city.

I pulled into traffic a couple of vehicles behind her, and felt the old familiar adrenaline rush that is the thrill of the chase.

Chapter 9

At the major intersection on the High Street, Stella Martin turned left. In spite of everything, she was heading to the slum area again tonight. I too swung left at the lights and followed her. The big difference was, traffic in her lane had slowed to a crawl as it followed a semitrailer, which appeared to be searching for an address in the light industrial area. As one of only three cars in the other lane, I was able to speed past Stella Martin's vehicle.

I turned off onto the street prior to the one leading to the derelict two-storey building. From about halfway along, the street I turned onto was lined by abandoned light industrial workshops. A former cabinet maker's building set back some distance from the street was fronted by a large concreted area to accommodate customer parking and to allow trucks to turn without disrupting traffic on the street. I drove in and parked close to the side of the building. Then, on foot, I picked my way around rubbish and over broken-down fences as I made my way through the block and onto the next street to watch the two-story building.

An old, now overgrown mango tree across the road and slightly further along from the two-storey building offered an ideal place for surveillance. It created a large area of dense shadow. Within that shadow, I discovered the stump of another tree felled long ago. It would provide a comfortable enough seat while I waited for whatever was going to happen tonight. Before I made myself comfortable, I needed to ascertain the current situation.

Across the road from my vantage point was a crumbling single-storey house. The remnants of a fence separated what was once the house's driveway from that of the two-storey place next door. I dashed across the street and started picking my way along beside the house. There was just enough moonlight to see where I was putting my feet. All went well until I was about halfway along the driveway. My shin contacted something large, metal and heavy, hidden in a patch of shadow. The object didn't move but I felt an egg developing on my shin. In the back corner of the yard, beside the fence, was a shrub that had become a straggly small tree. I eased my way into its dark shadow, and pulled myself up on the rickety fence until I could just see over the top.

Two vehicles were parked behind the building next door. One was an expensive sporty-looking model. I thought it odd they chose to reverse park at the rear of the cleared area, as opposed to nosed into the building. Perhaps more vehicles were expected, and required some management of parking arrangements. No sound came from the building, but a faint glow was evident in its back room. The light was so weak, it didn't extend beyond the doorway.

The little voice in my head told me this was an ideal place from which to watch what happened next door. My gut had other ideas, and insisted I get to hell out of there. My policy has always been 'when in doubt, stick with your gut', so I picked my way out to the street and dashed back to my mango tree over the road. The old stump proved not as comfortable as I'd hoped, but was better than standing up or sitting on the ground. In the end, I wasn't sitting there long enough for it to matter.

About five minutes after I planted my rear end on the stump, headlights appeared in the street. Stella Martin's car slowed. It turned onto the driveway of the derelict two-storey building and disappeared around the back. The uncomfortable tree stump was history. I was on my feet and poised ready for a hasty retreat if needed. The weight of my Glock in the pocket of my cargo pants was reassuring.

I waited – and wondered. What am I supposed to do now? What are they doing in there? How long will it take? Should I go back across the street for another look over the fence? They are bound to be in that back room, so I won't see anything by peering over the fence anyway. Still, the temptation to take a look was strong. After about ten minutes, I began to weaken. Venturing out from under the mango tree, but staying deep within shadows, I inched further along the block until I was opposite the two-storey building's driveway. What a waste of time, I told myself. All I could see was the driveway. I returned to the mango tree and my stump.

As I sought the most comfortable position on the stump, I thought I heard a sound. Forget the stump! I was on my feet again; ears straining for any sound from across the street. The seconds ticked by. No sound. No movement. I was lining up to plant my backside on the stump again when I heard it.

Soft and muffled somehow; maybe a car door being closed gently? It was followed by a series of soft, muffled thumps. A dog further along the street voiced its objection to being disturbed by the unfamiliar sounds. Then there was another sound; a different sound. My blood ran cold and the hairs on the back of my neck stood up. I inched further back in the shadows, until my back was pressed hard up against the mango tree's rough trunk.

Was it someone attempting to shout or cry out? Maybe it was just a loud response to a surprise or something funny. … Could even be someone stifling a cough, I tried convincing myself. I wasn't successful. It wasn't a cough, but that didn't make me feel any easier. A few more muffled thumps followed. My panic level almost hit the critical zone. My gut wasn't helping by telling me something unpleasant was happening in that building. Damn it! I had to try looking over the fence. I tiptoed out to the edge of the dense shadow … before beating a hasty retreat to press myself again to the tree trunk.

This time there was no mistaking it. That was a car door closing none too quietly. A powerful motor growled. Seconds later, a vehicle careened down the driveway at high speed. It roared down the street, before turning back towards the city.

Okay, that's one gone. Now, what about the other vehicle? As that question flitted through my mind, a bigger one elbowed it to one side: why hadn't Stella Martin left first? Shit; I don't like the way this is shaping up. Dare I risk crossing the road to look over the fence? If I do chance it, am I likely to be skittled in the middle of the street by the other vehicles leaving the building? A moment later, another car door slammed. The sound of another vehicle coming down the driveway put paid to any thoughts of crossing the street.

The second vehicle I'd seen there earlier followed the previous departure and headed back towards the city heart. Common sense told me all that remained at the building were Stella Martin and her car. My gut insisted I couldn't be sure of that. How did I know there weren't other people still in the building? What if one of those other vehicles had more than just the driver in it when it arrived? I was reasonably sure the two vehicles I watched leave were occupied by only their drivers, but that wasn't much help at this juncture.

For a few minutes, I was a mass of writhing internal turmoil and nervous energy. I prowled about under the mango tree. Sat on my stump and bounced up again. Snuck out to the edge of the shadows and checked the street for any signs of activity. Nothing… You would be forgiven for thinking, in a place with the ambience of a morgue, unknown vehicles roaring about in the night would generate some interest … but apparently they don't.

Time for desperate measures; I sized up the width of the street. How long would it take me to cross the street and be in the shadows in the yard on the other side? Only one way to find out. A couple of deep breaths and I raced across the street as though the devil himself was behind me. Avoiding the thing that attacked my shin previously, I made my way to the scraggly shrub in the back corner of the yard. A quick peep over the fence showed me what I expected to see there – well, more or less.

Stella Martin's car remained parked nose-in to the building. The soft light evident earlier in the back room had disappeared. I devoted a couple of seconds of thought to the matter. No light might mean nobody remained in the building. Perhaps Stella

Martin left in one of the other vehicles, and would collect her own car later. That idea didn't wash. I hadn't seen a passenger in either of the vehicles. Still, that might have been by design. Perhaps they didn't want anyone to see Stella Martin in one of those vehicles.

Argh hell; this was achieving nothing other than tying my stomach in even tighter knots. Nothing for it, I told myself. Go and find out. The idea didn't appeal and, being not one for playing the hero, the hesitation continued for at least another minute or two. While I stood there, my ears, and probably every nerve in my body, were on high alert for any sounds emanating from the building. Even the dog down the street didn't pick up anything. I turned and picked my way out of the yard and around the end of the fence to the entrance of the neighbouring driveway.

Sticking as close as possible to the wall of the building, I eased my way along to the back corner. A quick glance around the corner showed nothing in the backyard had changed since I last looked over the fence. Piles of junk and other rubbish made it impossible to stay close to the rear wall. I paused at the doorstep, more to try quietening my thumping heart than for anything else. The silence felt heavy and cloying.

A moment to prepare myself, and I was on my way in with my Glock in one hand and a torch in the other. No need to progress too far into the room to understand the sounds I heard earlier. Ignoring my first impulse, I stood glued to the spot and played my torch over every inch of the room. Then, it was time to give in to that initial impulse. I ran to the body sprawled on the floor in the centre of the room.

"Jesus; don't let her be dead," I implored the universe as, down on my haunches and struggling to find a pulse, I again scanned the room. My first attempt found none. I took a moment to steady myself before trying for the carotid. There it was; weak and a bit thready. But, she was alive. I placed my torch on the floor and swapped my Glock to the other hand so I could extract my phone from one of the cavernous pockets of my cargo pants.

For a few moments, I thought Ben wasn't going to answer. Then he growled, "Is this urgent?"

"Only if you're interested in saving a badly injured woman's life," I snarled back.

"Are you injured?"

"No, but someone I think is Stella Martin is in a bad way on the floor or that two-storey building in the slum area. If you're not interested, I'm calling the paramedics myself."

"Don't do anything. Are you safe being there?"

"As far as I can tell there's no one else here now."

"Are you armed?" I told him I was. "Good. Stay there. I'm on my way."

About the same time as I heard a vehicle bouncing its way along the driveway, I heard the wail of sirens approaching. "Are you still in there, Sonny?" Ben yelled. "I'm coming in, so don't shoot." As if I would – but I didn't say so.

Ben came and crouched down beside me, before trying for the woman's pulse. "Hmm; just about alive; the paras are on their way."

"Is it Stella Martin?" In the torchlight, I saw Ben nod, but he said nothing. Then he was on his feet again and moving away.

"I'll be back in a second. Don't touch anything or move her." I heard a car door open and close and, a moment later, Ben returned carrying a sizeable bag and a camera.

He photographed Stella from just about every imaginable angle before turning his attention – and his camera – on the rest of the room. I heard another vehicle easing its way along the rough driveway. Ben went out to meet the new arrivals, and was followed back into the room by two teal-uniformed paramedics. As the room was small, Ben, the two paramedics and their gear, and Stella Martin, occupied almost all available space. When the paramedics came in with Ben, I took myself outside to wait until they were done with the patient. I suspected it was going to take some time before they wheeled her out, so I made myself comfortable on an upturned rusty drum.

It felt like hours before I heard them trying to manoeuvre the gurney out through the restricted doorway, but it probably wasn't more than twenty minutes. Ben remained inside, and I heard him barking orders on a hand-held radio. As if by magic, a tall slim man in civvies strode around the corner of the building and disappeared inside. I assumed this was Ben's sole remaining member of his detective squad. After allowing him a few moments alone with Ben, I started back inside to see what was happening.

Ben met me at the door. "Best you don't come in and disturb anything further. Where is your vehicle? Is it close by?" I explained about leaving it in the next street and walking through the block to avoid any attention. "Okay, come on. I'll drive you back to your car. Then you must go home. I'll see you at your office first thing in the morning." There was no further conversation from either of us on the drive to my car, and nothing more than a cursory 'good night' when he dropped me there. I was barely out of his car before he was on his way back to the crime scene.

Going home wasn't what I wanted to do, but there were few other options. And, I didn't know what else to do if I didn't go home. So, I did as I was told.

A large single malt accompanied me to my home office. I opened my Martin case file and added my notes from tonight. Then, I fished out my phone and flicked through to the photos I took. So, this is Stella Martin. She was an attractive looking woman before someone worked her over.

Even in the short time after she was attacked and before I photographed her, the bruises had developed strong colour. She had a busted lip, possibly a broken nose, and an eye so badly damaged and swollen, she couldn't open it if she were conscious. As I printed out the photos to add to my file, I wondered what the rest of her looked like. Had they just worked on her face, or would her torso tell much the same story? Whatever mess she had gotten herself into, it involved dangerous people. Stella could count herself lucky she didn't end up like the previous woman we found there.

In spite of my best efforts to shut tonight's images out of my mind, it took sleep some time to arrive, and a rough night followed.

*****

As promised – or should that be 'threatened' – Ben followed me into my office about five minutes after I arrived this morning. He left me in no doubt it wasn't a social call, and went straight to the reason for his visit. "Tell me about your escapade last night. Start from when you left here, and leave nothing out, regardless of how unimportant it might seem."

In spite of what developed into a hair-raising event, it didn't last long. By nine o'clock, I was home again with a scotch and examining those shocking photos of a damaged Stella Martin. Recounting my story of last night took even less time; no more than a few minutes. As I finished my story, I jumped in with the question I'd wanted to ask since Ben's arrival. "How is Stella Martin this morning? And, where is she?"

"She is in hospital under an assumed name, and being guarded around the clock. They tell me her injuries are not life-threatening. She has a couple of broken ribs and a severe concussion. It goes without saying, I won't be talking to her for a couple of days or so."

"Did you find anything useful at the scene?"

"Nothing I would describe as 'useful', but I'm waiting to see what forensics tell us when they're finished with it. What can you tell me about the other two vehicles that were at the building?" His question reminded me of something. I grabbed my phone.

"Hang on a minute." I flicked through the photos to one I took prior to those of Stella Martin. It wasn't too clear with only the moon lighting the area. "These are the vehicles parked at the building before Stella arrived. Later on, I watched them leave. That one went first and, a couple of minutes later, the other one followed. I can't give you much information about the colour of them. I think the sporty-looking one was a pale colour; maybe something like sky blue. The SUV was dark, but I don't think it was dark enough to be black. It might have been more like a charcoal-grey colour."

"Can you print me a copy of the photo?" I nodded and sent it to my Wi-Fi printer. "And, while you're about it, I'll have copies of the other photos you took last night too." If I knew his mother, I'd have a word to her about his lack of manners. It wouldn't hurt to say please. Even so, I wasn't left with much option other than to print my photos of Stella for him.

That seemed to bring my interrogation to an end. Ben went to stand, and then changed his mind. "You could offer me a coffee before I leave. The coffee at my workplace is terrible."

"Ye-es, I could offer you a coffee – but only if you tell me about Trent Martin's current condition." There was his rumbling trademark chuckle, and it told me we were back to being mates again.

"When I checked yesterday afternoon, I was told he was holding his own. I queried what that meant, and was told it meant there had been no change. Earlier this morning I went in to check on Stella's condition – not that I expected any change. They told me she was as comfortable as she could be, and her vital signs were stronger. So, I asked again about her husband. This time, they told me there had been 'a surprising improvement in his condition overnight'. I asked for an explanation, but didn't get one. So, now you know as much as I do … And where is the coffee you were going to make me?"

He studied my photos while drinking his coffee but, as soon as his mug was drained, he was gone. Now I needed a coffee to help work out where-to-next with my investigation. Mindful I might have two new cases starting next week, I felt pressured to wrap up the Martin case as soon as possible. If I'm desperate, I suppose what comes out of the police investigation into Stella Martin's attack might be enough to provide her husband with some of the answers he wanted.

Chapter 10

Friday night saw a return to normal post-working day routine. Neither Ben nor I were working tonight. Ben arrived about seven o'clock. We put the day to bed over a drink and a chat to fill in time until the stew I made was ready. It was inevitable conversation would focus on both of our Martin cases.

Instead of just asking how my client, Trent Martin, was progressing, I now had both his and his wife's conditions to ask about. It was frustrating having to rely on Ben's second-hand reports but, as both husband and wife were part of ongoing police investigations, I had to accept that's how it would remain for a while yet. I asked the now familiar question, "Did you check on the Martins' condition this afternoon?"

"Yes, but there is not much to report. He continues to show slight improvement. Although they haven't said as much, I think they might be quietly hopeful he will pull through. On the other hand, there seems to be little change in Stella Martin's condition."

"So, she is still unconscious…?"

"I think she is in an induced coma. I'm not sure what the difference is. I still can't talk to her. They tell me it is to aid the healing process – to help ease the trauma or something. They probably will keep her that way for a day or two, depending on her progress."

"While that's to be expected, it doesn't help either of our investigations. Changing the subject, did you contact Pete Messell about borrowing one of his detectives?"

Ben gave a wry smile. "My ever so polite request met with a point -blank refusal. It appears his situation isn't any better than mine in that regard. As you pointed out, Ralston is in the grip of a major crime wave. About four days ago, one of Pete's detectives was shot and seriously wounded in the course of an investigation. He is likely to require a long recovery. Another of his detectives is on leave. Pete tried recalling him, only to discover the man was backpacking around Europe with his brother and nobody was sure how or where to contact him. It seems Pete is back being a detective in his spare time just as I am. He put in a request to Brisbane for a detective on temporary transfer, but hasn't had a response yet."

"Couldn't you try something similar? Doesn't the situation here warrant the temporary transfer of at least one detective to help out?"

"Our situation is not nearly as critical as Ralston's. I don't mean we don't need some help. Because they have a recognised crime wave, Brisbane is more likely to hear his plea than mine. So long as no other major incident occurs, we can muddle along with just the one detective until we receive two new appointees. The only major investigation here is the Martin case. It looks like I'll be working that one on my own until it's wrapped up."

"I know the opportunities are limited but, if there is any way I can help, let me know. I do have a couple of new investigations possibly starting next week. If I can finish my investigation for Trent Martin, I should have spare time to help you out. By the way, did they collect any useful forensics from Stella's crime scene?"

"They bagged or fingerprinted everything that stood still long enough. There wasn't much to be had, and how useful any of it will be doesn't look too promising."

There wasn't much left to discuss over dinner, or over coffee afterwards, so it resulted in an early night. Ben left at about nine o'clock. After unsuccessfully surfing TV channels for an hour or so for something worth watching, I was in bed with a book by ten o'clock.

*****

Saturday and Sunday dragged by without a breakthrough of any sort on either of the Martin investigations. I was becoming desperate. I half expected both my new clients to call on Monday to tell me to begin their cases. It's a shame they didn't ring me on Thursday or Friday. I could have been gainfully occupied on investigations – even over the weekend – instead of sitting around twiddling my thumbs waiting to talk to at least one of the Martins.

About mid-morning on Sunday, Ben lobbed on my doorstep. It was unlike him to arrive without calling first to make sure I was home. When I opened the door, his first comment was, "Have you got coffee on the go at the moment?"

A bit taken aback by the whole situation, I shook my head while searching for a reasonable reply. "No-o, I did think about coffee a few minutes ago, but I haven't done anything about it."

"Well, could you do something about it now, please?" How could I refuse such a desperate request?

We took our coffees and the cupcakes I'd bought the day before out onto the deck. After a few sips of coffee, and Ben was halfway through a cupcake, I judged the time was right to ask the question. "What brings you to my door in such a grumpy mood on this fine Sunday morning? Has there been a new development of some sort?"

"You could say that. 'Some sort' just about describes it. I went to the hospital this morning to check on Stella Martin's condition. They brought her out of the coma overnight, and allowed me a couple of minutes to talk to her."

"Don't knock it. That's a breakthrough. How did your chat go?"

"Oh, swimmingly… I 'chatted' – as you put it – and she kept her mouth firmly closed. If you need a translation: she refused to talk to me."

"No doubt you explained the folly of her behaviour…"

"I tried every approach I could think of to make her understand how precarious her position was, if we couldn't apprehend the people who attacked her. I also explained how we believed the same people who roughed her up were responsible for her husband's still critical situation. Nothing I did or said changed anything. She was determined not to talk to me."

After a minute or so of sitting in silence sipping coffee and munching cupcakes, the germ of an idea was starting to make its presence felt in the back of my mind. I gave it a mental nudge, and it developed into half-grown proposal. The only way to define it properly was to gives it oxygen. So, I did. "Ben, do you think she didn't want to speak to anyone, or was it more a case of her not wanting to speak to a big, burly copper?"

"I didn't do anything to intimidate her, if that's what you're suggesting."

"No, that's not where I was coming from. What if someone else tried talking to her? Another woman, maybe…? I'm not saying she would open up immediately to another woman but, with careful handling, she might loosen up and start talking."

"Where is this leading? I hear what you're saying but I'm not sure what's behind it. How would that work? And, do you have someone in mind for the job? I don't have any female officers I would feel confident to give such a task."

"Okay … I wasn't sure where it was heading either when I floated the idea but talking about it has helped it crystallise. What if I were to try getting her to talk about what happened and, more importantly, why?"

"At the moment, anything is worth a shot. I don't know why you think you might be successful, if she just doesn't want to talk about it. It's possible that, like the bloke in my cells at the moment, there are others she is more frightened of than us."

"Here's an idea from left field: what if I went in undercover and spent a bit of time gaining her trust, and generally working on loosening her up a bit?"

"How are you going to go in undercover?"

"You're the top cop in this area, can't you arrange with the hospital for me to be there as an undercover nurse, or some other type of staff person, who might come and talk to her from time to time?"

"O-o-h … Aah, I might just go and make a couple of phone calls. Don't eat all those cakes while I'm away."

"As if I would…"

What have I gotten myself into? I'm not sure how this is going to work – or if there is even a chance it could work. It's all down to the hospital now, and whether they will allow something like this. Would going undercover as a nurse work, or might it be better if I appeared to be one of the domestic staff; someone who brings the meals around perhaps? I was still mulling it over when Ben returned from making his phone calls.

"We have an appointment at the hospital in half an hour to discuss the finer details of how this is going to work. Prepare to be busy for the next few days. I don't know whether this has any chance of working, but it's the only option we have at the moment." Ben could be persuasive when he put his mind to it, and it looks like he's triumphed again.

Our meeting at the hospital went well. Ben refrained from being his usual officious self, and allowed me free-rein to present and discuss my proposal. The hospital readily agreed to my becoming an 'honorary domestic staff member' for a trial period of a week. The woman who runs that side of the operation was called to our meeting. I was introduced, and our plan explained to her. After only a few moments thought, she laid out how she saw my undercover stint could work – without arousing the suspicions of the other domestic staff, or anyone else. Not one to waste time apparently, she set-up an orientation session for three o'clock that afternoon to ensure I was ready to begin my new role first thing Monday morning.

By the time we left the hospital, it was almost lunchtime. We picked-up a couple of salad boxes on the way back to my place, and Ben stayed for lunch. He was concerned I hadn't thought through what I had let myself in for from tomorrow, and asked at least three times during lunch if I was sure about going undercover.

I tried reassuring him but, the third time he asked, exasperation got the better of me. "Ben, I don't know what more I can say to reassure you. I want to do this, and I will be all right."

"What about your own work? You can't just ignore your clients for however long this other thing takes."

"True; but my only open case at the moment is Trent Martin's. Yes, I do have two new investigations which might kick off in this coming week, but there are no definite dates for those yet. When they do commence, both will involve night work. I will be able to fit it in with my undercover work at the hospital during the day. Thanks to the yarn we concocted to explain my presence as a part-time casual domestic staff person, I have the flexibility to adjust my hours at the hospital to suit whatever else I have happening."

Ben left soon after one o'clock. I breathed a sigh of relief. Now I could sit quietly to think about how to present myself, not only to Stella Martin, but also to other domestic staff I might encounter. The time slipped by quickly, and I soon found myself fronting up for my orientation session.

Thanks to the manager of Domestic Services having thought out how to make it work for me, my orientation, though comprehensive, did not take long. I was soon on my way home again to prepare myself for my first undercover session at six o'clock tonight, when I would be delivering Stella Martin's evening meal. During the rest of the afternoon, I just about exhausted myself with constant mental rehearsal of the introductory spiel I would deliver with Stella's meal tonight.

Trepidation was my companion as I wheeled the trolley along the corridor to Stella's room. A uniformed officer lounged conspicuously in a chair opposite her door. I gave him a smile and a nod as I pushed the door open with my backside. In my best cheery, broad and unrefined voice, I embarked on what I hoped would be a fruitful undertaking.

"Hello love, I've brought your dinner." As I clattered the meal onto her mobile table thing, I kept up the patter. "Can you manage all this on your own, Love, or do you need a hand with anything? I'm only new and haven't brought your meals before, so you'll have to tell me what you'd like me to do … You know, if you need a hand with anything, I mean."

Her face initially remained blank and unresponsive. For a moment, I wondered if this was too early. Perhaps she hadn't fully recovered from her coma. But, I hadn't spent all afternoon rehearsing this evening only to draw a blank. So I soldiered on. I watched her face change as I continued. By the time I was almost finished messing about with her dinner, a confused look occupied her face. As I flapped open her napkin and reached over to spread it across her, I kept up the prattle.

"My goodness, Dearie, you have had a hard time. Car accident, was it? Hit the dashboard did we … or was it the airbag? Was another vehicle involved?"

She shook her head again. Out the corner of my eye, I caught her give a half-hearted shake of her head when I asked if a car accident caused her injuries. I ran with her response to the question about another vehicle being involved.

"Well, that's good isn't it, Love? If there wasn't another vehicle involved, it means there isn't another driver left dealing with his wounds too. Still, however it happened, you've done a good job on yourself. Now, like I said, if you need something, or you want a hand to do something, you just say. Don't be shy … Like, if you want your meat cut up for you, just say so. I'm happy to do that for you."

This time I received a slight nod and almost a lopsided smile in response to my offer of help. Come to think of it, she probably couldn't smile properly with her face in the state it was. Rather than lay it on too much on my first visit, as soon as she was ready to start eating, I said good night and told her I'd see her again in the morning.

Once I returned the trolley to the kitchen and changed out of my uniform, I was on my way home. While I expected to be hungry after spending time around food, I wasn't. I also wasn't aware of how tonight's performance had registered with Stella Martin. After pouring myself a drink, I took it out onto the deck to help review this evening's efforts. I barely made myself comfortable before I saw lights coming up my driveway. It was Ben.

"While I was at the hospital checking on Trent Martin's condition, I checked if you were still there. They told me you had gone home. I've brought Chinese for dinner if that's okay."

Of course it was okay, and the mention of it ignited my hunger. We didn't discuss my first undercover session until we retired to the lounge room after dinner. But, as soon as we sat down, the interrogation began. It seemed ridiculous, but I wasn't sure how my target audience had rated my performance.

"All I can tell you is that she didn't ask me to leave, or call for someone to chuck me out. Maybe that's a good sign. If I'm not kidding myself, I think it went okay. I think she was beginning to warm to me. We'll see what tomorrow brings. Maybe, by the end of the day, I'll have a better idea of how the operation is progressing."

In spite of the many questions being asked, there was little more I could add. Eventually, he accepted that was the case. It gave me the opportunity to ask about Trent Martin.

"They assured me he is continuing to make slow improvement. I'm sure they're right but, so far, I haven't seen any evidence of it. To me, his condition appears to be much the same as when he was admitted to hospital. To date, the only positive thing to happen with my case is placing you undercover in the hospital."

There's nothing quite like applying pressure to someone who really doesn't know what they're doing anyway. But, it was another early night, and tomorrow was another day that would start early with the delivery of breakfast.

*****

Everything went according to plan this morning, and I soon was pushing the trolley along the corridor to Stella Martin's room. After another cheery smile and a nod to the constable on duty, I was clattering Stella's breakfast out in front of her. Get the prattle going again, I reminded myself.

"Good morning, Love, how are you feeling today? You're not missing much being in here. It's a miserable day outside. Can you manage that fruit okay? You don't need me to help you with it? Okay, that's good. Do you have anything happening today; doctor's visit, physiotherapy, x-rays, anything scheduled?"

Stella shook her head and looked a bit downcast in response to my question. I quickly came up with a response I thought might help loosen things. "That's not good. It's a long day with nothing to do but lie here in bed all day. Do you have anything to read? I don't see anything on your locker. I could slip down to the shop for a magazine or a book."

She hesitated before shaking her head. Keep it going, keep it going, the little voice in my head kept chanting.

"It would be no trouble, Love. I could slip down as soon as I finish the breakfast run. You might need to tell me what you like to read though. If you leave it up to me to choose, you could end up with something you can't stand. Oh, I just thought of something else. I could pick you up some fruit as well while I'm down at the shop. Would you like me to do that? Like I said, Love, it's no trouble, and it might help with the boredom of just lying here."

A-a-h, at last a real response… She gave me a lopsided smile. It must've hurt because I saw her hand fly up to the side of her face. This time, the smile had travelled through to her eyes … well, to one eye, as the other one was still swollen closed. I reiterated my offer to fetch something from the shop downstairs for her, and added a bit more for good luck.

"Others in here have visitors come to see them; parents, kids, husbands, whatever. You don't seem to have any visitors. I know it's hard when you are a long way from home and all on your own. Well, you don't have to think of yourself as being on your own. I can help you, and bring you things."

"That's very kind of you, but I don't think I'd be able to read much before my one good eye started to complain. Why are none of the other domestic staff here so helpful and obliging?"

"Oh well, now, I don't know about that. Maybe they don't have time. I'm only new here. They put me on part-time casual because they are a bit short-staffed, what with people being on holidays, and a couple of others being off sick. My days are much better than yours I suspect. I come into work for a couple of hours here, and a couple of hours there during the day. Sometimes, it's easier to just stay here and read a book or something to fill in time between my shifts. So, you see, I have plenty of time to do things for the patients."

The day progressed slowly, but well in terms of my undercover project. I visited Stella again at morning tea, lunch, afternoon tea, and then dinner time. During my dinnertime visit, we had a little chat. Nothing of any consequence but it was a start. She asked how I filled in my day, and if the weather had improved. I asked her about her day. There were no surprises in what she told me. She was bored, and had slept a lot.

"Don't be concerned about sleeping a lot. It will help you recover. I don't know much about it, but I've been told the best thing to do when you're sick or injured is to sleep. So, you should keep doing that, and not worry about it."

My second full day on the job progressed well and I made further progress in terms of conversation. When confident we had established a reasonable connection, I decided to revisit something I'd asked her the first time I was in her room.

"I can't remember… Did you tell me it was a car accident you had?"

"No. No, it wasn't a car accident. It was just an unfortunate event."

"It must've been one hell of an event to leave you like this. What sort of an event are we talking about? Oh, I'm sorry. I shouldn't be prying. Take no notice of me, Love. You don't have to tell me anything. But, I do feel a bit concerned for you, what with all your injuries and the copper sitting outside your door. Do you feel safe enough in here? I don't know what happened to you, but I know it was bad. Even I can see that. And, it looks like the police share my concern that whoever did this might try again. Why else would they station a copper outside your door? What happens when he goes for a coffee? Even cops have to go to the toilet sometime. Who is minding your door when that happens? I'm sorry, Love. I shouldn't be saying these things. You're probably worried enough without me reminding you about it."

"There's no need to apologise. Thanks for your concern. You are right. I am aware of all that and, I have to admit, I am scared. I'd much rather be out of here; to just disappear to some place where nobody would find me."

"Yeah, that might be a good move … If you were well enough to be out of here. To me, you don't look like you're fit to be released any time soon. Anyway, if and when they do let you out, if you're still concerned about what might happen to you, surely the police might be able to arrange to hide you somewhere for a while."

She agreed that was a nice thought, but it was no more than a pipedream. I didn't pursue the matter. After a none too subtle check on the time, I made a hasty retreat, claiming I needed to return the trolley to the kitchen before a supervisor came looking for me. About ten minutes later, I keyed in Ben's number as made my way to my car. Yes, he was available tonight and would bring something for dinner.

Now, all I have to do before he arrives is work out how to sell the idea of stashing Stella Martin at some secret location as soon as she is able to be moved.

The suggestion didn't sound too outlandish … if you said it quickly!

Chapter 11

On Ben's arrival, our opening conversation dealt with the conditions of Mr and Mrs Martin. From Ben's point of view, although the doctors were telling him Trent Martin continued to improve slowly, he couldn't see any change in the man. I was happy to report Stella seemed to have improved. Her damaged eye had begun to open, although it still looked a mess … AND she had started talking.

"Oh, goody! But, has she said anything about what happened to her?"

"There's no need for that attitude. Okay, I get your frustration. Just because your case isn't progressing any better than mine, is no reason to take it out on me. Now, do you want to know what I've learnt today, or not?"

The half-hearted apology I received was more than I expected, but I didn't waste time cherishing the moment, racing on with a 'striking-while-the-iron-is-hot' approach instead. "She claims an *unfortunate event* caused her injuries. That snippet was forthcoming after I pushed her a bit."

"Well, in the strictest sense, you can't argue with her description. Did you happen to winkle anything else out of her?"

"I suggested the cop stationed outside her door indicated whatever happened to her was more than an unfortunate event. I asked if she felt safe. She stated she was afraid about her safety and wished she could go away and hide some place where no one could find her."

"She has every right to be frightened. The people who attacked her meant business. It was their second warning. Their first was the attack on her husband."

"Maybe their second warning was the body Stella found in that derelict building. What happened to Stella might be their third and final warning. If that is the case, she would be aware her next encounter with them might prove fatal."

"You could be right. Have you developed any bright ideas about how we might prevent it occurring?"

"Sort of… I wondered whether you – the Millhaven police – might know of a safe place. A sort of safe house where she could stay until what's going on is sorted out and the danger is eliminated."

"Has she mentioned her husband at all, even enquired after his condition?"

"No. No mention of him. It intrigues me. I can't work out whether it is because she isn't concerned about him, or because, by not mentioning him, she hopes to keep him safe from another attack. After all, she is in hospital under an assumed name, and might not want to start people wondering why she is interested in someone with a different surname."

"It might be a bit of both. While I don't think it was a close marriage, I doubt she would do anything to further endanger his life. Is there more to this bright idea of yours about a safe place to stash her?"

"That rather depends on whether you can arrange somewhere safe for her." Ben made a gesture I couldn't interpret, but took it to mean I should continue as if that were possible. "Okay, she appears to be opening up to me. You could try speaking to her to see how she responds to you now."

"I tried that this afternoon. It didn't get me anywhere."

"Hmm … in that case, I could try suggesting she apply a bit of blackmail."

"Eh…?"

"She wants somewhere safe to hide. With the right approach, you might agree to provide somewhere safe. Think about this scenario: she could refuse to talk to you unless and until you spirited her away to such a place. She would make it clear, she will not tell you anything until she is safe. Of course, you would fuss and fume about the attempted blackmail, before acceding to her demand. In that way she will feel she has the upper hand,

and is confident you will do whatever it takes to ensure her safety in order to solve your case. How does that sound?"

"It sounds like I need something to drink while I consider your proposal."

When I returned with a couple of glasses of port, he was deep in thought, and remained so after I put his glass down in front of him. Finally, he looked up and wiped a hand over his face. For the first time that evening, I noticed how tired he looked. I shouldn't be surprised. Ben had been trying to do two jobs for almost two weeks now. I felt concerned for him, and guilty about not being more sympathetic about his situation.

"You're right. It probably wouldn't hurt to try your approach. After all, what is there to lose? We're not getting anywhere at the moment. If it works, we'll be miles ahead of where we are now. And, if it doesn't, we won't be any worse off … but, your position as a member of the domestic staff at the hospital might have to come to an abrupt end."

After further discussion of how each of us would play our respective parts in the operation, Ben left early, and I also opted for an early night.

*****

On the way into the hospital this morning, I practised what I would say to Stella to bring our conversation around to my 'blackmail' idea. As I wheeled the trolley containing Stella's breakfast out of the kitchen, I still wasn't sure of my next move, and wasn't confident of pulling it off.

"Good morning, Love. How are you feeling today? I must say you look a bit better. That eye of yours is almost fully open now. …Still looks a bit of a mess though. You keep progressing like this, they will be looking to tip you out of here soon. Have they said anything about letting you out?"

This morning's cheery prattle didn't seem to lift her spirits. I had struggled not to catch my breath as I walked into her room. There was no mistaking it. The way she looked shrieked 'despondent'. It had me wondering what went wrong. The first thing to come to mind was the doctors had suggested she would be fit to leave soon. If this were the case, her future safety would be playing on her mind. It stiffened my resolve to do a hard sell of my blackmail idea. It took more prattling on about how she looked and how much she appeared to have improved before she confessed.

"Yes, the doctors think I might be fit to go home in a day or so. If only they knew. I can't go home. I can't go anywhere they can find me. While I don't feel so safe here, it is safer than out there." She finished speaking with a jerk of her head towards the windows. I understood she meant 'outside the hospital'.

"Last night, I thought about our conversation yesterday, Dearie, and how I suggested the police should be able to arrange a safe place for you to stay. I think you might need to bargain with them." I saw her eyebrows almost meet to cross the bridge of her nose in confusion. "My thinking was you might try making a deal with them. I don't know what. Do they want something from you, some information or something?"

"Ye-es, they want me to talk. To tell them who did this to me and what it was all about. But, if I talk to the police – or anyone else – I'm a goner. I can't talk to anyone about any of it."

"I see … But, if the police were to hide you somewhere safe, where nobody could find you, perhaps it would be all right to talk to them about it. I suppose I thought maybe you could make a deal with the coppers. If they guaranteed your safety for as long as required, you would tell them all they needed to know. That's sort of deal probably would put you in a good bargaining position. What do you think?"

"Maybe if… Argh, I don't know. Do you think it might work? I can see how it could give me some leverage. Anyway, I don't have many other options to try. Perhaps, next time that big copper comes to visit, I will try it on to see how he reacts. In the meantime, I'll give it some thought. I need to work out how to do it and what I'm going to say, so I'm ready the next time he is here."

"Good girl! You've gotta try something to keep yourself safe. Like you said, you don't have too many other options. Is the big copper you're talking about a regular visitor, or does he just come whenever?"

"He's been a couple of times, but not what you'd call regular. Yeah, I will think about it, and I will be prepared for the next time he visits."

Having sown the seed, there was little else for me to do, except leave her in peace to do her thinking. "I'd better be moving along. I'll see you later when I bring your morning tea. In the meantime, don't go wearing yourself out with too much thinking. Remember, you need rest if you are going to heal properly and fast."

With a couple of hours to spare between breakfast and morning tea, I went to my office in the city. As soon as I saw the red message light blinking, I felt my stomach start to tighten. First things first; I tried calling Ben to tell him Stella was ready to blackmail him. No answer, so I went back to my blinking read message light. I was sure it was one of my new clients telling me to begin work on their case. I was right. It was one of my clients, but I could relax.

Relative to my current investigation, it was good news. My client's spouse would not return to Millhaven until Friday. This meant I wouldn't start tailing him until the coming weekend at the earliest. It gave me at least three more days to wrap up the Martin case.

What did 'wrapping up the Marin case' require, and what are my chances of achieving an outcome by the weekend? It didn't require more than a few moments thought for me to realise much of what I needed to achieve now depended on other people. Stella needed to 'blackmail' Ben into stashing her somewhere safe. Ben needed to play the game and find somewhere suitable for an indefinite period of time. Then, the big one: Stella needed to start talking. Her story was essential for Ben to progress his investigation, and it was what I needed to wrap up my case for Trent Martin.

Depending on others to solve my case is not how I like to work, and not something I am familiar with. While considering how to manage my frustration at having to work my Martin case in this way, Ben called.

"I have about two minutes to spare. What did you want, and how urgent is it?"

"And a good morning to you too…"

"One minute and thirty seconds and counting... You had better speak fast."

A host of comebacks lingered on the tip of my tongue, but common sense prevailed. An image of last night's exhausted-looking Ben Richards flashed across my mind. Instead, I was polite and succinct.

"I think Stella Martin is primed and ready to blackmail you into moving her to a safe location when she is released from hospital, which may be as soon as tomorrow. That's what it will take for her to tell you what you want to know. Talk to you tonight about how things went with her."

With nothing else in my office demanding urgent attention, I arrived at the hospital a little early for the morning tea run. While sitting in the cool, shady courtyard close to the kitchen area, my thoughts turned to the second new client I expected to hear from this week. It was an insurance job requiring surveillance of a man injured in a workplace accident.

The insurance firm believed the man was angling for an insignificant injury to become a permanent disability. Nothing new in this story; I had dealt with dozens of similar cases in the past. I consider them 'bread and butter' cases, as they keep me busy during periods when other work dries up. Nevertheless, they can be a nuisance if I'm involved with something else at the time. The surveillance required tends to be around-the-clock, leaving little or no time to work other cases simultaneously. In this instance, not hearing from the insurance firm for a while yet might be a good thing.

Then, it was time for my next performance. Grabbing my trolley, I wound my way through the labyrinth of corridors to

Stella Martin's room. No copper greeted my arrival. I had a fleeting moment of panic until I saw him attacking the coffee machine at the far end of the floor. I backed into Stella's room, dragging the trolley with me.

A different looking woman greeted me. Stella was her usual uptight and cautious self when I brought her breakfast. Now, sitting propped up in bed, she beamed at me as I entered – albeit still with a lopsided smile. "Well, Love, you're looking brighter than when I last saw you. What have you been up to? You haven't won Lotto or something, have you?"

"Nothing quite like that; but it is all down to you that I'm feeling better about things. I thought about what you suggested I do the next time that copper comes to visit. I've even thought out what I'm going to say. Now, all I have to do is wait for him to come again."

"I suppose you could have a word to the bloke outside. Ask him to tell his boss you want to talk to him."

"No. No, I don't want to do that. I want to be… I want to play hard to get when he comes. I don't want him thinking I'm keen to do a deal, or I'm anxious to talk to him. That wouldn't work with the way I want to play it. No, I'll just have to be patient and wait until he decides to come. I'm sure, when they are ready to tip me out of here, they will let him know. I reckon it will bring him running to talk to me."

"You know, I think you are on the right track with how you want to play it. I'm sure he will see things your way. I hope they keep you somewhere nice after days of looking at just these four walls. I'll miss our chats when you go. But, it will be good to know you are on the mend and well enough to be let out of here."

So far, so good; everything is going according to plan. My only concern is Ben's being too busy to talk to Stella today. I don't want him to leave it too long before visiting again. She might change her mind in the meantime. Nevertheless, judging by his mood earlier this morning, I don't think I'll call Ben again today.

As it turned out, I didn't need to. After delivering afternoon tea to Stella, I stopped by my city office to check for new messages. Ben called to check if I would be home tonight. It was a brief conversation. I told him I wouldn't be home much before seven o'clock after delivering Stella's meal. He said he would bring something for dinner and would be at my place soon after seven. Although desperate to know if he went to see Stella this afternoon, I knew better than to prolong what was meant to be a short call.

Having to wait until I saw him tonight was going to be difficult to bear. I wasn't inclined to linger chatting to Stella when I delivered her dinner. I wanted to be home to wait for Ben. In the end, I shouldn't have worried about it. As I wheeled in tonight's squeaky trolley, I started to apologise for the noise it was making. The triumphant look on Stella's face stopped me mid-sentence.

"You are looking pleased with yourself, My Girl. What have you been up to this time? No, don't tell me. Let me guess. That big copper came to see you, didn't he?"

"He did … And, he took the bait." In her excitement, her voice was squeakier than my trolley. "I don't know much yet about how it's going to happen, but I think it might be late tonight or early tomorrow morning. So, if I'm not here for breakfast tomorrow morning, you will know what's happened."

"Now everything looks like it's going to be all right for you … you will be safe, I mean. You will keep your side of the bargain won't you? You will tell him what he needs to know to make sure you don't have to worry about not being safe ever again? You will, won't you?"

"Well, I suppose some of the stuff…"

"Listen here, My Girl. You had better stick to your side of the bargain and deliver as you said you would. I've seen that big copper. I don't think you should try messing with him. Don't do the wrong thing by him once he has you stashed somewhere safe. Remember, you will be depending on him for your life until the people who did this to you are safely put away."

I saw her face fall and her jaw tighten. The little voice in my head was urging me to rescue the situation – and quickly.

"Argh, I'm sorry, Love. I don't mean to be telling you how to do things. I'm not your mother, and you are an intelligent woman. You don't need me to lecture you. I'm sure you'll work it out for yourself. So, come on, this might be our last chat together. Let's make it a bit more cheery, shall we?"

My speech did the trick. Over the following couple of minutes of chatter, I saw her excitement return. But, I did want to be home when Ben arrived. I gave her a quick gentle hug and wished her all the best. Then, I straightened myself and put on my best stern face. "I've got to be going. There are people here who need feeding tonight. Now you get on and eat your dinner before it gets cold."

A few minutes later, I was in my car and heading for home, only to have Ben follow me up the driveway. While I went through to my office to dump my bag, Ben brought in our dinner. Its aroma wafting through to my office started my stomach rumbling. I didn't even know I was hungry before dinner alerted me to the fact.

The two roast dinners with all the trimmings disappeared in record time. I wasn't about to dawdle over eating. I wanted to move on to a conversation about Stella Martin and what happened this afternoon. Perverse by nature, once dinner was over, Ben wanted to talk about anything and everything else. At last, my exasperation got the better of me. "For God's sake, Ben, are you deliberately being difficult, or is there something about your meeting with Stella Martin this afternoon you don't want me to know about?"

"What…? If you wanted to talk about Stella, all you had to do was say so. Anyway, I thought she would have told you about our meeting when you delivered her dinner tonight."

"No. All she told me was that something might happen either tonight or tomorrow, and dinner tonight might be the last time I would see her."

"Well, that's about it. What more is there to tell? Oh, and she was right. You won't have to do her breakfast delivery tomorrow. Your stint as an honorary member of the domestic services staff is over. By the way, how do you feel about staying up late tonight?"

"Eh…? Why would I want to stay up late?"

"To keep me company and help keep me awake until about midnight. That's when we plan to transfer Stella from the hospital to her new safe place."

"Am I involved in the transfer operation?"

"Best if you are not. We want to keep the personnel and fuss involved to a minimum. There was a mini rehearsal at the precinct this afternoon. I'm confident it should go off without a hitch tonight."

"So, as far as you're concerned, my interaction with Stella Martin is finished for a while, is that how it is?"

"No. I hoped you'd be around for the interviewing part of the operation. What is happening with your two new jobs? Are you likely to have time to spare?"

"One can't start before Friday – probably the weekend at the earliest – and I haven't heard from the other one. So, yes, I have time to be involved. Will my being there prove difficult after my recent undercover stint?"

"It's to be hoped not. We'll play it by ear, but I'm hoping your being there might help her relax and feel more comfortable. I'll see how she settles in first, but my thinking is not to try interviewing her until sometime tomorrow. I'll let you know when, so you can be there when we are ready to kick off."

Most of the time until eleven o'clock was spent speculating on what Stella had become involved in and what – and how much – she might be prepared to share in return for her ongoing safety. Soon after eleven o'clock, Ben announced he needed to make sure everything was in place for Stella's transfer. Minutes later, I was alone in the kitchen loading the dishwasher. By the time I finished, and had showered ready for bed, it was midnight.

I thought I was too hyped-up over what tomorrow might bring to be able to sleep. I was wrong. The moment my head hit the pillow, I fell asleep.

Chapter 12

In spite of the late night, I was out of bed at my usual time, and wasted no time this morning making my way into my city office. While it was unlikely, after last night's events, Ben would start interviewing Stella early this morning I wanted to be sure I was ready when he decided to start. As I drove into town, it occurred to me Ben's strategy might be to make an early start, perhaps in the hope Stella's resistance would be low after her late-night and interrupted sleep.

By ten o'clock, it was obvious there was no early start. The clock seemed in slow motion all morning but, for the next couple of hours, I think it was even slower. By lunchtime I was just about climbing the wall, and was desperately looking for something on which to take out my frustration and impatience. With my admin tasks completed, and my file notes up to date, I resorted to buying a newspaper to help while away the time.

My phone rang as I unlocked my office door: Ben. I answered the call as I rushed to my desk to drop the newspaper and the salad roll I bought for lunch. In his now familiar mode of 'no niceties', Ben said, "I'll pick you up in about half an hour. Are you right to go?"

"Yep, I'm ready whenever you are. Just give me a call when you're on your way so I can meet you downstairs. Is there anything I should do or know beforehand?"

"Nah, I don't think so. I don't know how this will go today, and sometimes the first attempt isn't brilliant. I'll see you soon." He ended the call, and I was left with a salad roll and the newspaper to fill in the next half hour.

Twenty-five minutes later, Ben called again. "I'm on my way to collect you. Are you still right to go?" I reassured him I would be downstairs waiting for him.

We drove to a swanky-looking condominium at the marina. It tended to dwarf the other apartment blocks in the area. Even from out on the street, this one smelled of money; real money. As we parked and unclipped our seat belts, I let my eyes run up and down the many floors of the building. Yes, definitely big money involved here. Although unbelted and free to exit the vehicle, we both sat for few moments peering in awe at the building in front of us.

"Is this where you stashed Stella Martin; somewhere in this building?" Ben gave me a curt nod. "How on earth did you manage that? And, what's the security here?"

"I know a man who owns a penthouse, but prefers to spend his time elsewhere. He owes me a favour or two, and this is one of them. The money tied up in this place means the security is quite good. It's even better when it comes to the penthouse. During your last chat with Stella, did you gain anything useful – or that might be a problem – for today's interview?"

"Uhmm … Not sure … At first, I thought I detected a hint of something. But, I'm not sure whether there was a problem, or I was imagining it. Nevertheless, I gave her an earful for good measure."

"What? Oh, I see. You put the fear of God into her about what might happen if she didn't play the game?"

"No. I made sure she was well acquainted with fear of a particular copper – one about your size."

"Are you suggesting she might try to renege on the deal we struck?"

"Argh, I don't know. I hope not. If she does harbour such thoughts, my presence might make her think again. Shall we go up and get on with it?"

"I suppose it's the only way to find out what's going to happen." He scrambled out of the car with his phone to his ear.

We entered through a separate private entrance, and waited in a small foyer area as the lift made its way down to the ground floor. Ben explained, "It's a private lift servicing only the penthouse. A special key is required to operate it, and the officers on guard duty up there keep the lift at the penthouse level at all times when it's not in use by me or my officers.

The penthouse didn't disappoint. While it didn't run to gold plated taps and marble floors, such touches wouldn't look out of place in the apartment. A female constable met us in a small entrance foyer. Before taking us through to a sitting room, she told Ben Stella had spent most of the day resting in her room.

"Good; she still has some way to go with her recovery, and rest is vital. Now, as I remember, this place has a small library/ den type room."

"Yes, through there." The officer indicated a closed door leading off from the sitting room. Ben strode over and opened it. I caught a brief glimpse of a large wooden desk and a couple of high wing-backed chairs in what appeared to be a book-lined room. "Yeah, that will be ideal. Please fetch Mrs Martin for me. I'll take her through to the library when I'm ready. Once you've roused Mrs Martin, please ask the housekeeper to provide afternoon tea – or at least coffee – for three."

The officer strode off, and Ben turned his attention to me. "I think I'd like you to be something of a surprise element. If you wait in the library, while Stella is dealing with the shock of seeing you in there, I'll begin explaining your presence. If she intends being uncooperative, your presence should help change her mind."

Nothing in his suggestion made me inclined to argue. I made myself comfortable in one of the library's wing-backed chairs as Ben closed the door and went to stand in the sitting room. A minute or so later, I heard voices outside the door, followed by firm footsteps striding off into the distance across a beautiful parquetry floor. I assumed it was the female officer on her way to organise our afternoon tea.

"Come through into the library. We are less likely to be interrupted in here," I heard Ben say as he opened the library door. "I've asked for coffee to be brought in to us, so we might have to delay making a proper start on your interview until after it is delivered. I think we might sit at that glorious desk first to see if it's a comfortable enough place to work. By the way, one other will join us. I don't think introduction are necessary, are they?"

"You! Do you work here too?" As I rose from my chair so she could see me, Stella looked genuinely taken aback by my presence.

"No, I don't work here. But then, I didn't work as a domestic at the hospital either. I'm sure Superintendent Richards will explain." At least, I hoped he would, as I didn't feel inclined to try explaining everything to her.

Once we were seated around the desk, he did explain, and did a good job of it while Stella glowered at me the whole time. Perhaps Ben's idea of having me there wasn't so great after all. Ben picked up on the hostile vibes. How could he not? They almost were singeing my eyebrows. Then afternoon tea arrived, allowing the atmosphere in the library to settle a little. When all three of us had coffee and a slab of cake in front of us, Ben took charge again and sought to diffuse the issue of my presence.

"We placed Sonoma in the hospital under cover to help isolate you from any unnecessary visitors. Apart from the medical staff and me, no one else was allowed in your room, and that included the hospital's normal domestic staff. Sonoma developed a genuine concern for you. It was her idea for me to find somewhere safe to hide you when the doctors decided you should leave hospital. She's here now as a friend – to both you and me. And, don't worry about whether you can trust her. She is an investigator I've worked with on many occasions."

"Is this true? What do you have to say about it?"

"Everything he said is true. From the moment I saw you, I was horrified by what happened to you, and it was obvious you were fearful about your safety after leaving hospital. I wanted to help you. I do believe locking up whoever did this to you is the only way to ensure your future welfare. I suspect there is more than one person involved, and the whole operation – whatever it is – needs to be neutralised before you can be safe. So, you agreed to tell your whole story in return for being stashed here until it is safe for you 'out there'. The only way the police can achieve that is if you tell them everything. Don't start trying to play games. It's your life that's on the line here."

Her defiant attitude slowly wilted as I delivered my speech. By the time I finished, she looked quite subdued. Without looking up at me, she nodded a few times. Then, after a couple of deep breaths, she sat up and demanded of Ben, "So, where do you want to start?"

"Where else, but at the beginning," Ben said. "Why don't you start by telling me how you came to be involved in whatever resulted in your being knocked about so badly?"

"How and when did it start...? I've been asking myself that question. I think I can answer it now. What I can't tell you is why. I don't mean I won't tell you. I mean I can't tell you, because I don't know why; why me."

Ben indicated he understood and encouraged her to start her story from the point at which she thought it all began.

"I think it goes back to my stupid decision to attend a High School reunion with my former classmates. Some I hadn't seen since I left High School, while others I hadn't seen in quite a few years. I don't know why I went. I was in two minds about it from the moment I heard it was being organised. High School wasn't the greatest time in my life, and I didn't have any strong desire to return to my old home town. I went anyway, and, I would have had a better time if I stayed here at home."

"But now you think everything ties back to something at that reunion?"

"Oh, I know it does. What I don't know is why. I'm sorry. I'm being a bit vague. Okay, here goes. If it doesn't make sense, tell me and I will try to clarify."

We both nodded enthusiastically. Anxious to hear her story, I didn't feel inclined to waste time speaking, and I think Ben was of the same mind. Instead of launching into her story, Stella spent the next few moments staring into the distance. Ben's impatience was obvious when, in a bid to begin the process, he asked, "Did something significant happen at the reunion?"

"No. But, in my mind, it was the start of everything. I didn't have a lot of 'best friends' at High School. I had attended a different primary school from most of the others, so I was an 'outsider' from the start. They talked about past events and people they knew, and I wouldn't know who or what they were talking about. After High School, it seems most of my classmates remained in the same town, or at least in the district."

With nothing exciting happening in the story so far, I tried hurrying things along. "So, you regretted attending from the moment you arrived. But did anything specific happen?"

"A girl I hardly recognised was circulating through the crowd. When she spotted me, she rushed over and claimed me as her long lost best friend. She giggled and carried on about the things we got up to in 'those days', and the good times we had. Either I was suffering amnesia, or she was talking to the wrong girl. I had no memory of any of it. Then, she asked me where I was living now. She looked surprised when I told her Millhaven. No, I'm not sure she was surprised. It was more like she was acting. Anyway, at that point, they announced the official part of the reunion weekend was about to begin, and asked us all to hurry to take our seats in the main hall."

Stella stopped talking and appeared to be reliving the memories of the event. I tried bringing her back to her story. "That would have saved you having to make further conversation with the woman."

"It wasn't a problem anyway. As we walked into the main hall, a couple of other women indicated they had saved a seat for her. There were no other spare seats there, so I went further along and found one for myself. The session in the main hall was mostly speeches. Some former teachers took turns at recounting significant memories which stayed with them over the years. After the session finished, there was a guided tour of the school … 'so we could drool over the changes made since we were students there'. My 'friend' didn't come to find me after we left the main hall. As soon as the guided tour ended, I went back to my motel."

"Was that the end of the reunion's events," Ben asked before she had time to lapse into silent reverie again.

"The weekend's program continued. We were supposed to meet up again at a function centre in town for the official reunion dinner. Pre-dinner drinks from 6.30PM, and then everyone was to be seated for dinner by seven o'clock. I opted to give it a miss and ate in my room. Sunday morning's program was supposed to be a casual get together for more catching-up with old classmates. The weekend was to end with a picnic lunch in the grounds before everyone left for home. I checked out of my motel after breakfast as planned, but left for Millhaven straight after."

"Okay; nothing too scary happened at the reunion. The only thing of note was someone claiming to be your long lost friend – when they never were a friend. How does that relate to what happened to you?" Ben asked.

"It wasn't what happened at the reunion. It was what happened afterwards."

Ben shrugged and gestured for Stella to explain. She hesitated for a couple of moments. She seemed to be gathering her thoughts, or searching for the right words for her next chapter.

"A couple of weeks after the reunion, I was shopping on a Saturday morning and bumped into the same former High School student as claimed to be my friend at the reunion. She babbled on about her surprise when I told her I lived in Millhaven. She moved here a few months earlier and claimed not to have seen me around until that morning. I felt I couldn't refuse her invitation to go for a coffee. After work one day the next week, we went for a drink together. I didn't like her much and didn't enjoy her company at all but, no matter how hard I tried to put her off, she persisted."

"Do you think you were being groomed for something … there might have been an ulterior motive behind the friendliness?" I asked. It's how it sounded to me.

"Not at the time. I thought she hadn't made new friends yet

and was lonely in a new town. It wasn't until after the next 'event' that I wondered what was going on. Although, at first, I didn't realise I was being set up."

"Tell us about the 'event' you think was the defining moment in the woman's grand plan." Ben was becoming exasperated and it showed in his voice. I shot him a look and hoped he would interpret it correctly. It seems he didn't.

He responded with a frown and a slight shake of his head. Time for me to run interference. "I don't know about anyone else, but I could do with a long, cold drink of something. Do you suppose this establishment runs to iced tea or something similar?"

Conversation of no consequence filled the short interlude until the housekeeper delivered our iced tea. When our glasses were about half empty, Ben reignited her story. "You were about to tell us about that next thing you consider was a significant part of the story," he reminded Stella.

"A week later, she called me at work and asked me to meet her for coffee on Saturday morning. She said she wanted help with something. I agreed and met her at the coffee shop just before ten o'clock. Curious about what she wanted help with, I asked her about it while we waited for our coffees to arrive. She said she was getting engaged in about a month's time on the weekend of some special family event. There would be little time when she and her fiancé could go together to buy the ring. So, she wanted to look at engagement rings beforehand to work out what she liked in advance of their shopping expedition."

"She wanted your help to choose the ring…?" I blurted out in astonishment.

"Not exactly; she wanted me to go with her to look at what was available and decide which styles suited her hand. Although I felt useless, I went with her. I think the young man who served us was new to the job and a bit nervous. A tray of gemstone rings was in one of the display cases. At first, she thought one of those might be nice, and asked if she could try them on. He had to remove a tray of earrings from the case before he could remove the tray of rings. The earrings weren't on cards or anything. They were just laid out in pairs in a fan pattern on a silk-lined tray. As the lad took the tray out of the display case, he bumped it, and the earrings scrambled into a big heap. He put the tray of earrings on top of the display case so he could remove the tray of rings. The first couple of rings she tried on didn't fit. So, she asked if he had one of those ring gauge things to measure her finger and work out what size she need."

I didn't like where Stella's story was going, and sensed the obvious ending. Not wanting to interrupt her now the story was in full flow, I bit my tongue and she continued.

"The gauge thing was in a drawer over on the other side of the room. The young bloke went to fetch it, leaving the two trays of jewellery out on the case in front of us. As soon as he went to get it, she looked over her shoulder at the lad and whispered to me, 'I hope he doesn't mind, but I think I would rather have a diamond anyway… and the diamond rings are in that case over where he is. When he returned with the gauge, she apologised and said she had decided she preferred a diamond after all. He put the two trays of jewellery that were on top of the case back into the display case. As he locked it, he muttered something like 'I'll tidy that up later'."

Ben encouraged her to get to the point. "Did anything happen when you were looking at the diamond rings?"

"Not really. She tried on several, and particularly liked one. It was the most expensive one, but she asked it be put aside for her until the following week when her fiancé would come in to buy it. He agreed, put the other rings back in the display case, and we left. I kept wondering why she dragged me along too. She never asked my opinion or anything. It wasn't until the next day when I realised what had happened."

"Let me guess," I said. "You found your visit to the jeweller's had scored you a new ring?"

"No, that wasn't it. While I was looking for something in my bag, I found a pair of diamond and sapphire earrings that didn't belong to me. I remembered seeing them in the tray in the display case. I didn't put them in my bag, and I didn't see anyone put them in there. It didn't take me long to work out what happened, but I couldn't figure out why. Well, not until a bit later, that is."

"What did you do with the earrings?" Ben demanded a touch too sharply. Stella winced. I jumped in to try to save the situation. The last thing we needed now was for Stella to clam up.

"Finding those earrings must have been a shock. What were your thoughts at the time? Did you consider returning them, or going to the police? Did you confront your 'friend' about them?"

"My first thought was to return them to the shop. Then I realised how it would look, and the consequences if I did. I couldn't go to the police. How would they react when I told them *I just happened to find them in the bottom of my bag?"*

I continued the questioning before Ben could jump in to take over again. "I see. What about your friend, what did she have to say about it?"

"Nothing … well, nothing at first, because I couldn't contact her. I didn't know where she lived of where she worked. I didn't have her phone number, so I checked my calls log. The only ones I couldn't identify were those 'private number' calls where the caller's ID is withheld. After I checked their times and dates, I felt sure they were from her."

This time Ben jumped in ahead of me. At least now his voice had a more neutral tone. "But, that isn't the end of the story is it? You couldn't contact her, but she could call you. So, what happened next?"

At that point, the housekeeper knocked and came in. She asked if we would be staying for dinner. Her enquiry had us all checking the time. Ben said he and I would be leaving soon and there would be only Stella for dinner tonight.

Ben told Stella that was it for today, and reminded her to rest as much as possible. We would be back to see her sometime tomorrow morning. Her look of relief didn't go unnoticed.

Chapter 13

Leaving Stella to rest in the penthouse suite, Ben and I returned to our respective offices. Earlier indications suggested one of my new cases might kick-off tomorrow. I spent a few anxious minutes trying to work out how I might combine my two investigations.

The last thing I wanted was to miss out on Stella's continuing interrogation. While I knew I could extract details from Ben later, my need to be there was about more than hearing it firsthand. When Ben is wrapped up in what he is doing, he can become a bit rough. I don't mean physically, but he can verbally intimidate. Apart from still healing her physical damage, Stella remains psychologically fragile. She could sustain further damage if not handled carefully.

My concerns about handling two investigations simultaneously proved unfounded. My new client didn't contact me to confirm the surveillance target was back in town. So, at least Friday remained uncomplicated, and I could join Ben in the penthouse again tomorrow for the next enthralling chapter of Stella's story. With nothing else needing urgent attention, after texting Ben that I would be cooking dinner tonight, I called at the supermarket on my way home.

He phoned soon after six o'clock to ask what I was preparing for dinner. I knew he was checking which wine to bring. "Red wine would go down well. We're having lasagne tonight."

A few minutes before seven o'clock, he arrived brandishing a bottle of red wine in one hand and a container of fruit salad in the other. "That little deli next to the bottleshop makes tempting fruit salad. I thought it would be good after the lasagne … and probably better for us than TimTam biscuits with our coffee."

While we waited for the lasagne to finish doing its thing in the oven, we took our glasses of wine out onto the deck. There was a nip in the air and the night's dew already covered everything. Nevertheless, it was nice to be out in the fresh air after a day indoors. An animal of some sort – probably the neighbour's dog – ran through my rosemary hedge, launching a wave of perfume onto the night air. On such a crisp, clear night, the stars looked bigger and brighter than normal against the inky black sky. The tiny sliver of a new moon did not overshadow their brightness tonight.

There was no conversation; no need for it. With so much talk during the day, we both were happy to sit in silence sipping our wine in undisturbed peace. I shivered. A check on the time told me dinner should be ready. Ben remained alone with his thoughts on the deck while I did the last minute fiddling before we sat down to eat.

By the time we were halfway through our meal, it seemed the pair of us had returned to life. Conversation began in a slow and inconsequential way, and continued in much the same vein until we adjourned to the lounge room. Rather than remain seated at the table, our bowls of fruit salad and ice cream and our coffees accompanied us to the comfortable chairs.

Then, it was time for the inevitable conversation to begin. I plead guilty to having initiated it. "So, what do you make of Stella's story so far?"

"Interesting … Hers is a classic case of having been set up. The question is, set up for what? The hope is, all will be revealed in tomorrow's session. It's as well we finished when we did. It gave me a chance to follow up on the only real piece of evidence she provided today."

"I thought she told us plenty. What's this one piece of evidence you're talking about?"

"It was the bit about what happened in the jeweller's shop. From her description, I worked out which shop it was. I know that shop is well equipped with security cameras. So, I took myself along for a chat with the owner and staff."

"Was it the right shop? Did they remember the two women being there?"

"Yes. My guess was correct. Both the owner and the young staff bloke remembered the two women coming in that morning. As it turns out, the owner was none too impressed with their visit. It seems he came out into the store as one of the women was making a final decision on which diamond engagement ring she wanted. He remembers her asking for it to be put aside until the following weekend when her fiancé would be in town to pay for and collect it."

"That almost tallies with Stella's story, except she didn't mention the owner's becoming involved in the process. I suppose, to her, it didn't seem worth mentioning."

"Perhaps, but we won't mention it either. Let's see if the owner rates a mention as the story progresses. It appears the woman choosing the ring was nervous that it might inadvertently be sold during the week. To put her mind at rest and reassure her that, if the ring wasn't out in the display case, it wouldn't be sold, the owner took the ring in its box and locked it in the safe in the back of the store. When he returned to the front counter, the two women had left … And he was unhappy the young bloke hadn't secured a deposit for the ring before they did so. Neither woman has set foot in the shop since. He showed me the chosen ring – now back on display out front."

"You said the shop had security cameras. What about footage from the morning in question?"

"Two cameras cover the shop. One focuses on the entrance and its immediate surroundings inside the shop. The other one is mounted midway along a side wall. While it does provide coverage of the whole interior of the shop, its main focus is the display cases immediately in front of it. These are the ones containing the diamond jewellery, including the engagement rings. Those areas further away from the camera – such as the case on the opposite side of the shop where the gemstone rings are displayed – tend to be fuzzy images. Nevertheless, having had that explained to me, I requested the tapes to use as part of an ongoing investigation."

"I'll bet that confused the owner. He would be wondering what all the fuss was about. As far as he knew, he hadn't been robbed, so why were the police interested in what happened in his shop on that Saturday morning?"

"Yeah, he was a bit perplexed, but he had no problems with the police reviewing the tapes. The only problem was, he doesn't hold them. The security firm that installed all the alarms and cameras also looks after the tapes. They change the tapes on Wednesday and Sunday nights. I tried calling the security mob so they could dig out the tape I required and have it ready when I came to collect it. The bad news is: they close at 4:30PM, and no one was there when I called."

"Is that part of the story worth following up? Was it possible for the earrings to be removed from the display tray and placed in her bag while everything else, including the camera, was going on around them?"

"I know it sounds unlikely, but there are two things to consider. First, that's where Stella is convinced the earrings went into her bag. The other, and probably more important factor, is it sounds like a well-practised and slick operation. I just wish we knew the nature of that operation."

"I feel this will prove not to be some backyard gang, but something on a much grander scale. I realised a couple of moments ago, we still don't know the name of the 'friend' who claims Stella as her long lost High School bestie. Stella might not be able to find out anything about where she works or lives but, if you had her name, you might find out who or what she is."

After spending quite some time with Stella today, we still haven't gained much to work with. Maybe after tomorrow's session, we will have more clues to point us in the right direction. In essence, once I find out what she's involved in, the investigation her husband, Trent Martin, hired me to carry out will be finished, and I will be able to close the case before either of my new ones begins.

Along with the realisation that today's interview of Stella Martin produced a heap more questions to ponder, it also made for a restless night as I tried applying the 'what if' approach in the hope of opening new avenues to investigate.

*****

Ben hadn't indicated what time we might descend on the penthouse this morning, but I imagined he was as anxious to continue the story as I was, so I made a point of being in my city office a little earlier than usual. After all the routine first-thing-in-the-morning admin tasks were done and I had made yet another coffee, there still was no word from Ben regarding the time for today's interview.

He called at about 9:30AM. "I'm about to head off to talk to Stella. Are you coming today or not?"

What a silly question. Of course I would be there. After confirming I would meet him in the car park adjacent to the apartment block, I grabbed my bag and was on my way down the stairs and out the backdoor. A demonstration was taking place in the city heart. Traffic was held up, and queueing up along surrounding streets. It lined up past the entrance to my building's parking lot and, even if I could get my vehicle out onto the street, I wouldn't be going anywhere.

A taxi rank is located about half a block further along on the opposite side of the street. There were four cabs waiting for fares. Abandoning any thought of trying to drive to the apartment block, I jogged through the traffic to the other side of the street and along to the taxi rank. Cabs leaving the rank headed in the right direction to avoid the traffic chaos. I arrived at the apartment block as Ben was scrambling out of his car. His eyebrows rose up when he saw I was the taxi's passenger.

"This is doing things in style, isn't it? This private investigator lark must pay well. What have you done to your vehicle?"

"Good morning to you too, Ben. There's nothing wrong with my vehicle, except the traffic snarl in the city heart had me locked into the car park behind my building. Besides, the taxi ride is a business expense against my Martin investigation. Shall we go up to see if Stella is ready to talk to us this morning?"

After dealing with the usual security rigmarole, we were once more in the penthouse foyer. I could see Stella watching TV in the lounge room. In deference to his rank and authority, I let Ben go in first. Stella said she hadn't heard us arrive, but seemed happy enough to see us. After arranging with the housekeeper for coffee to be brought in, we took over the library again.

"Did you get some rest yesterday after we left?" I asked by way of a conversation starter. She nodded, so I continued. "What about last night, did you sleep well?"

"Yes, I surprised myself. Do you want to start straight away, or should we wait until after coffee arrives?" she asked Ben.

He smiled and said we'd wait until after coffee. I think it was a smile and not a grimace. I wished it would arrive, so we could get down to business. I don't doubt Ben was just as impatient.

After we had taken only a few sips, Ben launched today's session of Stella's interview. "Yesterday we discussed your 'rekindled' previously non-existent friendship with your High School classmate. What is that woman's name?"

"Lenny… Sorry, that's Lenore; Lenore Collins. Even some of the teachers were calling her Lenny by the time we left."

"Thanks. So, after the jeweller's shop episode, you didn't hear from Lenny for a while and you were unable to contact her. Is that right?" Stella nodded. "But she did contact you again?" Nodded confirmation again. "How long after the earrings event was that, and how did it happen?"

"It must have been three weeks… no, nearly four weeks later when I 'happened to bump into her' at the supermarket, and she suggested going for a coffee. My trolley was full of groceries, including a lot of cold stuff. So, I said no thanks, as I needed to go home to put the cold stuff in the fridge straight away."

"If you didn't have food to go into the fridge, would you have accepted her invitation?" I asked.

"I... uhmm … I'm not sure. While a part of me never wanted to see her again, another part of me demanded an explanation; wanted to know why those earrings ended up in my bag. During those weeks, it didn't matter how often I thought about it, I always came back to the same conclusion: she slipped them into my bag. Why? There had to be a reason, and she owed me an explanation. So, I don't know if I would have gone for coffee with her or not. If we were to meet up, I think I would have suggested somewhere less public, because I'm sure there would be a heated conversation."

Ben jumped in before I could ask another question. "Okay, so you didn't go for coffee. What happened after that? When was the next time that you did meet with Lenny?"

"It must've been more than a week later. She rang and asked me to join her for a drink after work at a wine bar. I was tempted to say no because I had to go home and prepare my husband's dinner, but he was working back that night and would eat in town. So, I agreed to meet her."

"A wine bar still is a fairly public venue, and sometimes not quieter than a coffee shop. Surely you didn't think that would be a good place to have it out with her?"

"After I refused the coffee invitation, I must've spent hours thinking about it. What I should have said, what I should do if she called again, all that sort of stuff. Anyway, what I decided was, if she called again, I would be pleasant and meek and mild. I'd accept her invitation, and be nice until I found out why she did it. After that, things might get a bit unpleasant. So, yes, I met her at the wine bar and tried to behave as an old friend would ... But, I *did* ask about the earrings while I was being *ever so friendly.*"

"Oh, I wish I had been a fly on the wall in that wine bar," I said. "I can't even picture how your meeting went, but I'm sure it would have been interesting to watch – and to overhear. What did she have to say about the earrings anyway?"

"She denied it. Would you believe it? She denied any knowledge of the earrings, said she had no idea what I was on about, and became upset that I seemed to be accusing her of something. I wasn't buying any of that malarkey. That's when the polite me disappeared and the other one took over. I told her to stop treating me as a fool. I knew she did it, and I wanted an explanation. Neither of us was going home that night until I knew what it was all about. After that, I suggested we go out to the car park where we could talk privately. She was angry, snatched up her bag, and strode out into the car park. I followed her out. It wasn't until I was on my way out, I realised being out there alone with her in a dark car park might not be the wisest move."

"Had she threatened you in anyway, or said or done anything, to make you think you might not be safe?" Ben asked.

"Not really; she was angry and called me a few names and accused me of trying to blame her for my theft of the earrings. But, when we at our table and I suggested going out in the car park, I didn't feel threatened – not physically threatened. The thought it might be a possibility struck me from out of the blue as I followed her out. It wrong-footed me a bit. I was unsure how to tackle it; whether to be all-out aggressive in questioning her, or more restrained."

The dilemma Stella faced is one I've encountered many times during some of my cases, so I could understand what was going on in her head at the time. "So, in the end, how did you approach it?"

"As we looked for a suitable place to talk, I decided to be to-the-point; forceful but not aggressive. Well, that didn't happen. When we stopped to talk, I exploded. It wasn't a pretty thing."

"How did she react? Did she threaten you?" Ben demanded.

"Threatened me…? No. She laughed in my face. Told me *she couldn't believe how stupid and naïve I was not to have worked it out by now.* Then she asked me how I liked the earrings, and did they suit me. She didn't threaten me, but her voice had become hard and cold. I started to feel frightened, but I didn't want it to show. While I was trying to think of what to say or do, she asked the question that nearly rocked me: *so, what have you done with the earrings if you haven't worn them, and what do you plan to do about them. I would think carefully about the answer to that if I were you."*

"So, now a threatening element had been introduced. Did you understand it to be a threat, and how did you respond?" Ben asked.

"Of course it was a threat. I tried to bluff it out; told her I was going to the police, and would tell them everything. She just laughed, and asked what I was going to tell them? Did I think they would believe a rubbish story about someone else slipping expensive earrings into my bag? They would believe I had stolen them and now, feeling guilty and a bit afraid, I had cooked up a story to save myself. I knew she was right, but what could I do. In the end, I admitted defeat, but demanded she tell my why she had done it."

"And did she … explain why she did it, I mean?" I asked.

"It took me a while to fully understand her explanation. At first, it didn't sound like she had told me why. Then I realised she had – and what she meant by it. All she said was: *I own you. We control you.* She only had one glass of wine, and couldn't be drunk. Maybe she had taken something. And, that 'something', combined with a glass of wine, had made her go a bit funny. But, she wasn't laughing anymore. Her face had set hard and there was something vicious about the way she looked when she next spoke. Her words chilled me right through to the bone:

Tomorrow night, seven o'clock, be at the little park off Kingston Street. Someone will meet you there, and you will find out the answers to some of your questions. Come alone. Don't even think about not turning up. And, don't even consider going to the police. Being arrested for theft would be wonderful compared to what might happen to you if you talk to them."

"After that threat, of course you went to the park to meet them, and you went alone," Ben muttered as he scribbled notes on the pad in front of him. "And what sort of reception committee was waiting for you in the park?"

"Yes, I went alone. I was terrified, but what else was I to do? I'd been told to come alone and, even if I hadn't been, I didn't want anyone else involved. At first, I thought it had been a cruel joke of some sort. There wasn't much light in the park but you could make out shapes. There was no one around. At least, I couldn't see anyone. Not wanting to venture too far into the park alone – just in case – I only walked in a few metres. Then I stood there looking around for a few seconds. I couldn't see anyone, and no one came to meet me. So, I turned and started back towards my car. A man appeared from nowhere and blocked my way. A voice from behind me – a gruff male voice – told me to turn around and keep walking further into the park."

"So, you knew there were at least two men. What did you do?" Ben asked.

"I faced the classic 'fight or flight' situation. My chances of winning a fight with two blokes were pretty remote, so I chose the flight option. Perhaps it was the wrong choice anyway. I used to play a lot of sport and I'm still a good runner. I thought I'd be able to outrun them if I made a good dummy move to start with. The bloke blocking my way must've anticipated it. He tackled me after only a couple of steps, and began dishing out a bit of rough treatment, until the other bloke told him to stop and to avoid marking me too much.

They marched me further into the park and shoved me down onto the seat at one of those picnic tables. If I went to the police about the meeting in the park, the jewellery shop owner would, by mysterious means, discover he was missing a pair of valuable earrings, and he might be given some clues as to where they went."

"Okay, so they baited the trap and now you were hooked. What did they say about why they went to so much trouble to put you in such a position?" I asked quietly. I felt sick at the thought of how Stella must've felt alone in the park at night with those men.

"Oh, they told me they didn't have anything too difficult in mind for me to do. All I had to do was collect some parcels one night and deliver them to somewhere, and on another night, I would have to go back to that last place to collect the parcels again and deliver them to somewhere else. I told them I didn't do drugs, and wouldn't get involved with drug running, not at any cost. The gruff-voiced one demanded to know if I'd heard anyone mention drugs. Of course I hadn't. They assured me they did not associate with those in the drug trade. Then I got my final warning: *keep your mouth shut, do as you're told when you are told and on time. Go home and wait for further instructions regarding when to begin work.* After that, they escorted me back to where I first encountered them. They stood there and watched me walk to my car and drive away."

Stella reached for a glass of water. I noticed her hand trembled and her breathing had become shallow and rapid. It was nearly lunchtime. I suggested Stella go and freshen up while we organised the housekeeper to rustle up lunch. She almost bolted from the room.

Ben snarled, "What do you think you're playing at? We were coming to the important part of the story needed to crack this thing wide open."

"She was about to breakdown. Best we leave her in peace to recover before we try for the remainder of the story. Having to take us through the next bit – the 'now' part of the story – might prove even more traumatic than where we've been so far. Again, maybe that next chapter will have to wait until tomorrow."

Then without any effort on our part, the housekeeper and our lunch suddenly materialised in the library.

Chapter 14

I spent Friday night dining alone – on left-overs – and enjoying every minute of it. As we left the penthouse after lunch, Ben agreed leaving Stella to rest for the afternoon was the right move. Ridiculous as it seems at this late stage of the interviewing process, he was all for spending some time tonight mapping out a plan for tomorrow's session.

In my mind, there was no doubt the move was designed to stifle, and possibly eliminate, my interruptions. As with so many other well-laid plans and good intentions, it didn't happen. Ben called just as I packed up to leave my city office. He probably would spend most of the night working a new crime scene. Once I demolished my 'dog's dinner'-like pile of left-overs, I shoved everything in the dishwasher on my way through the kitchen to my home office.

Right, now ready to start work, what did I have to add to my case file; what actual information? I fished the digital recorder out of my bag and found the relevant file. With my feet up on the desk, and a notebook and pencil resting on my midriff, I pressed play … and prepared to revisit two hours of today's interview. Part way through the exercise, I nodded off, and had to rewind to the last bit I remembered hearing.

Then, it was after ten o'clock. The recording had ended and I had a shortish list of points scribbled in my notebook. "A timeline, that's what I need", I told my empty office. For a timeline, you need actual dates to record along the line. There was my first problem: no actual dates. Everything was 'a couple of weeks' or 'a few days later'… not the stuff of timeline development.

After contemplating my notes without achieving anything, I decided to do something worthwhile – like going to bed. No sooner had I made the decision than I felt the flutter of vague and distant thought. Back to staring at my notebook again. Of course, there it was. I did have a starting date: the High School reunion. It only took a moment to locate the newspaper article where I found the first mention of Stella Martin.

With my case file open beside me, I drew a line across my whiteboard and entered the date of the High School reunion at its left end. Then, in my file notes, I found mention of Stella's first meeting with the 'friend' after the school reunion. It was a couple of weeks later and on a Saturday morning. Reference to a calendar soon had the next date entered. Applying much the same procedure, tentative dates for the jeweller's shop event and Stella's confrontation with the 'friend' were added.

"Yes, it's coming along well," I told the universe. After adding approximate dates for the other milestone events from our interviews, a clear picture of a well-practised operation began emerging. I stood back to consider my handiwork. Suddenly, I was aware of how Ben must be feeling about waiting until tomorrow for the next critical instalment of Stella's story. My timeline was halted until I had details for the gap between when she was recruited and when her husband was bashed and left for dead in a dark alley.

*****

Saturday mornings are for reading the weekend papers – unless I'm working on a case. This Saturday morning, I would be working on a case, but not until about ten o'clock if it follows the pattern of the previous couple of days. Ben's call interrupted me while I was eating breakfast and perusing the front page.

His voice was thick and raspy. "I've arranged to start today's interview at nine o'clock. You need to be in the carpark a few minutes before then, if you want to be involved." I confirmed I would be there. The call ended.

'Not much sleep last night', the little voice in my head suggested by way of a warning. Today could be tense and difficult. From past experience, I knew Ben would be difficult and short-tempered. I needed to tread carefully during todays' interview, or he might resort to having me removed. "Ah well," I sighed aloud, "so much for a lazy Saturday morning."

At fifteen minutes before nine o'clock, there was no sign of Ben or anyone else when I pulled into the carpark beside the apartment block. I locked my car and went and stood beside the door to the penthouse. Just as I was contemplating returning to wait in my car for Ben to arrive, he drove in.

"Come on. Let's get up there if this interview is to start in about four minutes' time."

Yep, definitely a 'handle with care' kind of day ahead. I wished there was some way I could warn Stella in advance of today's onslaught by a sleep-deprived bear of a copper.

She waited in the lounge room again, and the housekeeper hovered to see if we required coffee before we began work. Ben told her coffee would be appreciated as soon as possible. Coffee taken care of, we moved to the library and resumed our customary seats.

Today, Stella looked better than Ben did. She confirmed she again slept well. A stray thought flashed in from left field: how was her husband, Trent Martin going, and how did he sleep last night? Somewhere amidst that thought, another more concerning one thundered through from the back of my mind.

Not once during our interviews had she asked after her husband; not even the slightest enquiry regarding his condition or progress. Should I read something sinister into it, or ignore the matter until I talked to Ben about it later. Doing so proved easier said than done. The question continued to lurk in a corner of my mind. Perhaps I was making something out of nothing. Maybe she called the hospital on a regular basis to check on him. In spite of my best efforts to persuade myself there was nothing amiss, I wasn't convinced.

As soon as we savoured a few sips of coffee, Ben began the interview. "When we left off yesterday, you had been given a rough overview of what you would be doing, and were told to go home and wait for further instructions about starting work for them. How long after the encounter in the park was it before you heard from them again?"

"After about three weeks with no further contact, I hoped they might have forgotten about me. Then, one day as I was packing up to leave work, Lenny called. There wasn't a conversation as such. She just delivered my instructions and ended the call. I was to start working for them that night. My instructions were to go an address, use a code word to identify myself and pick up a parcel, which I then had to deliver to another address. In a way, I almost felt relieved. It didn't sound too bad. Not nearly as bad as I thought it might be. My only problem was leaving home just before seven o'clock to be at the first location on time. Most nights, at seven o'clock, we were still at the dinner table."

Stella paused. She seemed to be gathering her thoughts; trying to recall exact details of her first run. As I struggled to refrain from asking a question, Ben stepped in to prod her along.

"Ah yes, I can understand your problem. Before then, did you often go out at night alone during the week?"

"God no; neither of us ever went out on week nights; hardly ever went out on any night. So, you see how awkward it was for me. Anyway, I thought I would get around it by having dinner on the table a bit earlier than usual; fifteen minutes earlier. Wouldn't you know it? My husband decided to work back that night. So, there I was with dinner ready to go on the table early and no one to feed. Coward that I am, I sent him a text to tell him I had to go out for a while, but I would leave his dinner in the oven. A few minutes before I was about to leave, he called. I saw the caller ID, and ignored it, knowing full well I would have to deal with the matter later."

Again, another pause occurred. Ben, scribbling in his notebook, didn't seem to notice the delay. I decided to risk incurring his wrath, and did the prompting this time. "Are you suggesting your husband controlled what you did?"

"No, not exactly. My husband was very … conservative. What I mean is, he was a man of habit – of routine – who didn't allow anything to change the way he did things. We never went out; never went to the movies, or out to dinner. We were either at work, or at home. Sometimes, I did go out on a Saturday, but only to the supermarket to do the shopping, and then only if I hadn't managed to fit it in after work during the week. I'm not complaining. He was good at what he did. It's just… he fixated on his job and the work he did … was almost sanctimonious about it. Everything else was 'frivolous'; unnecessary. I was used to how he was; used to always staying at home."

Since I had started this line of discussion, I felt entitled to continue it. "So, telling him you were going out that first night must have upset him. It would disturb the established order of things in your home."

"When I came home, he was so angry. He started on about what the neighbours would think of my going out alone at night. It would be all over the neighbourhood. They would think I was a tramp. After my first 'courier run', I was uptight and frightened. Nothing unpleasant happened. I just picked up a parcel at one place and dropped it off at another. I wasn't in the mood to be told the neighbours would think me a tramp. I exploded, told him what I thought about our life – everything – and stormed off to bed.

An hour or so later, I still couldn't sleep. He came in, at his usual time, to go to bed. I told him to get out. The spare room was his from now on. He could live his life and I would live mine. We didn't speak for a few days afterwards. Oh, everything continued as normal: he had an early breakfast and went to work. I got up later and went to work. I came home, made dinner and had it on the table at the usual time. Dinner was eaten in silence. Then we both went to different parts of the house to fill in time until our respective bedtimes."

"With your 'courier runs' continuing on a regular basis, there was little chance for the situation on the home front to improve. Was there a truce at all?"

"Not really. It did settle down a bit. We became civil when we needed to speak to one another, but that was about the extent of the improvement. The number of times I went out at night didn't help the situation."

Ben decided to take charge of the interview again. "Do you mean you were obliged to make more courier runs than you anticipated?"

"I thought I might do a run whenever, or maybe as much as one run per week. At the time of the first run, I didn't realise there would be a set schedule. In the first week, I also had to make a second run. Then, the following week, I only had to make one run, but more time was required to complete it. That's how it continued. Sometimes, on the second week – the alternate week – I'd be told to make a second run. There was no chance to improve the domestic situation."

Ben sat tapping his pencil on the desk as he considered his notes. "So, life continued along those lines for some time. I assume things were going okay for you, or you would have tried to opt out. Is that a reasonable assumption?"

"No, not by any stretch of the imagination. I know it sounds simple enough: go to an address pick up a parcel, take it to another address and drop it off. But, unpleasant elements were involved. There were bad people. People who scared me. Some of the places I sometimes had to visit terrified me. I wasn't enjoying it, and only kept doing it because I was too afraid not to. I was constantly afraid, tense and uptight. It started affecting my health, and it impacted on my job."

"Did you contemplate doing anything about it?" Ben asked.

"All the time… I kept trying to think of ways to escape the mess. Ways of breaking free of the mob and their grubby business. It took a while, but then I couldn't handle it any longer. I told them I wouldn't do it anymore. When they reminded me I didn't have a choice, I told them I would go to the police if they didn't let me stop and they didn't leave me alone. They tried reminding me about the earrings. I just laughed, and said whatever the consequences regarding the earrings might be, I'd deal with them. But, while I was about it, I would make sure the police knew everything about the mob's operations."

"Jesus, such threats wouldn't go down well," I blurted out, and received a withering look from Ben for my trouble.

"You're right. The response was not directed at me, but at my husband. Regardless of how things were at home, he was my husband, and they threatened his life if I didn't continue. After a couple more runs, I announced I was only going to do the one run on the alternate week from then on. They would have to find someone else to do my extra runs. My husband almost lost his life because of my bravado. It was thanks to their handiwork he was in the alley where you found him. For the next week or so, I kept my head down; did what I was supposed to do. But, I kept thinking about it, and how I must try again to make some changes. I asked one of the people who received the parcels I delivered to pass on a message to the boss, to tell him I wanted to talk to him urgently."

Ben looked up from the notes he was scribbling and ran a hand across his face. "While it was a gutsy move, I'm not sure it was terribly wise. From what you've said, I take it you had no direct contact with the boss, or whoever it was, who was running the show. Did your message get passed on as requested?"

"Of course not. I shouldn't have been so stupid. When I hadn't heard anything by the next time I saw the man again, I demanded to know if he passed on the message. He laughed in my face, and told me in no uncertain terms how stupid I was. The only people I had contact with were those I encountered on my runs. I had no way of contacting anyone else. The only other person I had contact with was Lenny. I think she was what you might call 'my handler'. Whenever I had to make an extra run, or do something different, Lenny contacted me with the instructions. I guessed she was fairly high up in the hierarchy of the mob. It's why I approached that other bloke to pass on my message, rather than asking Lenny to do it. After that failed, the next time Lenny contacted me, I told her in no uncertain terms I needed to speak to the boss and, if they wished to continue their operation, he needed to meet with me."

"Do you have a death wish, or do you just like living dangerously?" Ben asked. "Did she pass on your message?"

"Yeah, she did. A couple of days later, she called to tell me the meeting was arranged. I wasn't to do a run on the night. Instead, I was to go somewhere else to meet the boss."

Stella became fidgety when she mentioned the proposed meeting. A thought slammed in from left field. The little voice in my head encouraged me to run it by her. I took care in constructing my question. "Had you been to the derelict two-storey building in the slum area before?"

My question drew startled looks from both Stella and Ben. Ben's face darkened as he prepared to speak. I cut him off. My question had wrong-footed Stella, and I wanted to pursue it while she was off-guard. "You believed you had a meeting with the boss in the derelict building in the slum area. But it's not how it played out, was it?"

"No-o," she whispered. I watched her wringing her hands together. She kept her eyes firmly focused on the desk top, and didn't appear inclined to say more. I wasn't about to leave it there.

"So, you went to the building. Went around to the back and went in. The boss wasn't there, was he?"

Stella gave a half shake her head, but kept her eyes on the desk.

"No, he wasn't there. Wasn't the only person you found in the building that night a dead woman?"

As I finished speaking, Stella gasped. From the other side of the desk, I heard Ben give a low growl. I chose to ignore him. My gut instinct told me Stella was going to be less than honest about the night in question. If I gave her the benefit of the doubt, I might suggest she tried blocking it from her memory because finding the body was so horrific. It was brutal to do this to her, but both Ben and I needed to know not only the whole story, but the truth. I softened my approach, and persuaded her to tell us what happened.

"I was stupid. I know better than to go to a place like that at night on my own. Still, I was determined to speak to the boss and, if it's what I had to do, then I would meet him at that building. First my husband – and I'm sure they thought they had killed him – and then Rosie. Only, in Rosie's case, they succeeded."

"So, you knew the woman whose body you found in the derelict building that night?" Ben asked quietly, his aggression disappeared.

"Rosie was another one of their 'girls' – another one of the couriers. I don't think the couriers were ever supposed to meet, but sometimes the gods deal you a lucky hand. One night, Rosie's car had a flat tyre on the way to make a delivery. A passer-by helped her change the wheel, but it meant she was late dropping off her parcel. We ended up making a drop at the same time. When we went to leave, I told Rosie I'd meet her at a little coffee shop on the north side, if she was interested in having a chat. She was a good operator. In case anyone was watching, I drove towards home, but then drove past our place and went to the coffee shop. After about ten minutes, I figured Rosie wasn't coming. I was about to leave when she arrived. She had driven all over town to create a convoluted route to the coffee shop."

"Was your meeting worthwhile? Did it establish a friendship of sorts between you and Rosie?" Ben asked

"We didn't become friends. In fact, I never saw or spoke to her again until I found her in the building that night. What I learnt from our meeting in the coffee shop was how Rosie also wanted out of the business the mob was running. She said she had already made noises about getting out, but didn't think anyone took her seriously. The difference between Rosie and me was, she didn't have any family or anyone close to her they could threaten – or worse."

"That night at the derelict building, do you think the mob intended to dish you out the same treatment as they gave Rosie?" I couldn't help myself. My question earned me another withering look from Ben.

"I don't think so. For whatever reason, I don't think they intended to kill me … not that night anyway. I think I was set up to find Rosie's body as a warning to scare me into toeing the line. Maybe they knew Rosie and I had talked. I don't know. But, I do know their plan backfired. After what they did to Rosie, I was even more determined to end my association with them … even if it meant my ending up on the floor of the derelict house in the same condition as I found Rosie… And, it's almost what happened."

Our interview had continued way past morning tea time without further coffee or sustenance interrupting proceedings. It was just after eleven o'clock, and too early for lunch. For a change, it was Ben who noted Stella's agitated state, and suggested we leave finishing the interview until tomorrow. He spotted the housekeeper hovering near the library door and beckoned her in.

"I know it's a bit early for lunch, but I think Mrs Martin might like something now before she goes to rest for the remainder of the day. There will be only one for lunch. My colleague and I are about to leave."

About ten minutes later, we were in the carpark. As he climbed into his car, Ben warned me to be prepared to work after dinner tonight. He wanted to run through everything we had on both of our Martin cases.

Chapter 15

On my way home, I called at my city office. Although it was Saturday afternoon and I wanted nothing more than to go home and put my feet up with the weekend papers, Ben's threat of working after dinner tonight meant I had work to do.

My Martin case file needed updating, including adding the notes from today's interview. The timeline on my whiteboard needed transferring to my computer. Once he saw the whiteboard, Ben would demand a copy. I could tell him to photograph it with his phone, but it wouldn't go down well. No, best I create it in my Project software and add today's information. Then I will be able to print copies for him and my case file.

There were no messages and nothing else requiring urgent attention to detain me in my city office for more than a few minutes before I was on my way home. As I turned onto my driveway, an idle thought floated to the forefront of my thinking: I hope he brings dinner tonight as there is nothing in my house to turn into a meal. I hadn't felt inclined to sacrifice precious time by calling at the supermarket on my way home.

After brewing a coffee and slapping cheese on a couple of crackers for a makeshift lunch, I took everything through to my office and began work. First task: listen to the recording of today's interview. As it played, I checked the notes I took against the recording. Then, I typed up my notes, added a copy to my case file, and turned my attention to my embryonic timeline. Once replicated on my computer, I added today's new milestones to both versions.

By the time I completed everything, it was almost six o'clock. I hadn't heard from Ben since we left the apartment block. I wondered about reminding him to bring something for dinner – and if he would be coming for dinner. It is possible he still might be involved in whatever kept him out of bed last night. Make another coffee first and then call Ben seemed the correct order of things.

While I was hovering over the coffee machine, Ben called. Yes, he was coming to my place tonight, and he would bring something for dinner. I splurged on a swipe of vegemite as well as cheese on another cracker and took it and a coffee to my office. Everything I needed to do before Ben arrived was complete except, there was something I needed to get my head around prior to our after-dinner session.

With no idea of what Ben intended doing or achieving tonight, I decided to make a note of the things I wanted to discuss. Rather than a series of notes, my efforts produced a list of questions. As I sat studying the timeline on the board, more seemed to almost jump off its surface at me. There were other questions as well. Questions about background information, and others which sought to establish possible emotional responses involved in specific situations or events.

By the time headlights coming up my driveway announced Ben's arrival, my list of questions had grown to two pages. Were any of them irrelevant or unnecessary? There wasn't time to worry about it. Ben and dinner had arrived – and I realised, in spite of my crackers, I was famished.

Dinner was a non-event. The selection of Chinese dishes was excellent, and we both tucked in with gusto. But, it appeared neither of us wanted to waste time on eating, preferring instead to spend time examining our Martin cases. With no demand for dessert tonight, and the post-dinner coffee in the lounge room ritual abandoned, we settled for a glass of wine in my office instead.

As predicted, as soon as Ben saw the timeline on my whiteboard, he demanded a copy. About a minute or so of silence followed as he studied his printout. Then it was down to business. In such situations, it's normal for Ben to take charge, to set the agenda and control the discussion. Tonight, he seemed at a loss about where to start. For the first time this evening,

I realised how haggard he looked, and remembered how little sleep he had last night.

Taking the initiative, I eased into my list of questions, starting with what I considered the easy ones. "Have you managed to obtain the CCTV tapes from the jeweller's shop's cameras?"

"No. The world is conspiring against me. I tried again today – and at least received an explanation. It appears the owner – or the bloke in charge, whoever he is – is the only one with access to the archived tapes vault. He wasn't at work on Friday, and doesn't work on weekends. So, my first chance to get my hands on those tapes appears to be some time on Monday. I admit to being a bit frustrated about the process. I want to lay eyes on this Lenny person before too much longer. I feel she is a key to this whole case."

"Yeah, I'm anxious to get a look at her as well. Why do you think she is a key player? Maybe she is just another of the mob's lackeys, albeit of a higher rank than Stella."

"Maybe… But, I'm going to borrow one of your standard phrases to explain it: my gut tells me she is something more. What else is on that list you keep looking at?"

"It's a list of questions. I don't know about their importance, but they are matters I am curious about. Right, moving down the list… how is Trent Martin progressing? We haven't spoken about him in days."

"I did talk to the hospital this afternoon. He is still doped up to aid his recovery, so I still can't speak to him. Nevertheless, they assure me his improvement is slow but continuous… And, no, they couldn't give me any indication of when I might be able to interview him."

"From the little Stella told us, it doesn't seem as though their marriage was bundle of laughs. In fact, it seems the marriage was in trouble long before Stella became mixed up with this mob. I can't determine the extent of the impact what happened to her husband had on her. It stands to reason she was quite shaken up by it, but why? Was it because she still cares about him? Or, was it due to being confronted with hard evidence of what the mob did to those who didn't toe the line?"

"While I was talking to the hospital, I checked whether Stella had enquired about her husband after he was first admitted. There was nothing while she was in hospital, and there had been nothing since she has been holed up in the penthouse. We have separated her from her mobile phone. It is safer she doesn't have it. With plenty of time on her hands, but without a phone, she can't call people to help fill in time. No doubt the mob have done their homework well and are aware of her friends and associates."

"Are you suggesting those 'friends and associates' are being monitored in some way for any contact with Stella?"

Ben shrugged. "Who knows? If we knew who they were and what they were up to, we might be able to answer that question and a whole truckload of others. Despite what she told us about the state of their marriage, I still find it intriguing she hasn't enquired after her husband's condition."

"I've been meaning to ask, are you going to continue the interview tomorrow morning?"

"Yes. Why wouldn't I? This investigation has dragged on far too long. I need to get to the bottom of it, and soon. I hope we can finish the interviewing tomorrow. Then, perhaps by Tuesday, and with the help of the CCTV tapes, we will be better informed and closer to wrapping up this case."

"To my way of thinking, establishing the identities of both Lenny and Rosie is important. I don't know why I'm concerned about Rosie, but it bothers me she remains a Jane Doe on a slab in the morgue. Something just occurred to me. When Stella told us about meeting Rosie at the coffee shop on the north side, she talked about Rosie having driven all over town to avoid being followed. What sort of car was Rosie driving? Did Stella notice anything specific about the car: colour, model or make, its plates…?"

"Good point; we haven't explored the car with Stella. We'll ask about it tomorrow, but I'm not confident she will have anything to tell us. Any other bright ideas you might like to share?"

"It's not on my list, but something else occurs to me: what about those two vehicles at the derelict building the night they attacked Stella? I wondered whether a traffic camera somewhere might have picked them up after they left the scene."

"I plead guilty to sloppy investigative procedures. No, I haven't given them another thought. Good question though… I'll start someone checking out camera footage tomorrow."

"Don't beat yourself up about it. You're a one-man team on this case, and much of your time has been spent interviewing Stella. Are there still no new detectives likely to be posted here soon?"

"Not a glimmer of hope I'm afraid, but I have asked for temporary assistance from Brisbane. I'm hoping, either Monday or Tuesday, I'll receive word of a couple of detectives on their way to Millhaven. The upside to borrowing a couple from Brisbane is the-powers-that-be will get off their backsides and find me at least a couple of permanent replacements, so they can have their temporary replacements returned as soon as possible."

"Here's another thought; at the appropriate point of tomorrow's interview, ask Stella about those two cars parked at the derelict building the night she was worked over. They were parked behind the building when she arrived. I know it was dark, but she must have noticed something about them. She would have been on high alert at the time, and would have assessed everything around her."

"I'll add it to my list of questions to ask."

While many of my questions hadn't been addressed, Ben looked so wrung out, I felt concerned for him. Although it was only eight o'clock, we should call it a night. "Ben, you are exhausted. Go home and get some sleep."

He went to put his glass down on my desk. It seemed to slip out of his hand, almost missing the desk. "On second thoughts, you are too tired to drive. The bed in the spare room is made up.

Go and fall into it. I don't want to see you again until tomorrow morning."

"I can't go to bed like this. I haven't even had a shower."

"There's a towelling robe in the cupboard in the spare room. It will fit you… and this establishment does run to a shower. Do as you are told. Go… shower, and then go to bed."

The fact he didn't reject my offer of a bed for the night was surprise enough, but I was astonished when he left my office without further encouragement and did as he was told. I finished cleaning up in the kitchen and then, once I knew he had gone to bed, I too showered and took to my own bed for an early night.

*****

While I was trying to untangle my eyelashes to open my eyes this morning, I heard Ben moving about. I was out of bed in a flash and, wrapped in my bath robe, I went to investigate what he was up to in the kitchen.

"Good morning. I don't know what you have for breakfast these days, but I thought I should at least get the coffee happening. By the way, that is a fantastic bed to sleep in." Relief flooded through me at finding a much chirper Ben rummaging in my kitchen cupboards.

"Where the hell do you keep the vegemite? I think I've looked in every cupboard and haven't found it."

"That's probably because it is in the fridge."

"Who keeps vegemite in the fridge?"

"Well, obviously I do. Because I don't use enough of it, a jar lasts me a long time." I received a grunt in response as he opened the fridge and reached for the vegemite.

Geez, perhaps it's just as well our relationship all those years ago didn't result in some living-together arrangement. Or, maybe it is both of us having lived alone for so long is the problem. Regardless, breakfast occurred in peaceful harmony. After which, Ben rushed home to shower and change before going in to work … and I allowed myself a leisurely hour to flip through the weekend papers before preparing to head to the apartment block for today's interview session.

Having agreed to start the interview at nine o'clock again, I pulled into the carpark about ten minutes ahead of time. Ben almost followed me in. We started work right on nine o'clock. Five minutes later, coffees arrived to cause a few moments of faffing about. Then, we were settled again, and even Stella appeared keen to begin.

Today, Ben began in a different way. It had me wondering if he discovered something I didn't know about. "Before we move on with your story this morning, is there anything you might have remembered overnight in relation to the events we covered yesterday?"

"I don't think so. While I don't remember everything I said, there weren't any 'lightbulb' moments after you left. If you think there are gaps or something was missed, you will have to ask about it."

Stella's comments weren't enlightening, and Ben didn't pursue the matter further … leaving me mystified by the question. I hoped patience might produce results as the morning progressed.

"Okay, let's start. When we left off yesterday, you were telling us about having found Rosie's body on the floor in the derelict building. Was your meeting with Rosie at the coffee shop, the only time you met or spoke to her?"

"Yes … well, no, not really. I didn't speak to her again. It was only two days later when I found her dead. I think she tried calling me the day after our meeting. I was checking all my calls before I answered them, and didn't answer any with blocked caller ID, or whose ID I didn't recognize. It meant I wouldn't answer any further calls from Lenny, as her calls just showed they were from a private number … along with all the other nuisance calls we receive these days."

"Why do you think Rosie tried to call you?" Ben appeared to be deep in thought as he asked the question.

"It wasn't until after … after I found her body, I realised the call might have been from her. When the call came in, the caller ID looked strange. So, I ignored it. After what happened to her, I remembered that caller ID. Somehow, something about it suggested it might be Rosie. Although I knew it was pointless trying to call Rosie, I tried the number. It didn't answer, but it could be due to all sorts of reasons."

"Please think back to the night when you met Rosie at the coffee shop. I assume Rosie was driving her own car?" Stella confirmed Ben's assumption with a nod. "Good; what can you tell me about her car; anything at all you might remember?"

"Her car…? Uhmm… It was nothing special I don't think; some make of small sedan. It was red – a bright red, not one of those dark reds. To me, it looked fairly new. I don't remember it having any pin striping or other fancy additions."

Ben was tapping his pencil on the table again as he glanced through his notes. Rather than let the silence drag on, I was about to ask a question when he stopped tapping and jumped in ahead of me.

"Do you think Rosie was her real name, or was that just something she decided to go by rather than use her right name?"

"No-o, I'm fairly sure it was her real name. I've never thought about it. There didn't seem to be anything odd about Rosie being her name. Come to think of it, it either was her real name or she was very attached to the name. The plates on her car also had that name: Rosie90."

After scribbling a hasty note, Ben said, "If the '90' on the number plate referred to the year in which she was born, it would make her about thirty now. Do you think it's about the right age for the woman you knew as Rosie?"

"Again, I never thought about how old she was, but ye-es, now you ask, I think thirty could be about right."

"Okay, great. Now we're going to talk about cars again," Ben announced. Stella rolled her eyes at the prospect. Ben ignored her. "I know this probably is somewhere you don't want to revisit just yet, but I do need to talk to you about the night you were attacked in the derelict building." Stella drew in a deep breath before giving Ben a half-hearted nod.

"Talk me through what happened after you turned onto the street where the derelict building is located."

"I knew which building to go to, so I just drove straight up to it." Stella closed her eyes. I suspected she was reliving in her mind the night's events. Without opening her eyes, she continued speaking. "After my previous visit, I was feeling nervous. I paused for a moment or two before turning onto the driveway to go around to the back of the house. It's a terrible driveway. I suppose I was hoping to delay the inevitable by trying to pick my way carefully along it.

When I arrived at the back corner of the house, I could see a pale glow inside, but it didn't spill out onto the backyard. I parked nose-in to the rear wall of the building, but didn't turn off the motor or get out of the car. For a few moments, I just sat there scanning as much of the area as I could see. No one was waiting outside. So, I got out of the car, and stood beside it listening for anything happening inside. Then, there wasn't anything else to do but go in and supposedly meet with the boss to tell him I wanted out, and it didn't matter what happened, one way or the other, I would no longer be working for them."

By the time she finished speaking, Stella appeared quite agitated. It wasn't surprising given this was the first time she recounted the details of the night of her attack. I wasn't surprised the memory was so raw. She dropped her head onto her chest, and sat with her hands clasped on the table and her eyes closed.

Ben allowed her a few moments before quietly resuming the interview. "I understand how difficult this is for you, but I can't begin to explain how important it is to investigate not only what happened to you, but also what happened to Rosie and your husband. Do you feel up to continuing, or would you prefer another coffee break before we continue?"

"Perhaps a coffee break… It will give me a chance to get my head together again before you ask me more questions."

I volunteered to go in search of the housekeeper for morning tea. She was in the kitchen and had most of it prepared. Back in the library, I told the other two morning tea was on its way. Stella looked better than when I went in search of the housekeeper, but I suggested she might like to take a few minutes to wash her face and freshen up.

Morning tea was dispatched without undue waste of time, and Ben soon resumed interview mode. "Stella, I want to take you back to when you first arrived at the building. You drove around to the back, parked up against the rear wall, and then sat there checking out the backyard for any sign of threat. What was in the backyard? I don't want to know about all the junk and rubbish there. I'm interested in anything significant or unusual you noticed."

"There wasn't much else apart from junk and rubbish. The only other things besides me and my car were two other vehicles. They were reverse parked as far back as possible in the cleared area of the yard. Apart from those, I can't say I noticed anything else worth mentioning."

"You're doing great. You said there were two cars there. Can you describe them for me?"

"Well, the light from inside the building didn't extend outside, so where they were parked wasn't lit up, but the good moon allowed me to see them quite well. One caught my eye straight away. It was an expensive-looking sporty convertible. I was going to say it was the sort you'd see a lad about town driving around in, but that doesn't quite fit. A bloke probably wouldn't choose a powder blue vehicle. At least, I imagine they'd pick something more of a bloke's colour – whatever that might be."

"Those are the exact details we need to know. Now, what about the second vehicle parked there, what can you tell me about it?"

"It was one of those big SUV type cars. I think it was new – I mean, I think it was a recent model. It's a bit hard to explain, but its contours were sort of rounded, rather than being square and boxy. It was a dark colour, possibly black … No, not black, it was grey, or maybe something like midnight blue."

Stella pressed her eyes tightly closed and seemed to be attempting to recall something. Ben allowed her time, and it paid dividends.

"Damn! I know both of those vehicles had personalised number plates. You know the sort containing a smart-arsed message of some kind. I've tried, but I can't recover what I saw on the SUV's plates. And, I don't really know what was on the sports car's plates, except the word 'stud' was part of it. I'm sorry, but I can't remember any more at the moment. Maybe if I think on it for a while, more details will come back."

Again, the morning had run away from us and, after a late morning tea, it was almost lunchtime. Ben decided the three of us would lunch together today, and sent me off to instruct the housekeeper accordingly. We filled in time until lunch arrived by discussing how Stella was recovering, and what she thought of her present accommodation. There was no bad news in any of it, so all of us were in reasonably high spirits by the time the housekeeper arrived with lunch.

As soon as we finished eating, Ben and I left. On the way down from the penthouse, Ben said he had work to do this afternoon and might be late arriving for dinner tonight. With a whole afternoon to myself, I suggested I might make a curry for dinner … And made a detour to the supermarket on my way home to ensure a curry was possible.

Chapter 16

The spicy perfume of my curry greeted Ben as he came through the door. "I hope that won't take too long to cook. The smell of it has me just about drooling in anticipation."

He didn't have long to suffer. The moment I saw his lights coming up the driveway, I put the rice on to cook, and the naan bread in the over to warm through. We took long glasses of pale ale out onto the deck while we waited. It was a glorious crisp, clear night, but the air had a nip to it. Icy pale ales probably weren't the best suited drinks for the deck tonight, but neither of us complained. Ben's only comment was, "The aroma of that curry seems stronger and even more tantalising out here."

In spite of a more than adequate lunch, we both appeared half-starved by the time we sat down to eat. No conversation intruded until we dispatched significant portions of our meals. For want of greater inspiration, leftover fruit salad and ice cream followed the curry. I did top it with a slurp of Bailey's Irish Cream liqueur to make it a little more interesting. Serious discussions began as soon as the fruit salad disappeared.

"Ben, what's your approach for tomorrow's interview of Stella? While we are gathering useful stuff from her, the process is slow and frustrating. How much more do you think she is able to be to tell us?"

"That's the unknown factor in this exercise. I'm impressed with the extent of her recall, but we are starting to explore the period surrounding her trauma. Her self-preservation mechanism might blank out some details of what happened in the building. It might leave her with nothing more than a few vague, shadowy recollections. All we can do is try to extract as much as possible from her memory banks. It's possible the process of scouring those memories might help unlock key information she isn't aware she holds."

"Do you have a particular line of enquiry for tomorrow? And, are you planning another nine o'clock start?"

"Er, no, probably not. I'll visit the security firm's office first thing after they open. I want to collect the recording from the jeweller's shop CCTV camera on the morning Stella and her friend, Lenny, were there … when the earrings conveniently found their way into Stella's bag. The office opens at eight o'clock, but I want to view the recording before we talk to Stella."

"So, what do you think, maybe ten o'clock, or later?"

"I'll aim for ten o'clock, and see what happens."

"What about the vehicle descriptions Stella gave you, is there any chance you might be able to track them down?"

"Since this afternoon, I've had my sole detective going through footage from the traffic camera along that end of High Street and from the cameras at the major intersection. The approximate timing of their departures from the derelict building you provided should help narrow down the footage he has to view. And, I've asked the sergeant in charge of Traffic to chase up those personal plates Stella gave us. I was hoping to hear something from him by now … maybe by tomorrow morning."

"While I won't see it before we talk to Stella again, I would like to see the recording from the jeweller's shop sometime. I suppose, like you, I'm curious to see what this Lenny person looks like. It's possible I've seen her in the city heart on occasion. How are you going to approach tomorrow's interview? Stella only has what happened in that building left to tell us."

"Yeah, I think 'go in gently' might be best. We will have to play it by ear; adjust how we go according to her response."

I nodded my agreement as I ran tomorrow's possible interview scenario through my mind. Over the last few days, Stella had proved she is tough, and made of sterner stuff than I thought, but tomorrow might test her resilience. Ben's voice cut through my thoughts.

"What about you, are you available for the interview tomorrow, or will you be starting a new case?"

"A new case…! It would be good to know what was happening in that regard. I expected one or both of my new cases would start this weekend. Here it is Sunday night, and I haven't heard a peep from either of them. I don't mind. If they began as expected, I might have to curtail my involvement in Stella's interview. As tomorrow might see the interviews completed, starting either of my new jobs, or both of them, won't cause problems."

There was no opportunity for further discussion. Ben's phone chirped and, after checking the caller ID, he wandered out onto the deck to take the call. I guessed it was about work. Less than five minutes later, he returned but was preoccupied with whatever the call was about. I sat in silence and let him be until he was ready to talk. A few moments later, he seemed to realise where he was, and I was with him.

"Sorry; something has come up. I should check on it. When I know how things are going and what's happening in the morning, I'll call you about the timing of Stella's interview."

Minutes later, I watched his taillights disappearing down the driveway. As I finished cleaning up in the kitchen, I replayed tonight's conversations through my mind. Nothing riveting eventuated from the evening. A tinge of disappointment accompanied the realisation. Maybe tomorrow will reveal more about this mess involving Stella, and maybe Ben and I might be a lot closer to wrapping up our investigations.

Tomorrow is another day, and an unknown quantity. With nothing else I could do to progress my case tonight, I indulged in an early night.

*****

Monday-itis ravaged me this morning. Perhaps 'depression' might be the correct term for it. Not having wrapped up the

Martin case was starting to gnaw at me. The uncertainty about what was happening with my supposedly new cases wasn't helping. With today's episode of Stella's interview likely to begin later in the morning, I felt no compulsion to rush into my city office.

"Shake yourself, Sonny!" I chastised myself aloud. "What is wrong with you? Get up, and go in to work." My stern talking-to was of no use whatsoever. Yes, I could be in my city office at my usual time this morning, but then what? What did I have to do today? "Well, I could jolly well call those two new clients to find out what the hell is going on," I told me and my kitchen.

Chastising wasn't a waste. It wasn't professional of me not to follow up on those new clients. Perhaps their situations had changed, and they no longer were going to be new clients. If it were the case, and I wrapped up the Martin case within the next day or so, I could take a few days off. Maybe go up to my beach place and relax. The little voice in my head reminded me not to get ahead of myself. It told me I knew better than to make plans before I was in possession of all the facts.

I picked up my bag, and headed down the driveway to join the seething mass of early morning peak hour traffic. One lane was closed. Traffic was moving at the rate of about a mile a month. While I needed to pay attention to what was going on around me, a small part of my mind was off doing its own thing. It was running through a basic inventory of facts relating to the Martin case.

By the time I reached my office, I had created a couple of tasks to do which might fill in time until Ben called about today's interview with Stella. After checking emails and messages, I picked up my bag and headed onto the street. The morning was fresh and crisp and provided a pleasant walk around to the office supplies place in the next street.

Colleen Jenkins was helping a customer choose a new office chair when I found her in the back corner of the display area. I was happy to wait, and signalled her not to rush. The customer made a decision about her preferred chair. After sending the woman to wait near the checkouts, Colleen sent a young lad to fetch one of the chairs from the building's stockroom. Colleen's nervousness was obvious as she came to talk to me.

"Is everything all right, Colleen? You seem a bit concerned about something."

"Yes, I can show you something that might suit. Come with me and I'll show you what we have."

She led me to the rear wall of the display area where collapsible tables were stacked against the wall, and then proceeded to mime explaining the virtues of each model to me. I didn't have to be a genius to recognise subterfuge. "What's going on, Colleen? Would you rather I wasn't here?" As I asked my questions, I played along, pointing to the different models as I spoke, I hoped I gave a reasonable performance of a customer querying the advantages of the various tables as I pointed to them in turn.

"I can't be seen to be talking to you if you're not a customer. I could come to see you at lunchtime – or after work if you prefer. But, I can't be 'chatting' to you in here."

Given the uncertainties of my day, after work seemed like the best option. "I was on early start this morning, so I finish work at about four o'clock this afternoon. I'll come straight round your office."

After a few moments of standing scanning the tables we supposedly were discussing, I tried for my best rendition of an undecided customer who was going home to think about which model to purchase. All the way back to my office, I mulled over what happened in the office supplies showroom. In the sales area, if employees were talking to someone, they were expected to be selling, and not just chatting. But, there was something else going on there this morning; something with a sinister tinge to it.

Bugger! Four o'clock is hours away, and I'm in danger of dying of curiosity in the meantime. Why was Colleen on the floor trying to sell furniture anyway? She is supposed to be Trent Martin's offsider, and should be in her office bean-counting or whatever assistant accountants and their offsider's do. A disturbing possibility tried wriggling its way through to the forefront of my thinking. I managed to keep it at bay, but it remained lurking in the background.

Still, my visit to the office supplies place wasn't a complete waste of time. It made me think of something else I should do: see if the hospital is kind enough to tell me how Trent Martin's recovery is progressing. Back in my office and with a fresh cup of coffee beside me, I called the hospital. I expected to draw a blank.

When I was put through to the appropriate ward, the nurse on duty remembered me. She was on Stella Martin's ward the previous week and, although she was unsure about my involvement, she agreed to discuss Trent Martin's condition with me.

"As of this morning, he has been taken off all medication. It might take another day or two for him to become lucid again, so we will continue to monitor him until he is able to talk to us."

"Once he regains consciousness, will I be able to talk to him – even for just a couple of minutes?"

"He remains under police guard. So, you wouldn't be able to see or talk to him without police approval."

"No, of course not. I'll have the necessary authority put in place today."

After thanking her, I ended the call, only to have my phone ring immediately. It was the new client I expected to hear from last Friday. It seems things were not going to plan. The target I was to follow would not return to Millhaven now until later in the week, possibly as late as Friday. I would be let know the moment he arrived back in town.

Okay, it looks as though I can take a few days off, but not enough to accommodate a trip up to my beach house. A couple of lazy days at home wouldn't be too hard to suffer. When I returned from talking to Colleen Jenkins, I noticed the message light on my answering machine was blinking. I listened to the message.

My other new client asked me to return her call. The law of averages said everything was going too well this morning. This one had to be bad news. The client answered on the first ring. There was a bit of a development – a hiccup really, she advised apologetically.

This case supposedly was about an insurance claim relating to a workplace injury. Mention of a 'hiccup' tended to confirm the call would be all bad news. Instead, the news was intriguing, quite intriguing.

"News we received this morning tends to indicate the person we wanted followed has disappeared. Since his injury, he has been assigned a housekeeper who comes in one day a week to take care of those things his injury prevents him doing for himself. She comes in every Thursday. By Wednesday at the latest, the man orders groceries to be delivered on Thursday morning, so the housekeeper can bring them in and put them away for him. Before she leaves on Thursday afternoon, she takes out the rubbish bin and leaves it for the truck to empty early on Friday morning. Then, later on Friday, when the housekeeper goes into town to do her own shopping, she drops by the man's house to bring in the bin."

Most of it was of no consequence to me, except for the bit about his apparent disappearance. I discovered the housekeeper called the insurance firm first thing this morning to register her concerns. When she went to work on Thursday, the house seemed deserted. There was nothing in the fridge and no rubbish in the kitchen tidy. No one came home during the time she was at the house. She put the bin out as usual, and called again on Friday morning to bring it in. No one was home, and she realised the usual grocery delivery on Thursday had not occurred. It tended to confirm her suspicion nobody had been in the house for a while. When she drove past on Saturday night no lights were on in the house. As soon as the insurance firm opened for business this morning, the housekeeper called. Subsequent investigations suggest the man did a flit sometime early last week.

And then there was only one – one new client, that is. Unless and until the insurance firm located their missing man, they were no longer a client. I knew things had to turn sour sometime this morning, and I found myself hoping it was the only bad news I'd receive. I couldn't help wondering if something might go wrong with Stella's scheduled interview. As it was almost ten o'clock, and it was likely Ben would call within the next little while, it seemed pointless to start anything.

Eleven o'clock came and went. I had just about read the ink off today's paper. Maybe there wouldn't be an interview today; not this morning anyway. For a few moments, I toyed with the idea of going in search of something for lunch, but decided to wait until midday. If I hadn't heard from Ben by then, it was likely there would be no interview today, and I could pack up and go home for the rest of the day.

His call came at about ten minutes before the deadline. "Are you ready to go? I'll pick you up in about five minutes. No point in taking two cars. Lunch will be ready when we arrive. I'm on my way."

I seemed to develop six arms and legs going in different directions as I madly dashed about trying to rinse my coffee mug, set the answering machine, check the contents of my bag, lock the office and be downstairs waiting for Ben, all within about two minutes of his ending his phone call. It does not take five minutes to drive from his office to the parking lot behind my building. As I let the back door of the building slam closed behind me, Ben nosed his way into the parking lot.

As a conversation opener, I commented, "I thought today was cancelled when it was so late and you still hadn't called. Are there problems I should be aware of?"

"There are always problems but, no, none of today's problems relate to the forthcoming interview. Everything conspired to delay me today. When I went to collect the jewellery store's CCTV recording, the boss hadn't arrived at work yet. The very embarrassed receptionist explained although the office opened at 7:30, the boss usually didn't arrive until at least nine o'clock. I wasn't going to hang around until then, so I went back to the office to see how the boys went with tracing those two vehicles Stella described for us."

"Don't tell me; they didn't have any good news for you, did they?"

"Well, yes and no. They tracked down the plates on both of those vehicles and could tell me who the supposed owners were. I made a few phone calls. One of those owners doesn't exist, and never did exist as far as I can determine. That's the SUV I'm talking about. The other car, the convertible, involved a more complicated story."

"Of course it did. It would be far too simple if you could just call the owner and sort it out in a few minutes." He shot me a look I took to mean I should refrain from being quite so flippant.

"It appears the blue convertible is involved in a property settlement tug-of-war subsequent to a recent divorce. Ownership of the vehicle is being questioned."

"As far as your investigation goes, does it matter who owns it?"

"Not if that's all there was to the story, but it would also be too simple. The ex-husband locked the vehicle in a secure storage facility building. Security was a bit lax. Nobody noticed the break-in for a few days. When the security guard noticed the damaged roller door, he called the ex-husband, who rushed over. The vehicle was gone, along with other items the man seems quite attached to, but reluctant to tell me about."

"Okay, so the ex-wife – or more likely her current romantic interest – broke into the building and the wife now has the car."

"Yeah, it should be so simple, shouldn't it? Both parties are now blaming the other for 'spiriting away' the car."

"Oh good; was there a happy resolution to the situation?"

"The detective I spoke to was still investigating the case, but he was inclined to think an independent third party was involved, and neither the wife nor the husband had the vehicle."

"So, this was a straightforward case of a stolen vehicle. That won't make it easy to find out who has it now."

We ran out of time to discuss the vehicles or anything else, as we had arrived in the apartment building's carpark. After the usual faffing about with the security systems, we were met by the housekeeper and ushered into the dining room, where the table was set ready for lunch. She told us Stella had gone to freshen up and would join us in a few minutes.

Chapter 17

Lunch was an event over which none of us was inclined to waste time. Only the occasional comment intruded. Then, it was back to the library to get on with the serious part of the day. Ben opened the interview by inquiring about how Stella was holding up through the interview process. He indicated that, depending on how much ground we covered today, this could be our last interview session. In response, a strange look flitted across Stella's face.

If anything, I would expect her to be pleased it was almost over. The look I saw cross her face indicated something else. I detected a hint of fear – uneasiness – in that look. It was fleeting and it seems Ben didn't notice it. I couldn't let it go by without exploring what lay behind it.

"Stella, I thought you would be happy we wouldn't be annoying you every day, but something tells me that's not how you feel. Do you think there is more story to tell; more than we are likely to cover today?"

"No, I don't think so … Argh, I don't know. I don't know what you want to know, or how much more I know. All I know is, I want the nightmare to end. I want your investigation to be successful, for people to be put away… for this whole mess to be shut down and for nobody else to be killed; for no one to live in fear for their life."

Ben fidgeted on his chair and shot me a warning look. I had held up proceedings for long enough. I responded with a smile, and relaxed back into my chair to signify my withdrawal from the conversation. He wasted no time resuming command.

"Stella, on and off through this interview process, we have mentioned your fellow high school student, Lenny. Apart from the fact Lenny is now living in Millhaven, you don't know much about her life now, and don't recall seeing her around town before the high school reunion. As we don't know who she is, or what she looks like, we're unaware whether we've seen her around town either. Could you describe her to us? Start with any significant features she has."

"Uhmm … I'll try. She is about as tall as I am, and slim – one of those straight up and down sort who never develops any curves. So, she doesn't look curvy, as much as well-muscled now. I mean, she looks like she keeps fit; works out at the gym. That's strange. I can't recall her being into anything physical; never played any sport as I remember."

"That's a good start. Apart from looking fit, is there anything else about her appearance, anything to help pick her out in a crowd for instance?"

"She's easy to spot. Just look for her hair. She has this thick mop of dark red hair. When we were at school, it was only a bit long, down to her shoulders maybe. Now, it is really long – and it looks thicker. I remember it used to have a bit of a wave. Now she wears it dead straight, and a bit severe looking. It has a thick heavy fringe and then falls straight down beside her face and down her back. I suppose, I'd describe it as spectacular; not necessarily nice, but eye-catching."

Ben continued scribbling in his notebook after Stella finished speaking. I risked another withering look from Ben and jumped in. "If she is a redhead, I imagine she has the fair skin associated with such colouring – and possibly a few freckles too."

"Yes, she is fair skinned. Your mentioning freckles reminded me she had a sprinkling of freckles in her younger days. They weren't evident at the reunion and I don't remember seeing them any time we've met since then. It's probably thanks to the make-up available today."

It was time for Ben to exert his authority again. "Is there anything else you can add about Lenny to help us identify her?" Stella shook her head. "Then let's move on. When we left off yesterday, you had arrived at the derelict building in the slum area and discovered two other cars parked out the back. You parked nose-in to the building and, after checking the back yard, you went in through the back door. Let's return to that moment. What did you see as you stepped inside?"

"Because the door was jammed partially open, you couldn't see much when you stepped over the threshold. It required a couple of steps to be able to see around the door. And then you couldn't see much anyway. There was a small lamp on a box in about the middle of the room. It wasn't a powerful light; only giving off a sort of yellowish-orange glow that didn't light up the whole room."

"My apologies for the interruption, but who was there waiting for you in the room? How many people, and what can you tell me about them?" Ben spoke in almost a whisper. This was taking Stella back to the most traumatic period of the episode. The last thing either of us wanted was for her to breakdown when revisiting the situation.

"This is going to sound ridiculous. You'll say it's my mind's self-preservation mechanism in action, but I don't know how many or who were in the room. I thought about this last night, after forcing myself to replay my memories of what happened after I stepped into the room. I managed to 'see' the scene again. The lamp was a battery-operated torch. It was small, only a few centimetres tall – maybe ten or twelve centimetres. They placed a sort of screen behind it. I don't know what it was made of, but it formed an arc around the sides and back of the lamp. As a result, everything behind the lamp remained in darkness."

"Are you saying you didn't know there were people in the room?" Ben asked.

"No… I knew there were people there. When I first stepped into the doorway, a man's voice told me to come in. There was more than one person there. As I took those few steps to enter the room, I heard barely audible murmuring from somewhere on the other side of the room. From what happened later, I know there were two of them."

"How did your 'meeting' with those people progress once you were in the room?"

"That's the bit I'm not clear about. I know it all happened quickly. I didn't see it coming. Look, I'm not a fool. I knew it wasn't going to be a pleasant chat. I suppose I was naïve enough not to expect what did happen … even after I saw what happened to Rosie. It was as though they materialised out of the darkness; one on either side of me. Then I was on the floor being punched and kicked. Nobody spoke – not a word. According to my memory, it lasted a short period of time, maybe only a minute or two. I think it was the punch to my face – the one that busted my eye – that did it. Everything started to spin. Blackness descended. After that, I don't remember anything until I woke up in hospital."

Stella sat clasping and unclasping her hands in her lap. I couldn't tell whether her eyes were focused on her hands, or whether they were closed. Whatever was going on in her head had nothing to do with her presence in the library, or our being there with her. Ben gave her a few moments to settle again before asking anything else.

"I can understand how the speed at which the situation escalated took you by surprise. Did you hear anything while you were in the room – apart from the initial murmuring? Did neither of the men speak, not even to one another? I know this might be difficult for you, but please try running your mind back over what happened every second after you entered the room. Let your mind focus on any sounds, whether it was speech or otherwise."

It was magic to see and hear Ben in action. His voice was low and persuasive. I felt myself being sucked into the conversation, even though I didn't have a clue what went on in that building. It was difficult to tell how Stella was coping with it. She still hadn't lifted her eyes from her hands in her lap – just continued to sit there gently nodding her head.

Almost as if jabbed with a pin, her head jerked up, her face frozen in surprise. I felt my pulse quicken. My stomach tightened. Had we pressed too hard? I risked a sidelong glance at Ben. He remained relaxed, as if nothing had happened, but he remained silent. I knew he was waiting for what came next before deciding whether to press on with the interview or call it a day.

A minute or more elapsed before he spoke again, and then still in the same soft soothing voice. "What happened just then, Stella? Did you remember something? Do you think you could share it with us? Don't be afraid. Whatever it is, we will understand. We are not here to judge, or give you a hard time about anything. Would it help to talk about it?"

"I'm … I'm not afraid… It's just… well, I remembered something. Something I didn't think I knew. It just popped into my head. As clear as you like, there it was. I don't know where it came from or how it happened, but I had no recollection of it until just a moment ago. They did speak. Both of them spoke when I first stepped into the room. I still don't know how many people were there, but two men spoke."

"Do you recall what they said?"

"Not their exact words. One said something along the lines of, nobody likes people who make threats. Then, the other one told me I knew what happened to people who didn't play the game properly – who rocked the boat – but I seemed to be a slow learner. Then, the first one chimed in. He said something about because I was such a slow learner, now they would have to teach me a lesson, and *it was a pity I wouldn't be around long enough to learn from the lesson.* I think the blood froze in my veins then. I went into shock. It's probably why I was so unprepared for what came next – so incapable of defending myself."

"So, the next thing to happen was when the two men jumped you and handed out your 'lesson'?"

Stella nodded. "Yeah, that's what happened. That's how it went down. Huh, how I went down – in a great heap."

"What can you tell me about those men? You suggested they were in the dark side of the room when you came in and, therefore, you couldn't see them. When they grabbed you, they had to step around into the light. Did you see them?"

She bit her lip for a few moments before answering. "Ye-es, they seemed to materialise out of the darkness, swooped in and grabbed me. It was quick. Before I knew it, I was on the floor and couldn't really see anything properly." Another pause and more chewing of her lip before she continued. "They wore dark coloured clothes. Black I suppose. I can't tell you more than that."

"Okay, so their clothes were dark – probably black. What about their faces? Their faces should stand out against a dark room and the black clothes."

"No-o … No, they didn't. That's it! I didn't see their faces because they had something over their heads. They were like ski masks. But, again, they were dark-coloured and probably black. It was like two black apparitions came out of a black room and grabbed me. Come to think of it, I didn't even see their hands. Maybe they wore gloves too. I can't say I noticed gloves; don't remember the feel of gloves on my skin."

I tried to catch Ben's eye. Stella's breathing had become rapid and shallow. It wasn't surprising she had become distressed. The interview couldn't continue. Ben had to stop now; walk away and give her time to recover. He didn't even glance at me … time for more direct action.

"It's time we took a break." Ben snapped his head around towards me. His look was fierce.

Sorry Ben, I told myself, this time you are going to have to listen to me. "This has been a distressing session for Stella. She needs to take a break. Perhaps we could organise afternoon tea while Stella goes to splash some water on her face, and all of us need to relax for a few minutes until it arrives." Ben went to argue. But, I too have a vast repertoire of fierce looks. I shot him one of my best. It startled him… But it did the trick.

"Sonny is right, Stella. Let's take a break for a while. You go and relax or do whatever you want. We'll call you when afternoon tea is ready."

Instead of bolting for her room as I expected her to, she nodded a couple of times but remained seated for a few moments. Then, as a woman much older than her years might do, she leaned on the desk to support herself as she eased herself upright from her chair. "Yes, thanks, I will take a break," she said before leaving the room on somewhat unsteady legs.

"She is all right, isn't she?" Ben hissed at me as soon as he thought Stella was out of earshot. "I thought she was handling it okay. Did I miss something? What happened?"

"There was no one thing responsible for her distressed state. The tension was building the whole time you took her through her attack. It just continued to build until she was almost at the point of collapse. We said we would organise afternoon tea. We should do so, but I don't think you should continue the interview afterwards. Anyway, how much more is there she can tell you? She said the attack only lasted a minute or so before she lost consciousness. I know Stella wasn't at the house for more than a few minutes when the first of those other cars roared out of there and was soon followed by the second one."

The housekeeper had afternoon tea mostly laid out on the tea trolley when I went to find her in the kitchen. She said she was nearly ready to bring it in, and it would only take about five minutes to finish preparing everything. I asked her not to do that. No explanation was required when I asked her to wait another fifteen or twenty minutes before finishing preparations for afternoon tea. She understood, and only asked how Stella was holding up. What could I tell her, other than Stella was feeling a bit weak-kneed at the moment.

About twenty-five minutes later, afternoon tea was wheeled into the library. As she unloaded the trolley onto the desk, I told Ben I would call Stella. In a firm voice, the housekeeper told me to sit down. She would call Stella to afternoon tea. It appears my offer had threatened to trespass on the housekeeper's territory.

While waiting for Stella to appear, we discussed whether to continue with the interview today or not. It was a few minutes later before Stella returned. She looked wrung out and decidedly pale. I caught Ben's eye and gave him a faint shake of my head. There was no way the interview could continue today.

Afternoon tea was a mainly silent affair. None of us appeared interested in conversation, and spent the next twenty minutes or so simply going through the motions of spreading jam and cream on scones and sipping coffee. As the performance drew to an end, Ben stretched back in his chair and announced he thought we had done enough for one day.

"You don't have to stop because of me," Stella said quietly. "You should finish gathering all the information you need. Don't worry about me. I'll be fine. Let's just get on with it; get it over and done with."

"Thank you, Stella, but I don't know how much more information there is to gather. Once they dished out your 'lesson', they left you unconscious on the floor. There is no more you can tell me. I thank you for being brave enough to take me through this last stage of your involvement with that mob. We will leave now so you can rest. It's unlikely we'll be back in the coming days, unless we encounter something we think you might be able to help us with. It is possible though, other fragments of memory might come back to you in the meantime. If that should happen, please tell the housekeeper you wish to talk to us. She will make sure we come to see you.

As nice as this place is, I don't doubt it's going to feel a bit like being in prison as the days drag on. I will do all I can to wrap this investigation up as quickly as possible. Until then, this is the safest place for you. Do you have any argument with any of that?"

"No, and thank you. I know this is the best place for me. And, you are right. I really do need to rest now."

After we left the penthouse, I spent an hour or so in my office taking care of emails and messages before leaving early for home. I could have stayed in my office and updated my case file there but, for some inexplicable reason, I just wanted to go home. So, as soon as I was home, I went through to my office, dumped my bag, and opened my case file. The next hour and a half was evenly divided between typing up notes to add to my file, and thinking.

If I'm honest, I was hoping inspiration – some bright ideas – about how to proceed with the investigation might miraculously occur to me. I was out of luck. It didn't matter how many times I read my notes, it was a straightforward story with no hidden bits or mysterious grey areas suggesting further avenues to explore. It appears Stella became a proverbial pain in the backside for the mob, and they seem to have definite – and final – ideas on how to deal with such matters.

At about six o'clock, Ben called to ask what I might like for dinner. I hadn't given it any thought. I felt as though I'd eaten food all day. The first thing to come to mind was fish and chips. He seemed delighted with my choice. As I went for a shower, I realised my tastebuds were looking forward to a fish and chips dinner.

Refreshed and feeling a bit brighter after my shower, I poured myself a long glass of mineral water, tossed in a couple of lime slices, and took it out onto the deck. The clear, crisp air of these cooler days produces gorgeous sunsets. Unlike the spectacular fiery reds and golds of summer sunsets, these evenings produced intense pinks, and mauves graduating to almost purple as twilight creeps in. Lost in the beauty of nature's palette, I let my mind roam free as I enjoyed the show.

It was inevitable it would return to Stella, her story, and the mess now threating her life. What does the future hold for her? An already damaged marriage doesn't seem to have much chance of survival after recent events. Her lack of interest in her husband is obvious in the fact she has never once asked after him. My thoughts turned to her husband, my client Trent Martin.

A brief thought about whether he had regained consciousness yet flew through my thinking. It took my focus off Stella and planted it firmly on my client. What of his future? I imaged it might still be too early to tell if he sustained any permanent impairment as a result of his injuries. Would he be able to return to work, or would he spend the rest of his life burdened by some disability which prevented it.

Thoughts of Trent Martin and his employment at the office supplies firm brought Colleen Jenkins to mind. When I returned to my office this afternoon, one of the messages on my answering machine was from Colleen. She had to work late and couldn't make our arranged appointment, but she would call tomorrow to make a new time. I sensed something unpleasant happening there but, for the life of me, I couldn't see how it could possibly be connected to Stella's situation.

Such thoughts shunted my mind back to Trent Martin. Would he still have a job after he recovered? After he ended up in hospital, I suspect some form of 'hatchet job' was being cooked up in-house against him at the office supplies place. Curiouser and curiouser… And, how does he feel about Colleen Jenkins? How she feels about him is all too obvious. Maybe the feeling is mutual. Maybe the way he is towards his wife might have something to do with the fact he would rather be with someone else, Colleen Jenkins for instance.

Ben's arrival saved me from myself. He called from the kitchen to announce dinner had arrived and did I want to eat inside or out on the deck? The air had become a little too chill, so I suggested inside would be better.

Goodness only knows the extent of the web of intrigue my mind might have woven if Ben hadn't arrived when he did.

Chapter 18

As I dumped handfuls of salad mix from a packet onto plates and distributed the fish and chips, Ben sliced wedges of lemon. I sensed an air of excitement about him, and decided to gently ease into finding out why. "How did the rest of your afternoon go? Did you get much done? It must be hell trying to run the precinct when you are spending so much time interviewing Stella."

"They seem to manage all right without me looking over their shoulders, but you're right. There are a few things starting to build up, and some of them will soon start screaming for attention. Nevertheless, there was a bonus in spending time in my office this afternoon. As soon as we finish dinner, I'll show you what I have."

His comment ensured we didn't dawdle over our food. As soon as our plates were empty, we adjourned to my office. As I waited for my computer to wake up, Ben handed me a memory stick. I gave him a questioning look. "A clue as to which file I am supposed to load would be useful," I suggested as I inserted the stick into a USB port.

"There is only one file on it. I'll come around to sit beside you so we can watch it together."

"No, don't bother. I'll put it up on the big screen so we can watch it in comfort. What are we watching anyway?"

"It's the recording from the jewellery store's CCTV from the Saturday morning when Stella accompanied Lenny to look at engagement rings."

Okay, now the screen had my undivided attention. Footage from the store's entrance camera rolled across the screen. Nothing was happening. No one came or went. I was about to ask whether this was as much as it would provide when the

174

camera caught movement approaching the doorway. Then, clear images of Stella and another woman filled the screen. Our eyes were glued to the screen as we watched the two women glide into view and then out of reach of the camera.

"Damn! It didn't give us much of a look at Lenny."

"Be patient … Here comes the next bit. It's from the other camera in the shop; the one on the wall behind where the engagement rings are displayed."

"Hmm … It does have good coverage of most of the interior of the shop. There they are." Stella and her friend walked into shot and strolled across to a display case on the opposite side of the room. "Right, good; this is when they first came in and went to the case with the gemstone rings and the tray of earrings."

Silence reigned as we watched the images scroll across the screen. We saw the young assistant remove the tray of earrings from the display case. He set it down on top and a little off to the side, before retrieving the tray of gemstone rings and placing it on the top of the display case in front of the two women. Images for the next minute or two showed the women with their backs to the camera. What we could see of Lenny's movements suggested she was trying on rings.

Then, the big moment: the young assistant reached over and took hold of the tray. His intention probably was to return it to the display case.

"This must be where Lenny decided she'd rather have a traditional diamond after all," I murmured more to myself than to Ben.

Sure enough, Lenny turned to face the camera and pointed towards it. "Yes… there, she indicated she wants to look at the diamond rings."

"Shut up and just watch the recording," Ben snarled at me. "We might want to freeze and rewind this in a moment. How do we do that?" I assured him I could manage it.

Just to satisfy my curiosity, I rewound briefly and then froze the frame of Lenny turning towards the camera and pointing to the diamond rings. The image was clear enough, but maybe the distance robbed it of some detail. It captured a tall, slim pale-faced woman with a severely cut mop of dark, straight hair cascading down each side of her face and over her shoulders. Would the image allow me to recognise the woman in a crowd? The short answer: probably not. The only giveaway might be her hairdo.

With nothing more to be achieved from studying the frozen image, I clicked the button and set the recording rolling again. "Ah, yes, much better," I whispered.

The two women walked towards the camera as they moved to stand at the case with the diamond rings. Then, Lenny looked up into the face of the young assistant as she pointed to one of the rings on display. I froze the recording again and studied the face hiding under all the hair. …Attractive, but with a hard edge to it somehow. I decided she would stand out in a crowd, and it wasn't just because of the hair. I started the recording rolling again, in slow motion this time.

"Wouldn't it be great if they were coloured images?" I mused. "We'd be able to see her mop of hair in all its glory." The monochrome images on the recording just showed it as 'dark'. If you didn't know it was supposed to be red, you would be forgiven for thinking it was dark brown or even darker.

"Impressive…" Ben murmured as the recording reached its end. "So cool and confident … Not a hint of any nervousness about what she was up to, and poor Stella looked vaguely bemused throughout the whole performance."

Ben was right on all counts. Knowing what we know now, Lenny's performance was Oscar nomination stuff. I was running the images through my mind when Ben's voice caught my attention.

"Don't turn it off, there's more to come. I asked the tech boys to isolate some images for me and enhance them a bit. The bit of the recording about to start now shows their efforts with those images."

They had done a remarkable job. There were several shots of Lenny's face from slightly different angles, every one clear and sharp. She was an attractive woman. For some reason, I struggled to take my eyes off those shots of her. There was something about them … And not just that she was so attractive.

"You could print those shots if you like. They might prove handy for confirming identification when you're out and about in the city heart," Ben suggested. I was already on my way to the printer to load photographic paper.

After retrieving the printouts, I perched on the end of my desk and studied them. I heard Ben chuckle.

"It doesn't matter how long or hard you stare at them, they are not going to tell you any more than they already have."

"Wha…? I'm not so sure. There's something about this woman."

"Are you suggesting there is more to her than an attractive and a talented actress?"

"I don't know what I'm suggesting. All I know is my gut keeps telling me to look more closely. Speaking of looking more closely, should we go back to when the women first came into the shop to see if we can pick up when the earrings went into Stella's bag?"

"No need … There is one last extract on the stick. Bring it up on the big screen please."

Again, Ben's tech boys had been busy. It showed a segment of the footage when the two women were standing at the display case with the gemstone rings. They slowed the footage down so it advanced frame by frame. Right, there was the frame where Lenny turned towards the camera on the other wall and pointed to the diamond engagement rings. Hang on; there was something about how she did it.

"Ben, watch this bit when I replay it. There is something about how it happens."

With Ben now focused on the big screen, I rewound two frames and pressed play again. As the next frame came up on the screen, I froze it. "Look, watch this," I hissed at Ben.

"See what Lenny does? As she is about to turn around, she sort of shuffles a short distance along to her right. There's nothing funny about the way she does it. It might be she was repositioning her feet to turn around without tripping. But, as a result, Stella has to scuttle out of the way. Stella takes a couple of steps further along in front of the counter. The manoeuvre put the tray of earrings slightly to the left of Stella, but almost directly in front of Lenny's right shoulder."

Although I wanted to roll onto the next frame to scrutinise what happened there, I needed Ben to confirm he understood what I was pointing out to him. It seemed to take him an eternity, but probably only a couple of seconds, before he confirmed the point I was trying to make.

"Yeah, I see how the little dance rearranged Stella's proximity to the earrings. I think the next frame shows her turning to the camera on the opposite wall I wonder what her right hand was doing while she was about it."

A click of the button and the images rolled onto the next frame. Yep, there was Stella turning towards the camera. I peered at the image on the big screen, not sure whether I had seen something or not. Ben was way ahead of me.

"See, there … The slight movement of Lenny's shoulder consistent with her having reached for something."

Once you knew what you were looking for, it stood out like the proverbial. Lenny had reached for something, and the only 'something' remaining on top of the display case and close to hand was the tray of earrings. I confirmed Ben's observation of what happened.

"Right, now move on to the next frame … And the next one. There! Stop it. Did you see what Lenny did?"

Yes, I did see what Lenny did. After turning and pointing to the case with the diamond rings, in one swift movement, Lenny turned to face front again, before pivoting to her right to half face Stella. She seemed to grab Stella around the left bicep as she waved her left hand towards the diamond rings. Throughout the whole movement, Lenny looked excited, as though she had just experienced some revelation.

"That's when it happened, isn't it?" I murmured to Ben. "It was as she reached over to grab Stella's arm, she let the earrings drop into the bag gaping open a bit as it hung over Stella's left shoulder."

"O-oh, yes; it's one part of the mystery solved. There can be little doubt now the whole series of events were designed to set-up Stella; to create leverage with which to force Stella to work for them."

"I agree, Ben, but why Stella? Why not any other woman in Millhaven – even me or Emily, for instance? Why single out Stella? Is there something in their history which drove Lenny to select Stella?"

"Looks like I'm going back to interview Stella sooner than anticipated."

"Well, I didn't want to say this before but, now you're talking about more interviews with Stella, there is something else we haven't addressed yet. I think the 'something else' might be the linchpin in this whole operation."

"Are you telling me I don't how to do my job ... that maybe I've lost my touch?"

"Of course not. It's just viewing this footage has allowed other questions to develop. Apart from the question of 'why Stella', the other big question coming to mind is: what was in those parcels she ferried back and forth around town?"

"Christ, I haven't asked about those, have I? She hasn't told us what was in them ... has she? Did I miss something along the way?"

"The answer is 'no'... but, now you can tell her how the earrings got into her bag, you have a bargaining chip if she should prove reluctant to share the information."

Having gained all we might from the CCTV footage, we stopped to make coffee on our way to the lounge room. We sat in silence; each of us dealing with our own thoughts, until I posed the next question.

"Where to from here, Ben? What's the next move?"

He shrugged. "The only thing I'm sure about is going back to talk to Stella again. I was hoping the CCTV footage, and whatever we found out about those two vehicles from the derelict house, might progress my investigation before I returned to speak to her again. As that's not the case, I'll think about setting up another interview for some time tomorrow."

"Ben … Don't ask me to explain what I'm going to tell you … Just listen please. There is something about the woman that's ringing a bell for me. I don't know what it is, or why it is, but my instinct is telling me to take another long, hard look at her. It's suggesting there's something about her I should be seeing, and I'm not. Argh, I suspect this is going to keep me awake for much of the night."

As Ben opened his mouth to say something, his phone chirped. I was pleased it did, because the look on his face suggested he was about to rubbish me for my comments about Lenny. He took the call out on the deck. I used the time he was out there to clear away after dinner and stack the dishwasher. When he returned, he looked tired, and I was concerned for him. He has looked that way far too often lately.

"Gotta go; duty calls. I'll give you a call sometime tomorrow morning to let you know what I'm doing about Stella." Then he was out the door, and I stood watching his tail lights disappearing down the driveway.

In spite of all we had done tonight, it wasn't late – and I wasn't ready for bed. I wandered back into my office and picked up the printed images of Lenny's face. "Who are you, and why is there something familiar about you?" I demanded of the printouts as I fanned them out on my desk. While standing bent over the desk studying them, the germ of an idea started to form. I glanced over at my computer. Ben hadn't taken his memory stick with him. Aah, now there's a possibility.

Moments later I was seated behind my desk and waiting for my Photoshop program to open. Then, it was a simple matter of importing the best image of Lenny's face. Not being an expert at using the program, it took me a while to get my head around how to do the things I wanted to do. It was the better part of an hour later before I took a breather and congratulated myself on having reduced the image to the first stage of what I hoped to achieve. Removing the mop of hair from down the side of her face and over her shoulders, for someone who knew what they were doing, probably would take five minutes. Lenny's naked face, minus the rest of her head, was a bit unnerving. What was left on the screen was eerie. I felt compelled to rush on with what I wanted to try.

Time slipped by unnoticed. I must have tried at least a dozen approaches, each one ended up looking more ridiculous that the last. It was almost two o'clock. My neck and shoulders hurt and my eyes struggled to focus. Try one last thing, I told myself, and then call it a night. So, I did.

In truth, I'm not sure what I did or how I achieved it. Mind in neutral, I was messing about waiting for a bright idea for something else to try. And then, there it was. There was a familiar face looking back at me. It wasn't Lenore (Lenny) Collins. It was a problem – a major problem. Without thinking, I reached for my phone and keyed Ben's number.

"What…?" he barked almost as soon as it started dialling. "Do you know what time this is?"

I mumbled a few words by way of a cack-handed apology for waking him, and admitted I hadn't checked the time, before ending the call. "I am sorry. I'll talk about it tomorrow."

"No you won't. You'll talk to me now. As for waking me up … I was about to head home. Has something happened? Are you all right?" Concern had crept into his voice.

"I'm okay…"

"Then, what happened to cause you to ring me at this hour?"

"You will need to see it for yourself but … I found Lenore Collins, only she isn't Lenore Collins – not anymore anyway … and I think you might have a problem."

"Just what I need at this hour of the morning: another problem, and someone speaking in riddles. Well, if I'm still out of bed, so are you. I'll be at your place in about ten minutes."

After a stroll around the deck to wake me up a bit, I cranked up the coffee machine. The first cup was ready to pour as Ben pulled up outside. It hadn't taken him ten minutes – but I don't suppose anyone was going to arrest him for speeding when he had been up all night working a case. He grunted by way of thanks as I handed him a mug of coffee.

"Well, where is it? Where is this thing I need to see?" he demanded as I made myself a coffee.

"Have a look at what's on my computer screen. I'll join you in a moment."

As I headed for my office, I heard his reaction to the image on my screen. "Bloody Hell! … Can that be right, or have you lost your marbles?"

"What do you mean? And, there is no point in shooting the messenger. What do you want to know about the image you're looking at?" To prove I hadn't doctored the face in any way, I showed him the progressive images leading to the final version now on the screen.

"Do you recall what Stella said about when her 'friend' Lenny Collins moved to Millhaven?" he murmured as he stared transfixed on the image on the screen.

My case file was open on the desk. I flipped to my transcript of our first interview with Stella. "Yes, here it is. At the reunion, Lenny told Stella she moved to Millhaven 'a few months ago', and then went on about still not knowing anybody there."

"Well, that bit fits, and is reasonably close to the truth."

"Ben, she is the police officer I've seen around city heart on a few occasions, isn't she?" He nodded and slapped his hand down hard on the desk in disgust. "So, what happens now? I mean, as the top cop in this region, what do you have to do about it?"

"There's only one thing I should do: call in the flying squad to sort it out."

"Who are they, and why do you need to call them in?"

"They are the internal investigation mob who needs to be called in whenever there is a bad smell about a police officer. I think I'm getting more than a whiff of bad smell from this image on your computer screen. Before I talk to them, I need to be bloody sure of what I'm going to tell them. I can't hold off telling them about my suspicions for too long without being seen as complicit in whatever's going on. I think we might have twenty-four hours at the most to get a handle on this thing."

He stood up and picked up his half empty mug. "Do you think we might have a port with this?" he asked as he waved his mug at me.

I poured two glasses of port, and we took them and our remaining coffee through to the lounge room. Within minutes, Ben was slumped down in his chair and struggling to keep his eyes open. I wasn't doing much better.

"Ben, the spare bed is still made up from the other night. Why don't you go and fall into it for a few hours?"

"I need a shower."

"… And the towelling robe is still hanging in the cupboard in the spare room. Go and have a quick shower and then fall into bed."

It was a quick shower. By the time I had shut down my computer, rinsed the mugs and glasses and stacked them in the dishwasher, Ben was on his way to bed. Later, as I made my way to my room, light snoring came from the spare room.

While I didn't know what time Ben needed to be at work in the morning, I was quite sure neither of us would be too bright and rearing to go when we surfaced tomorrow.

Chapter 19

It was early. The sounds of movement in the house woke me. Alert, I was out of bed before I remembered Ben had spent the night. Throwing on a robe, I went to see what was happening, and encountered Ben as he emerged from my spare bedroom.

"Sorry… I was trying not to wake you. I should be going before the neighbourhood comes to life. God knows what they are thinking after my car has been parked outside for a couple of nights lately."

"If they are giving it any thought at all, they might be thinking I've finally got a life. So, now the matter is dealt with, would you like breakfast – or at least coffee – before you leave?"

"Only if you are sure you are not going to be run out of the neighbourhood for conducting a house of ill repute."

"What a shame that won't happen. It would liven up the place no end for at least a couple of days. Now, what would you like for breakfast?"

Unaccustomed as I am to preparing breakfast for anyone, the morning started well. Ben's taste in breakfasts mirrored my own. Then, after a second coffee, he was off home for a shower and fresh clothes before going into work. After he left, I went into my office.

Everything remained spread out where we left it not so many hours ago. After adding my Photoshop efforts to Ben's memory stick and packing everything into my oversized tote bag, I joined the throng of early morning commuters heading into the city. My office phone was ringing as I unlocked my office door.

"It's Colleen Jenkins, Miss Whittington. I apologise for calling so early, but I was hoping to see you after work today. I'm due to finish at four o'clock again today. It's unlikely I'll be told to work late two days in a row."

I made the appointment. Then, as I unloaded my bag, I searched my memory banks for a clue as to why I wanted to talk to her in the first place. Unlike Ben, I had consumed only one coffee so far this morning. Perhaps another cup would help my recall. It was still a blank as I placed the mug on my desk and dropped onto my chair.

The coffee worked its magic after only a few sips. Total recall returned. To avoid a possible repeat performance when she arrived this afternoon, I scribbled myself a few notes about the topics I wanted to discuss. I had all but completed my usual morning admin tasks and was reading the last email when Ben called.

"I'm planning to head to the penthouse at about eleven o'clock. I've asked the housekeeper to prepare an early lunch, and not to mention today's visit to Stella. While I have no idea why, for some reason, I feel taking her by surprise on this occasion might be a good thing."

So, with my calendar empty until eleven o'clock, buying a newspaper made sense… And, buying a newspaper meant passing the bakery selling all those amazing sweet treats which are so suitable for morning tea. I returned to my office with today's paper and enough tasty morsels to provide morning tea for several people. In spite of their siren call from the bench in my kitchenette, I resisted temptation until a little after nine o'clock.

I was standing by the bench trying to decide which to eat first when Ben strode into my office. "Is that freshly brewed coffee I can smell?"

"Yep, and I'm in danger of bouncing off the walls if I continue consuming it at the rate I am this morning. I assume you have time for a cup?"

"…And some of whatever is in those boxes to go with it." I told him to choose his own sugar fix while I made his coffee.

Settled in my ancient lounge chairs with a decadent morning tea spread out before us, I risked wrecking the pleasant interlude by asking a question to which I wasn't sure I wanted an answer.

"I'm sure the lure of coffee and cake didn't bring you to my office. So, why are you here? Have you brought news of another disaster that has befallen us?"

"No… I came to see if you brought in the memory stick I left in your computer last night. So, did you?"

Donning my best disappointed look, I quipped, "Oh well, if it's all you've come for…"

"The stick – and cake and coffee of course…" And there was the familiar deep rumbling chuckle.

As I handed him the stick, I asked how he planned to tackle today's interview. So far, the only question I knew was on the agenda was what was in those parcels Stella ferried back and forth. Of course, where they came from, and where they went, would be of interest as well. If Stella knows the answers to those questions, today's interview is unlikely to take long to complete.

"Well, I plan to start by asking about the courier service she provided: what she carried and the locations involved. Then, I aim to ask pointed questions about who her contacts were at each of the places she mentions."

"What if she doesn't know the answers to your questions? I mean, yes, she will know what locations she visited. But, she might not know about the contents of the parcels, and there might not have been a specific contact at each place. Maybe she just turned up, and whoever was around at the time handed her the parcel – or accepted the package when she brought one back. Of course, there also is the other possibility. It's possible she might be too frightened to give you any of the details you want."

"I hadn't overlooked the possibility she might refuse to provide answers – at least, honest and accurate answers. If I feel she is not playing the game properly in return for our efforts to keep her safe, I shall resort to shock tactics to loosen her up a bit."

"What constitutes 'shock tactics', and am I going to feel happy about being involved? Should I maybe skip today's interview – just in case?"

"No. You will want to be there. Anyway, I'm counting on your involvement."

"Why? What's my role in all this?"

"It's only if I'm forced to employ shock tactics. If it goes bad, and she collapses in a great heap or anything, I'm counting on you to support her. To look after her as someone who has become a close friend would do."

"That just about decides it. I think I'm too busy today to attend Stella's interview."

"Too busy doing what? Drinking coffee and eating cakes? Don't be such a wimp. Nothing will happen. You know how to talk to her better than I do. She doesn't get such a defiant look about her when you explain things."

"Probably because I don't bark and demand – or threaten…"

After a glance at his watch, Ben was on his feet. "I have a few things to do before we see Stella. Do you want me to pick you up when I'm ready to leave for the penthouse?"

I declined his offer. It seemed wise to take my own car today. It meant I could leave at any time it suited me. Ben insisted on taking me, and I relented. By the time Ben left, there wasn't much time before he would collect me to head off to the penthouse. Perhaps in the hope of finding new clues to open up other avenues of questioning for Stella, I filled in the available time studying my case file … and the copy of the jewellery store's CCTV footage I copied for my own use. Nothing inspiring emerged from any of it. The only thing worthy of note was Stella's performance on the CCTV footage. From the moment she entered the store, she looked bewildered. Even during Lenny's exaggerated excitement as she tried on the various rings, Stella continued to look like an unrehearsed bystander press-ganged into being there, rather than a participant.

The housekeeper met us on our arrival. She informed us lunch would be on the table in about five minutes, and Stella was resting in her room. Ben asked the housekeeper to call Stella first. I silently heaved a sigh of relief. When the housekeeper told us Stella was in her room, I half expected Ben to tell me to fetch her. My gut was telling me I didn't want to be complicit in today's events … well, no more than as a spectator at best.

True to her word, we were in the lounge room only a matter of minutes before the housekeeper announced lunch was served. Today, Stella seemed reserved – even uptight – and had not responded to the conversation Ben and I tried to engage her in. Yes, she was surprised Ben was there today, after indicating yesterday he might not visit again for a while. Her surprise quickly turned to something else. She withdrew into herself. It was as though she pulled down the shutters and erected a defensive perimeter.

Bringing my own car today looked increasingly as though it would have been a wise move. After Stella failed to join in conversation over lunch, I was almost convinced I wanted an early escape. This was not the Stella we interviewed over the previous few days. There was a sullenness about her today. What had happened during the less than twenty-four hours since we were here yesterday? It was almost as though she had eavesdropped on conversations between Ben and me during the intervening period, and decided she wanted no part of what was proposed for today.

In keeping with our usual procedure, as soon as we finished a quick lunch, we moved to the library. Ben already was showing signs of growing frustration. His voice had hardened, and his speech was cutting and to the point. It was not a good way to begin today's interview, and was unlikely to achieve results – not the ones we hoped for anyway. I needed to intervene before the situation worsened.

As soon as we finished eating, Ben announced it was time to move to the library. His statement produced an abrupt reaction from Stella. Without a moment's hesitation, she sprang up from her chair and strode off in the direction of the library. Ben scrambled from his chair and went to follow her. I caught him by the arm and held him back.

"Go and talk to the housekeeper or one of the other police officers for a few minutes. Give me some time to talk to her alone. If we don't sort out what's bugging her today, we might as well leave. We are not going to achieve anything with her the way she is at the moment."

The irritated look I received suggested he wasn't going to comply. Then, he nodded and marched off to find one of the police officers on guard duty. I took a deep breath to relax myself before joining Stella in the library.

"Ben will be along soon. He's talking to the police officers on duty. Stella, I'm quite concerned about you today. Has something happened? You are not your usual self. Is there something I can do to help you? Talk to me, please."

"Why has he come back today? Yesterday, he said that was all for a while, and today, he's back here again. No doubt, he has more questions to ask me. What more can I tell him? I've told him everything I know. Instead of wasting more time talking to me, why isn't he out there rounding up the people who are threatening my life? All I'm seeing so far are more questions, and no progress with investigating those people and what they're up to."

Okay, so there's more than a small amount of frustration on the other side of this equation as well. All I have to do is come up with some clever way of persuading her to participate in today's interview. Maybe the 'give him one more chance' approach might help.

"Yeah, I must admit being back here today surprises me as well. Nevertheless, I know Ben and how he works. He wouldn't return today unless there was something important he needed to ask you. His investigation must seem as though it's dragging on without much result, and it must be hard for you being holed-up in this penthouse for days on end. Stella, please hear what he has to say today. Yes, I'm sure he will have more questions, but I have no doubt they are critical to his investigation of your case. You're free to make your own decision, but I recommend you participate in today's interview. After it's over, make up your mind how you want to play it in future. How about it, will you at least hear what he has to say?"

She gave a dismissive toss of her head before turning to face me. I felt her eyes boring into my face as she considered my request. Then, at last, a sigh of resignation and a nod, "All right, I'll see what today is about. I don't believe I have any more to tell him but, because you've asked, I'll go along with it – just one more time."

It took me a minute or so to find Ben. I hurried ahead to lead him into the library. As we walked in, I said, "It took me a while to find him. He was yapping to one of his blokes," It was my attempt at lightening the mood. I hoped Ben sensed it and played along.

"I wasn't 'yapping'. I was checking on what has been happening here."

"Even I could tell what's been happening," Stella spat at him. "Nothing … that's what has been happening around here – nothing."

"And it's a good thing too," I responded quickly. "Now, come on; let's get this show on the road. I have other things to do today. So, Ben, it's over to you. What do you want to talk about?"

"Well, I realised I hadn't asked Stella if she knew what was in those parcels she was ferrying around town. You said they told you it wouldn't be drugs. Did you find out what was in them?"

"Not really; I wasn't game to have a look, and they made sure they didn't open them in front of me. So, I never had a chance to find out what was in them, but Rosie said she knew."

"How big were the parcels?" Ben asked. "Were they, say, the size of a shoebox, or larger? And, were they heavy?"

Stella laughed. It was the first time I'd heard her really laugh. "God, no, they were nothing like that. They are about the size of a cigarette packet, and they were light. Most of the time, they felt like they were empty but, if you shook them, something rattled inside. Oh, maybe I should clarify… That describes the parcels I picked up from different places around town and took to the central address. The parcels I picked up on the alternate week for delivery to various locations were a bit bigger and heavier."

"How much bigger, can you give me a rough idea of the size?"

"Uhmm …Maybe the size of a tub of margarine. Yeah, that's about right. When I said they were heavy, I meant they were heavier than the ones I'd handled the previous week. Even those bigger parcels probably didn't weigh more than a couple of hundred grams."

"On the alternate week, when you collected the parcels and delivered them to the various locations around town, were those locations the same as the ones you collected parcels from the previous week?"

"Sometimes; I would have parcels to take back to where I'd collected them from previously, but there were parcels for other places as well. Places where I didn't normally collect from, and I only delivered to them on occasions."

While Ben was still scribbling his notes, I jumped in with a question to keep things rolling along. "Earlier in this interview, you said Rosie told you she knew what was in the parcels. Did she share her information with you? Did she tell you what was in them?"

"Aw, she said they were credit cards. I don't know how she knew, or why she thought that's what was in them. It didn't seem right to me. I can't explain why but, somehow, it didn't seem like credit cards to me. All right, maybe the bigger parcels on the alternate week might have contained credit cards. I really don't know what was in them."

Ben elbowed his way back into the conversation. "What did these parcels look like: were they little boxes or paper bags? Were they wrapped in some way?"

"I think there were little cardboard boxes inside, but they always were wrapped. Most of the time they were wrapped in brown paper but, sometimes, they used gift wrapping paper, and tied the parcel up with coloured ribbon to make it look like a present. The parcels I delivered back to the various locations in the alternate week were always wrapped in brown paper. Sometimes they were tied with string, but mainly they just used adhesive tape to secure the wrapping."

"Other than Rosie, did you meet any of the other couriers, or even glimpse other people who might have been engaged in the same type of activities?"

"No, and I think it was by design. As I told you, it was only by chance I met Rosie. I don't doubt there were others. Maybe they worked on different nights to avoid contact."

"And you never met any of the main people who were running the show?"

"The only person I met was Lenny. And, I suppose you could say I 'met' the two blokes who knocked me about in the derelict house, but I can't tell you anything about them."

"The central location seems a key factor in the operation. Did its address change at all, or was it always at the same location?"

"After the first two weeks, what we are calling the 'central location' remained the same. When I first started, it was located on the outskirts of town. Then, after two weeks, it changed to a different location in the same area. It remained at the new address after that."

"From memory, could you give me a list of the places you visited? It doesn't matter if you miss a couple, as long as it provides us with a reasonable idea of the types of places involved."

Ben withdrew a pad from a drawer and pushed it across the desk to her. After scrabbling around in another drawer, he found a pencil and handed it across. Silence reigned for the next few minutes while, punctuated a few times by brief periods of staring off into the distance, Stella scribbled a list of locations for Ben.

"I think that's all of them," she said as she pushed the pad back to Ben. "There might be an odd occasional location I've missed. See this one down here. It's the central location we've talked about."

There was no attempt by Ben to hide his surprise at the length of the list. After a couple of minutes of studying Stella's list, during which Stella and I maintained our silence, Ben looked up and smiled at Stella. I saw her physically relax … which left her unprepared for Ben's next question which wrong-footed her.

"So, how well did you know Lenny when you were younger?"

"I only knew her when we were at High School. She wasn't in any of my classes, but you knew who people were. We didn't move in the same circles. There was a group of girls our parents probably called racy – or promiscuous. They wore all the latest fashions – skin-tight and showing as much flesh as possible – and seemed to be allowed to do things girls much older than us did. They all had boyfriends; older boys who had left High School and had their drivers licences. As I remember, a few of them had motorbikes – another thing our parents didn't approve of. I can't say I ever had anything to do with those girls, and I don't remember ever having a real conversation with Lenny. We might have said hello a few times, but no more. It's why it was so strange when she claimed me as a friend at the reunion."

"What changes have you noticed in the Lenny of today, compared to the girl from your High School days?"

"Apart from her claiming me as a long-lost friend…? She is different... but, as I said, I didn't know her well back then. I suppose we all change as we get older and experience more of life. Her personality seems to have changed. Don't ask me to explain what I mean. All I can say is she seems to have changed. She's become harder in some way. Although she tried to come over as bright and giggly, there is something else underneath all the show she was putting on. Something not happy, but dark and tight; menacing almost."

The interview screeched to a halt when the housekeeper knocked and came in to announce afternoon tea would be ready in about five minutes. Stella went to freshen up before it arrived. Ben and I sat in silent, deep thought until coffee arrived.

Chapter 20

Before Ben resumed Stella's interview after our coffee break, I checked my watch. Coffee had been a little early, probably a result of lunch also being earlier than usual. I had to be back in my office by four o'clock when Colleen Jenkins finished work for the day. It wouldn't take her five minutes to walk from the office supplies building to my office. With no idea how much longer Ben might spend on today's interview, I was beginning to feel nervous.

While it was only 2.45PM, I wanted to be heading out of the penthouse in another forty-five minutes at the latest. I knew I should have brought my own car. I told myself that's what cabs were for, and I could still leave whenever I wanted. It didn't ease the tightness developing in the pit of my stomach. Besides, I don't know how much longer Ben can continue with Stella. Even after our coffee break, she still looked close to collapse.

In a bid to prod things along, I encouraged Ben to move on with the interview. "So, Ben, do you have any further questions for Stella today? It doesn't sound as though there is any more she can tell us about the operation she found herself embroiled in."

"No, I don't have further questions about the couriering of parcels, but I do have something else to discuss with Stella. Actually, I would like her thoughts on something."

"Well, it will be a change from the constant questions. Let's get on with it. What is it you want to discuss?" Stella's voice and body language seemed to say 'bring it on'.

"Right … but first, Stella, I need to show you something I meant to show you earlier."

Ben partially opened a folder and slipped something out. He glanced at it, then slapped it down on the desk in front of her. I caught my breath – and hoped no one noticed. It was a printout of an image from the jeweller's shop CCTV footage. The image was a clear shot of the two women's faces as they turned towards the camera on the opposite wall. Stella went rigid at the sight of it. She sat there staring at it without once lifting her eyes.

"Do you remember the day?" Stella gave one weak nod in response. "It's from the CCTV camera on the day you went to look at engagement rings with Lenny. The day the earrings mysteriously ended up in your bag. Do you agree you are one of the people in that photo?" Another half-hearted nod without taking her eyes off the print. "Good; now who is the other woman in the photo with you?"

The little voice in my head suggested it must be the most ridiculous question he could ask. We both knew Stella had gone to the jeweller's shop with Lenny. Why was Ben wasting time asking such a question?

Confusion was written all over Stella's face when she finally tore her eyes away from the photo and looked up at Ben. "I told you, I went there with Lenny. It's Lenny in the photo with me; Lenore Collins, if you want to be precise."

"I suppose you recognised the hair. Her long mane does stand out a bit."

"This is only a monochrome image. If it were coloured, you would see her hair was dark red, just as it was when we were at High School. So, what's this all about? Did you find out something about the earrings?"

"Yes, we have identified where Lenny slipped the earrings into your bag."

Stella appeared to physically deflate. "Thank you. Thank you. Now I can hand those earrings in and Lenny and that mob won't have a hold over me anymore."

"Well, that's not true, is it? Now, they have another, more powerful, hold over you: the trafficking in illicit goods you have been involved in. No, don't protest, we understand the circumstances. Nevertheless, the mob you worked for would see it as a strong hold over you … if you had behaved yourself and not rocked their boat by threatening to go to the police."

She laid her head in her hands on the desk. I saw and heard a couple of sobs before she looked up at Ben. Stella's face was streaked with tears. "What can I do? Is there no way out of this mess for me? Help me, please."

Ben squirmed. He wasn't any better at dealing with bawling females than I was. Again, he opened the folder in front of him a little way and slid out something. He placed it face down on the desk and covered it with one of his great paws.

"I'm going to show you something, and I want you to study it closely. Then, I want your opinion about it."

Then, Ben picked up the item from under his hand and looked at it for a moment as if checking it was the correct item he wanted to show her. In one swift movement, he flipped it over and slapped it down on the desk in front of Stella. This time I was sure my gasp was audible.

Stella stared at the image Ben placed in front of her. Her mouth hung open slightly in surprise.

"Okay, Stella, what are your thoughts on the image. Do you see anything familiar about the person in the photo?"

Only a soft strangled croak came out as she tried to speak. I reached over and filled her glass from the carafe of water in the centre of the desk. She gulped down about half a glass without taking her eyes off the photo. Ben drummed his fingers on the desk in a bid to regain her attention. I thought she was about to crumple into a great heap when she looked up at Ben. The emotions were all there: shock, disbelief; horror almost.

"It's … It's Lenny – Lenore Collins," she stammered. "Okay, what have you done to her? She looks so different. Why did you change her?"

"So, you think the woman in the photo looks like Lenore Collins. Are you sure about her identity?"

"Yes … You've changed her hair, but she is Lenny."

"Now, that is interesting. You might be surprised to learn the woman in the photo is Shayna Kent, a Police Constable attached to the Millhaven precinct."

"Wha… What have you done to her? I don't understand … What are you telling me? Does Lenny have a sister … or a twin maybe?"

"No. I'm not suggesting anything like that. It seems your friend Lenny has remade herself at some point after High School and went on to become a copper. I haven't had a chance to look into her background yet. Do you know or suspect anything about this change?"

"How could I? Until the reunion, I hadn't seen or heard of her since High School. She looked like Lenny at the reunion and has done so on the few occasions I've seen her since. The only difference I noticed was her freckles had disappeared. I put their disappearance down to make-up, but I suppose it could have been the result of some expensive cosmetic treatment. Still, I can't reconcile the Lenny from back then, with Lenny, the police officer with a different name. She struck me as an unlikely police recruit. Are you sure this is the same Lenny as the one in the CCTV image?"

After Ben's reassurance the woman in the photo was Lenny, Stella descended into a troubled silence. I stole a discreet glance at my watch: 3.30PM. Damn! Just when it was becoming interesting… It was time for me to leave the other two to continue the interview without me. As I scraped my chair back from the desk, the sound was deafening in the heavy silence of the library. Ben looked up in surprise.

"What's up? Where are you going?"

"I have to go back to my office. Someone is coming in at four o'clock and I need a few minutes to prepare for it. You continue on here. I'll call a cab."

"We're finished here for today … unless you have something more to ask or say, Stella."

"Me…? No, I… No."

"Okay then, we'll call it quits for now. I might be back in the next day or so. It will depend on how my investigation goes in the meantime. Stay safe, and think about all we talked about today. Maybe it will help you remember something you weren't aware of at the time."

Then, we were out of there and on our way back into the city heart. We travelled in silence until we pulled up in the carpark behind my office. Colleen Jenkins would be finishing work in about five minutes … unless they asked her to work late again and there was another message waiting for me upstairs. As I scrambled out of his car, Ben said he would bring something for dinner tonight.

My answering machine wasn't blinking at me, so I felt reasonably confident Colleen would arrive soon. I checked my case file to refresh my memory, and to find the note I made of the things I wanted to ask her. It was a brief note comprised of only two questions. Good; it should mean Colleen's visit will be short. Perhaps a quick check with the hospital on my client Trent Martin's condition might be useful before she arrives. There was a knock on the door as I reached for the phone. Too late… Colleen Jenkins had arrived.

"Thank you for seeing me but, first, I wanted to apologise about the way I spoke to you yesterday. I didn't mean to be so rude and I'm sorry about all the play acting, but…"

"I understand, Colleen. I shouldn't have tried to talk to you during your work hours, but that's history now. While I wanted to ask you about a couple of things, I felt you wanted to talk to me as well."

She sat with her eyes glued to her bag on her lap as she kept twisting its strap. Her attack on the strap was so rough and forceful, I feared it would break before she left my office. As she seemed reluctant or unable to initiate meaningful conversation, I decided to launch into my questions.

"Colleen, do you often work on the floor selling furniture and supplies? I thought you were Mr Martin's office assistant."

"I had never been out front until this week. Old Brannigan stormed into our office at the end of last week and told me to clean out my desk. I wouldn't be working in the office in future. It sounded like he was firing me, so I asked him if he was giving me the sack. He denied it and said that, as Mr Martin wasn't there anymore, there wasn't anyone for me to assist. They weren't terminating me; just moving me to a new position."

"It seems a bit of a radical move, but I don't know how your office set-up works. Was it because, with Mr Martin out of the office, there was nothing for you to do there?"

"No, that wasn't the case at all. Because Mr Martin wasn't there, I was doing the whole lot myself; my job and his. It was hectic and I was really busy all the time, but nothing was overlooked. Everything was done. And done properly without errors, even if I do say so myself."

"Well, now you're out on the floor, how are they managing to do the work you and Mr Martin used to do?"

"Brannigan had two people working in his office with him. A secretary-type woman and a young clerk. He gave Mr Martin's work to the young clerk, and Brannigan and the woman took care of the work Brannigan was supposed to do. So, with a bit of re-organisation, Mr Martin's office was no longer required … and nor was I."

"So, with a bit of clever manoeuvring, they closed down Mr Martin's office and moved you to the sales staff. I can understand why you thought they were going to fire you when Brannigan told you to clear out your desk. Why didn't they? Wouldn't sacking you be the more logical thing to do if they found they had a staff member surplus to requirements?"

"Yes, a while back, that's what they would have done. In the last couple of months or so, there's been a fair bit of industrial unrest within the place. The union used to have a weak presence there but, in recent times, it has become a lot stronger. There have been several instances when management has been forced to step down when the union took it to task for improper activities against the workforce. In the past, management had no hesitation in sacking people… even good, loyal and long-term employees who did their job well but, for some reason, fell afoul of management."

"So, you believe, because of the current climate of industrial unrest, they couldn't sack you, and simply moved you to where you wouldn't be happy."

"Well, I don't know if that's right, but it's how I see it. When the union started making its presence felt, Mr Martin urged me to join. I was reluctant to do so. But he kept at me, and I did join – and I'm pleased I did! After what Brannigan did to me, the union is now keeping a close eye on what happens to me. It seems what the company did is contrary to our enterprise agreement."

"You said when Brannigan came in and told you to clear out your desk, he told you *Mr Martin wasn't there anymore.* What did you think he meant?"

"…Mr Martin was gone and didn't have a job there any longer."

"You didn't think he might have meant only while Mr Martin was in hospital and off work?"

"No, not after what I heard."

"Perhaps you should tell me about what you heard."

"It's more like something I overheard. It was the day before he sent me to the sales department. I was on my way to file some invoices when I saw something I didn't think looked right. I stopped to read it, to see if I could make sense of what I saw. It was while I was standing there outside Mr Brannigan's office reading the invoices I overheard the last part of his phone conversation with someone."

"I see. So, what did you overhear?"

Colleen stopped attacking her bag, and switched to scratching around in it instead. Her search of the bag's contents produced a small notebook, which she flipped through to a specific page. She then quoted from her note.

"He told the person he was speaking to: *They stuffed it up. But, he is in a bad way and likely to die. It's still good news for us, as it will avoid any possible further trouble.*"

"You assumed what Brannigan said was in reference to Mr Martin?"

The tears had welled up in her eyes as she repeated Brannigan's conversation. She fought to hold them back. My question had her in danger of losing control, but she swallowed hard a couple of times and then took a deep breath – no doubt to steady her voice – before her unexpected vitriolic reply.

"Who else would he be talking about? There were no other employees in a bad way and likely to die." She looked uncomfortable about her outburst, but I was grateful she didn't apologise for it. An apology would just start her tears flowing.

"What could he be referring to when he mentioned avoiding having to deal with any trouble?" I tried to make the question sound conversational.

"In Mr Brannigan's case, it could mean anything, but whatever he meant by it would not be good news for somebody. I don't know if I should mention this or not, but maybe I should. While I don't know what was going on, or what he was doing exactly, I think Mr Martin suspected something was not quite right. He was doing a bit of quiet digging on the side into whatever it was. He never mentioned what he was doing to me. It seemed as though he was trying to keep whatever he was up to hidden from me. We have worked closely together for quite a while. I can read him like a book."

"Maybe it's a good thing you can. Do you have any ideas about what he might have been investigating?"

"Yes… well no, not really. I mean, I don't have any real knowledge or evidence, but I think he found something amiss in the accounts. As I said, I don't know what he was looking into but, if there were something wrong with the accounts, I can think of a few things it might be."

"You and Mr Martin seem to have a very close working relationship. It's obvious you liked the man. Did he ever talk about his wife or his marriage?"

"Of course not; it would have been most improper for him to discuss personal matters such as those with me. He was always a polite, and a proper gentleman. Still, you didn't have to be too bright to work out things weren't too good at home for him. Oh,

I don't mean he said anything about it. It's more like inferences I picked up at different times. I really miss working with him. He was so good to work for, and he was teaching me so much about the job."

"Well, remember the old adage about while there is life, there is hope … Hope things will turn out well in the end. The best advice I can give you is to keep hoping for his recovery, and for this mess at work to be sorted out quickly. I must ask though, is there anything in particular from today's conversation you want me to do?"

"Not really; I just wanted to apologise for the other day and to tell you all I know about what appears to be going on at work. What I want you to do is the same as I wanted you to do the other day: find out who did this to Mr Martin and make sure they are brought to justice."

Colleen had nothing more to tell me, and I had no further questions. After she left, I felt I should try to spend at least some productive time in my office. I had extensive notes to type up, and quite a long tape to transcribe. It had gone 6:30 by the time I finished and dumped everything I needed into my bag. About ten minutes after I arrived home, Ben arrived and came in laden with our dinner.

It appears he had decided tonight was pasta night. Unable to decide what to choose, he opted for a selection of dishes, and brought both the red and white wines to go with them. Rather than allow dinner to go cold, a few minutes after he arrived, we sat down to the serious business of dispatching the food. In spite of our valiant efforts, leftovers went in the fridge for another time.

Once we were settled in the lounge room, our focus turned to our Martin cases. I opened the discussion. "What was your assessment of this morning's interview? Did it achieve what you wanted?"

"As much as I could have hoped for; yes. I had hoped to follow up on a few things after I returned to my office this afternoon, but other matters requiring more urgent attention took precedence. The upshot is, I didn't get to follow up on any of it. What about you, did you manage to achieve anything worthwhile today?"

"Stella's comments about Lenny, and her shock when you showed her the photo of Constable Kent were interesting. I suspect both our cases now rest on discovering more about the constable who used to be Lenny. Aside from that, my late afternoon appointment was with Colleen Jenkins." I saw Ben's eyebrows draw together as he tried to work out why the name sounded familiar. I put him out of his misery. "She is the young woman who was Trent Martin's assistant at that office supplies place. Also, I think she is someone who wants to be more than a friend of Mr Martin's, if she isn't already. There is no doubt in my mind, her glowing words about him stem from something deeper and stronger than friendship. I'd like to know whether it's reciprocated by the other party."

"Okay, now I remember who she is. Did she have anything interesting to tell you?"

"Oh, I think so. And, I think there may be something of interest to you in what she had to say. I didn't see the list of places Stella drew up for you during today's interview, but I'm wondering whether the office supplies business is one of the names on the list."

"Hang on a minute. I'll just slip out to the car to fetch my file. My hands were full with dinner, so I left the file in the car."

During the several moments he was gone, I moved our coffees to my office and cleared a space on my desk. When I heard him returning, I called out, "I'm in the office. I've moved us in here so we can spread things out on the desk to avoid slopping coffee all over them."

Moments later we were sitting on opposite sides of the desk with our case files open in front of us. "Who goes first?" I asked.

"I will. Here is the list of businesses Stella gave me. You might like to photocopy it first, and then we can deal with Colleen Jenkins' information."

Chapter 21

While Ben sat studying the transcript of my interview with Colleen Jenkins, I fetched fresh coffees and glasses of port. As an afterthought, I tipped crackers on to a small plate and added a couple of cheeses I found in the fridge. I didn't need anything to nibble yet, but tonight looked like developing into a long session. Ben was still poring over the transcript when I carried the tray into my office.

"Ben, please clear a space on the desk so I can unload this tray without spilling something." As I unloaded the tray, I saw his eyes light up.

"You must be psychic. I was feeling like something to chew, but I couldn't work out whether I wanted something sweet or savoury. I think you've nailed it with the cheese and crackers."

As he spread a goodly dollop of triple-cream Brie on a cracker, I felt it safe to ask a question without interrupting the process. "What do you make of Colleen's comments?"

"Is the office supplies place where Colleen works on the list Stella gave us? I don't remember seeing it."

"No. That's why I wanted to check the list. The office supplies place is not on it. Now, I think about it, it makes sense for it not to be on Stella's list."

"How did you come to that conclusion?"

"We know Stella wasn't their only operative. There was Rosie, and it is likely there were others as well. It's possible they've replaced Rosie by now. Although the office supplies place isn't on Stella's list, it might be on one of the other operatives' lists. Perhaps the mob considered it unwise to have Stella visiting the place where her husband worked, and where she might be known to some of the employees. The question arising from my train of thought is whether all of the couriers operated on the same nights, or if they were scheduled to work on different nights? We know on at least one occasion, Rosie worked the same night as Stella. Was it an aberration – and exception – or did she always work the same nights as Stella, but at a slightly different time?"

"Good thinking – and a couple of good questions … to which I don't have answers." Ben appeared deep in thought, before cocking an eyebrow at me and voicing some of his thoughts. "I get the impression you think the office supplies place might be involved in the mob's operation. More to the point, you suspect Brannigan somehow is involved. Am I close to the mark?"

"Yeah, I'd say you were spot on. Not only is your interpretation in line with my thinking, I'm almost convinced Brannigan knows what happened to Trent Martin and why. While I've no doubt Trent Martin was who he referred to in his phone conversation, what I'm not sure about is whether Brannigan was implicated in what happened. Colleen suggested Trent Martin was digging into something dodgy he thought was happening there. If my client's activities threatened a cushy operation Brannigan had running, might he initiate moves to end it?"

"As I said: psychic. Our thinking seems perfectly aligned on this one. I'll give some thought to how we might confirm any of our thoughts. There are too many unknown elements in the equation so far. We don't have a possible identity for the courier. We don't know the day or time of visits to the business. And we don't know who the contact is within the business. Is it one dedicated staff member, or is it whoever happens to be around at the time?"

"My first thought was the visits would happen at night; not late at night but after the staff went home. Maybe it had something to do with why Trent Martin worked late so often. As part of his investigation, he was hoping to catch something while it was happening."

"You might be right. We could ask Stella if she knows anything, but I doubt she does. My only option might be to set up surveillance on the place after dark and wait for something to happen."

"What about those other places on Stella's list, will you check them as well?"

"I didn't plan to. What makes you think I should? We know Stella won't be visiting them again any time soon … or ever, if we can close down the mob."

"Isn't it likely they've replaced her with someone else; another operative to take over her list of places. What about the address of the central location, is it still current? They've lost Rosie and now Stella. Would they consider it safe to continue to operate out of the same location, or would they play it safe and move their headquarters to a different address?"

"Another good question… I suppose it is possible they'd move their operation to a new venue on the off chance someone – like Stella for instance – shared what they knew with the police. From my point of view, and given my few resources available, I think my first priority is to concentrate on the known. Who knows? If one of the known sites comes good, we might be able to bust the whole thing wide open without having to deploy resources to the unknown, in the off chance we might learn something."

"It sounds like you have no new detectives likely to arrive any day soon."

"Correct… And the one bloke I do have is being run ragged. It wouldn't surprise me if he applies for a transfer to a precinct offering 'normal' working hours. A further restriction on the manpower I have available for any surveillance work is the apparent involvement of Constable Shayna Kent in the operation. People see rosters. People talk at their desks and in the lunchroom. It would be impossible to keep it under wraps and not have her find out what was happening."

"Yep, it would be a problem, and it gives us something else to add to the nice-to-know list: what is the constable's role in this? Is she just another person the mob has a hold over, or is she a major player in the operation?"

"We're doing it again aren't we: coming up with loads more questions to which we have no answers? May I have a copy of this transcript so I can dwell on Colleen's comments when I'm feeling a bit brighter? I do share your thinking on this one. The comments she made could well prove vital in cracking this case."

We both sat alone with our thoughts as the printer spat out Ben's copy of the transcript. As soon as I gave him the printout, we both tidied up our folders before closing them to signify our night's work was done. I loaded mugs, glasses and plate onto the tray and headed for the kitchen. Ben followed me out and continued on to the lounge room. I expected him to gravitate towards the front door in preparation for leaving, but it appears he wasn't ready to go yet. If I'm honest, I was feeling a bit jaded, was desperate for a shower and bed, and would be happy for him to go home.

"Ben, I'd offer you another coffee, but I think you've had enough to keep you awake for the rest of the week."

"True; but you could offer me another glass of port. Yeah, that would be good. Just a glass of port and then I'll be on my way. I just want to sit for a moment and think about what we've achieved tonight. Did we achieve anything? I mean anything apart from a whole heap of questions we can't answer?"

"Ask me after I've slept on it and am a bit more clearheaded. My gut instinct is telling me we moved closer to something important tonight. I just wish it would stop being so cryptic and tell me exactly what that is."

Not much later, I waved Ben off on his way home. It took me no time to shower and fall into bed. I was tired. It was mental tiredness, rather than physical. I soon realised mental tiredness doesn't induce sleep.

*****

At some point during the wee hours of the morning, at least one thing became clear. In reality, I now had two clients: Trent Martin and Colleen Jenkins. While they both might lead back to the same underlying problem, at this point, they were two separate clients with two separate cases.

The only good thing to happen was the news my other new case was unlikely to begin for at least another couple of days. That realisation led to another breakthrough in my thinking. Ben might not have the manpower to carry out surveillance on what he called 'the unknown', but I did. I had no night surveillance work lined up and, therefore, I was free to do a bit of nosing around on my own.

Where better to start progressing my investigations than with the office supplies place? There was a note of caution attached to that thinking: how to acquaint Ben with the fact I would be working a case at night for the next few days, without having him suspect which case it might be.

Leaving for my city office a bit later than usual this morning meant I missed the early morning traffic-crawl into the city. It also meant making a leisurely start to the day by buying a newspaper and visiting the bakery before going up to my office. Finding no red light blinking on my answering machine was almost a relief. I wanted time to myself ... time to think and develop strategies relevant to my existing cases. Ben hadn't indicated he intended talking to Stella today, so I should be able to spend the day in my office.

By ten o'clock, I had dealt with all of the usual admin tasks, and read everything of interest in today's newspaper. The mind-in-neutral procedure for making coffee allowed my mind to roam free. When I returned to my desk with my fresh coffee, I knew I would leave the office early this afternoon. Not much sleep last night had left me a bit below par. I needed a nap this afternoon if I was going to be spending time on surveillance tonight.

I sent Ben a text to let him know I would be working this evening. It was safer to send him a text than calling him. A message meant I avoided a grilling about some new case which required me to work tonight. Then, with my feet up on the desk, I studied Stella's list of the places she visited as part of her courier runs. I kept coming back to the address of the operation's central location. Would there be any activity there during the day? Regardless, daylight hours were the best time to see what a place looked like.

Eyeballing the place this afternoon was unlikely to help my investigation in any way, but it seemed the right thing to do. Call it being across all the information available about the mob's operation. I checked the address on Google Maps, and was surprised to find it situated in a cul-de-sac. It didn't make sense for a dodgy operation to be working out of somewhere which didn't provide an easy getaway in the event of a raid. But, its location might suit me to perfection.

After a chicken and salad roll for lunch, and yet another cup of coffee, I locked my office and headed for home by way of a tour of a lesser known area. The address was on the outskirts of town, in an area bordering semi-rural properties. As I crawled along the street, I tried to create the impression of someone trying to locate an address in the area.

At the entrance to the cul-de-sac, I stopped and checked a sheet of paper I held up on the steering wheel. "Don't panic," I murmured as I peered around me. "I'm just checking my map." Nobody was around, and nobody would have heard me anyway. But, I thought it helped give a touch of authenticity to my impersonation of someone lost in suburbia. Then, after a few moments, I turned into the cul-de-sac and made my way slowly to the end, where I again went through the 'checking my map' routine.

Stationary in the turning area at the end of the cul-de-sac, I alternated between looking at my map and checking the houses along the street. The address I was interested in was the third house from this end. While delivering my Oscar-winning performance of someone lost, I made sure my dashboard camera was recording. I had positioned my car in the turning area so the camera pointed directly at the house in question.

Time to go... One last look along the street, before throwing my 'map' onto the passenger seat and giving myself a head slap for having become lost. I drove out of the cul-de-sac at maybe a whisker above the legal speed limit. Then, it was a convoluted route from outer suburbia to home and a welcome nap for a couple of hours.

Woken from a deep sleep by my phone, I had no idea of the time, what day it was, or where I was. As I grabbed the phone and checked the caller ID, I worked at moistening my mouth enough to be able to speak. It was Ben. He picked up on my not yet having completely joined the real world.

"Sonny, are you all right? Where are you? Talk to me, Sonny."

"I'm fine and I'm at home. I had things to do at here so I came back after lunch. Did you want something?" He seemed confused by my question. "You called me. I wondered why you called. Nice though it is to talk to you, I imagine you're far too busy for a casual chat. So, why did you call?"

"Eh? Oh yeah, I read your text about working tonight. Have you started a new investigation? I mean, I wondered whether you were still working your Trent Martin case, or if you closed it and had moved onto something else."

"Nothing so simple… I'll be multi-tasking for the next little while, but my Martin case remains ongoing. Have you had a breakthrough with yours, or were you calling about another interview with Stella?" My brain had kicked in again and I realised the most likely reason for his call was something to do with his Stella Martin case.

"When I go back to talk to Stella depends on when I receive some information I'm waiting for. I'm hoping it might be sometime tomorrow. If you're busy with a new case, will you have time to be at the interview when I arrange it?"

"Of course I'll be there. My Martin case is still open, and everything Stella tells us is relevant to the basic question Trent Martin asked me to investigate."

"Okay, I'll keep you informed. I take it you are on surveillance tonight. Are you likely to work late?"

"That's a good question. I should know before eight o'clock whether it will develop into a late night or not. Was there a reason you asked, or was it just a casual enquiry?"

"A bit of both I think. I like to know when you are working nights. It allows me to be prepared for when you call for help. Apart from that, if the information I'm waiting for comes through, I thought we might kick it around tonight and see where it leads us in terms of planning another interview with Stella."

"I'll call you if I look like being home by eight o'clock."

Tempting though it is to abandon tonight's surveillance plan, Ben might not receive his information today, and it would be a wasted night. I decided to stick with my original plan to stake-out the office supplies premises. While it was nothing more than an assumption, if something happened there tonight, it would be between seven and eight o'clock. If that was the timing of Stella's courier runs, my hope was other operatives ran to the same timetable. Whatever happened, I didn't need to be in position until just before seven o'clock.

The last couple of hours of the afternoon, I planned to spend preparing for tonight's operation, although not much planning was required. It would be a straightforward matter of watching the place for an hour or so. After a few moments thought, I decided to leave my car in the carpark behind my office and proceed on foot to the observation point. Then I realised I had a problem.

Off the top of my head, I couldn't think of a good place from which to observe any after-hours' activities at the target location. A map was no use. I needed to see the physical location. Maybe some planning was required… and, perhaps it should start now rather than later. After checking all the gear in my 'surveillance kit', and adding a bottle of water and couple of muesli bars to the bag, I was heading into the city again.

I turned onto the street prior to mine and drove slowly past the office supplies building. Nothing in the immediate vicinity suggested a good place from which to carry out surveillance.

After driving around the block and parking behind my office, I cut through the block on foot to emerge on the next street opposite tonight's target. I crossed the street and ambled past the building. Still nothing inspired me.

Narrow vehicle access ran along one side of the building and around to the rear. It was too narrow for trucks, and probably intended for ordinary passenger vehicles coming to collect previously ordered supplies. So, how did the firm bring in its supplies? Trucks had to access the rear of the building from somewhere around here.

My ambling took me to the end of the block. I turned the corner and kept going. At the next corner, I hesitated. I thought it too far from the target location but I reminded myself trucks had to access the rear of the building somehow. I turned the corner and began strolling along the street. This was the third street back from the centre of town and was less 'city heart' than the previous two.

Not a bustling business area, I passed a backpackers' hostel, a newsagent and a small (not many stars) motel. Then, there it was: a wide laneway running from the street back and along the centre of the block behind the businesses. The shop on the other side of the entrance was empty. A faded *For Lease* sign was the only thing gracing its plate glass frontage.

Loud music, bright lights and youthful voices emanating from the backpackers' hostel filled the street. The illuminated *Vacancies* sign hanging on the front wall of the motel had a few gaps in its letters where, presumably, bulbs needed replacing. The building, like its sign, looked tired and unloved. With other more upmarket accommodation nearby, this motel was unlikely to see much action tonight. What this street had to offer suited me fine.

Nobody was visible in the street now, just as probably nobody would be around later to notice someone come along the street and slip into the darkened laneway. I stepped quickly into the shadows and picked my way along the wide laneway running through the centre of the block. This lane provided access to the rear of the office supplies building and other businesses facing onto the other street. It was perfect for my needs … but it was still a little too early to be in position.

After picking my way out onto the street again, I power-walked back to my car. It is handy to have your vehicle close by when you are working on foot – especially if something goes wrong and you need a quick getaway. I grabbed my jacket off the back seat, scrambled into the car, and stuffed the jacket into my surveillance bag on the front passenger seat. Evening traffic streaming along the street prevented me exiting the parking lot behind my office. Time was slipping away. I became nervous.

A miraculous break in the procession occurred when traffic was held up by an incompetent driver trying to reverse angle park in front of a building a few doors up from where I sat waiting to escape. I charged out through the gap, made a U-turn around a garden bed in the centre of the road, and dodged traffic to pull up two streets further away from the city heart. A line of parking bays in front of the motel was too good to ignore. Without choosing, I parked in a bay about half way along the line.

Although my sweater had long sleeves, as soon as I stepped out of the car, I felt the chill night air bite. I applauded my wisdom of keeping that big old jacket in the car for just such situations. With my bag over my shoulder, I stood on the pavement for a few moments checking for any signs of life out and about in the neighbourhood. Nothing seemed to have changed since I was there earlier. The impending cold night would help keep people indoors.

Once again, I stepped into the darkened laneway and navigated my way along towards the rear of the office supplies building. While some light spilled out into the lane from the hostel and the motel, it amounted to no more than a couple of patches of lighter shadow in an otherwise dark corridor.

In spite of the darkness, I felt exposed and vulnerable. A small extension had been tacked onto the rear of a building up ahead. The particularly dark area between the extension and a nearby industrial skip provided perfect cover. I slipped into the darkened space, and placed my bag on the ground at my feet, before studying the building opposite me across the laneway. I was positioned immediately opposite the backdoor and loading dock of the office supplies building.

Before turning off my phone, I checked the time. It was just seven o'clock. "Right, let's see if my hunch pays off," I murmured to the night.

Chapter 22

Time became an unknown quantity as the cold seeped through my boots, freezing my feet on its way up into the rest of my bones. Like an annoying child demanding to know 'are we there yet', the little voice in my head kept asking how much longer. By the time I was in position, my nose already felt frozen. Now, it kept running. It gave me something to do, but I was in danger of running out of tissues.

I decided to risk checking the time, and scrabbled around in my jacket's voluminous pocket for my watch. "Is that all?" I whispered. Its luminous dial told me it was 7.30. If I stuck to my original plan, I still had another half hour to wait before I could go home. As I shoved my watch back in my pocket, headlights shone up the narrow lane beside the office supplies building. "Show time!" I whispered.

Since I took up my position, light was visible in only one upper storey window in the rear of the office supplies building. At about the same time as the headlights appeared in the lane alongside, more lights came on in the building, including one above its rear door, which lit up the loading dock area. A small model sedan with bright green metallic paint drove up to the dock before making a meal of turning around in the narrow space in front of me. After much backing and filling, it faced the right direction to be driven back out along the side of the building ... or out onto the back street.

While the manoeuvring took place, a man came out and stood on the dock. He kept the light at his back, making it difficult to see his face. I slipped my hand into my bag and dragged out a small pair of binoculars. My digital recorder had been recording since the lights appeared in the lane. With my free hand, I brought it up close to my mouth and whispered. "Well, well; it appears old Mr Brannigan is working late tonight."

Brannigan gave the driver a small parcel. Even with my binoculars it was impossible to tell whether the driver was a young woman or a lad. Skinny, and with short cropped hair, the driver could pass for either gender. I hoped the driver's departure would take the vehicle past me and out onto the street behind. A closer look might help me decide about the driver. The driver had other ideas, and drove out the way he came in. Probably in the hope of avoiding attention, the small sedan, with only its parking lights on, inched its way along the side of the building and out onto the street.

By then, Brannigan was nowhere to be seen. I was so focused on the driver, I hadn't seen him go back inside, but I had seen the light above the dock, and the one immediately inside the backdoor, go out. On replaying my memory banks' record of the scenario on the loading dock, it appeared Brannigan handed over the package, turned on his heel and went back inside, all in the one swift movement.

As I stood reflecting on what happened, the sole remaining light visible, the one in the upper floor window, went out. Brannigan had finished for the night and was going home. No cars were parked at the rear of the building, so he wouldn't come out this way. While it was safe enough for me to remain in the shadows long enough for Brannigan to leave the building and be on his way home, there were things I needed to do and places I needed to be.

It took only seconds to stuff the binoculars and recorder back into my bag and strap on my watch, and then I was right to go. Taking care not to stumble over or bump into anything likely to create a noise, I slipped out of my hiding place and onto the main laneway. Feeling reasonably confident I was alone, I broke into a run, only slowing to a walk just prior to stepping out of the lane and onto the street. With nobody in sight anywhere on the street, I jogged to my car, unlocking it as I went.

There was no hope of following the little green sedan, but I figured I knew where it would go at some time tonight. That's where I went too. Outer-suburbia was quiet. TV screens, visible through windows as I drove along the street, suggested residents opted for a night in, rather than being outdoors in the cold. A vacant block a short distance past the turn into the cul-de-sac seemed the best place to park. It was helpful the house prior to the block was in darkness. I pulled into the kerb in front of the darkened house.

My brisk walk back along the street to the entrance to the cul-de-sac helped offset the chill. Trees planted along both sides of the cul-de-sac and no street lighting, except for a solitary light at the turning area at the end, were helpful too. Maintaining a pace I hoped mimicked someone out for an after-dinner stroll, I made my way towards the turning area. In spite of the lack of street lighting, and no one being out and about, on such a clear night, the moon lit up the area more than I liked.

Tonight, the trees were my best friends. The areas of shadow they provided were not large and were spaced some distance apart, but they were all I had to avoid being seen. As I neared the end of the cul-de-sac, I could see the green sedan parked in the driveway of the address I had scoped this afternoon. I hurried the last fifty metres to the end of the street. Although the only street light was in this area, there was an open area behind it.

No homes nestled around the semicircular turning area. Instead, a high, well-manicured hedge surrounding its perimeter separated the cul-de-sac from the adjacent nature reserve. My dash to cover those last metres ended with me throwing myself through a gap in the hedge. Once upright again, I took out my phone … and congratulated myself on having turned it on again on my way here. Keeping it hidden as much as possible under my jacket, I flicked through to Ben's number and set it dialling.

"I thought you were working tonight. Oh, of course you're working and something has happened. I'm a bit busy at the moment. Can it wait?"

His being a 'bit busy' explained Ben's terse comments when he answered his phone, but I wasn't about to waste time retaliating. "No, it can't wait … not if you want to see what's going on at the 'central location' we've been banging on about for the last few days. I'm watching the place now, and a delivery has just been made."

"We're on our way. Do nothing and stay out of sight."

What did he think I was going to do? While I'm not averse to taking a bit of a risk now and then, I'm not stupid. There could be dozens of not particularly nice people in that house. Amid such mental ranting, an unsettling thought elbowed its way to the forefront of my thinking. The driver of the green sedan had been in the house for a while, and there had been no sign of him during the time I was in the cul-de-sac. The car was there when I arrived, and was still there about fifteen minutes later. It did not gel with the impression I gained from Stella's comments about how the system operated. Her description suggested an operative arrived at the location, dropped off the night's packages, and was on their way again in fewer than five minutes. There was a bad smell developing about tonight's operation.

In what seemed like only moments after my call to Ben, I saw the dark shape of a patrol car ooze almost imperceptibly from nowhere and park across the entrance to the cul-de-sac. It had no lights and, with the wind blowing over the top and away from me, it seemed to arrive without a sound. As I stood marvelling at its stealthy arrival, my phone vibrating in my pocket startled me: Ben.

"Where are you?" a voice hissed in my ear when I answered.

I whispered a succinct description of my location. A couple of moments later, Ben materialised beside me.

"Anything new happen since you called me?" he murmured as he assessed our target location.

"No, nothing; but I am concerned about the welfare of the driver of the sedan parked in the driveway. Going by what Stella told us, the driver has been in there for far too long to be just dropping off a few packages. I noticed you sent a vehicle to block exit from the area but, are you a lone warrior, or did you bring troops with you?"

There was no reply. By the time I finished speaking, Ben had disappeared. I found myself wishing I was armed. On his own, he didn't stand a chance of dealing with whatever was going on in that house. Unarmed, I wasn't much help to him. My stomach had gone from being a roiling mass to feeling like a solid lead ball.

My tension didn't ease any when I spotted dark figures moving silently towards the house. I couldn't count how many, but it was irrelevant. No matter how many there were, I was sure there wouldn't be enough to deal with the scenario I imagined was about to unfold. It took me a minute or so to accept the reality of my situation: there was nothing I could do to assist. My only possible contribution might be to take down anyone trying to make a break for it through the nature reserve.

For a few moments, nothing happened. Those dark figures around the house appeared to be standing still, frozen in position. Then, all hell broke loose. There was the sharp crack of splintering timber as a ram smashed open the front door. Above the ensuing pandemonium, I heard Ben's voice, yelling for everyone to stay where they were and not to move.

A figure rushed out past the shattered door now hanging at a crazy angle on its broken hinges. The moment I saw him heading for the door, I flexed my ankles and made ready to move to intercept him if he bolted this way. I need not have bothered. He hadn't taken more than three paces outside the house before being tackled and brought to ground by one of Ben's officers. Things were not going well inside the house … but, maybe that depends on from whose point of view you assessed the situation.

Crashes and yelps, and a whole host of words not normally heard in polite society disturbed the previously silent street. Is everyone in this neighbourhood dead, deaf, or just away from home tonight? The racket coming from the house was loud enough to be heard above the pulsating music from the nightclubs in the city heart on a Friday night. So, why hadn't any of the residents come out to investigate?

My mind was diverted from such thoughts by movement that erupted from outside the far side of the house. A figure made a dash for the green sedan on the driveway. The only two officers visible out front of the house were dealing with the bloke who ran out through the front door. I took a couple of steps towards a gap in the hedge as I prepared to rush over to lend a hand. Common sense hit me like a thunderbolt.

What did I think I was going to do? Now the two officers had cuffed the bloke on the ground, what were they going to do with him? There was no paddy wagon waiting at the ready; no vehicle of any sort, except for the patrol car blocking the entrance to the cul-de-sac. I stopped and moved back to my original position behind the shrubbery as the second escapee dived into the green car and fired it up.

Clouds of gravel flew in all directions as he raced down the driveway. After bouncing over the gutter, he swung the vehicle around. Then, with a squeal of tyres, he made his getaway. More screeching of tyres occurred when he stamped on the brakes as the police vehicle blocking the exit loomed up in front of him. The two officers sitting in the patrol car weren't too quick off the mark.

With the green car almost brought to a halt, the driver abandoned it. He flung open his door, sprang out and galloped back along the street. It was unlikely he would return to the house. It left him with only one possible option for his escape: through the nature reserve on foot – and past me. A somewhat comical situation developed. The young driver – obviously fit and fast –made good progress along the street.

By the time the two officers from the patrol vehicle emerged onto the street, the driver of the green sedan was more than halfway along the cul-de-sac. Burdened by all the gear they carry, the two officers were not closing the gap between them and their quarry. There was no question about it. The driver was heading for the hedge I was hiding behind. As he drew nearer, he spotted the only skinny gap in it. I saw him swerve to aim his run for that gap.

It was time for me to help out. Moving quickly to stand beside the gap, I stuck my leg out across it. I was barely in place when the driver tried bulldozing his way through the hedge. Unhappy about the way they were being treated, some of the offended branches smacked him about the face as he pushed past. Finally breaking through, he stumbled over my outstretched leg. He didn't go down as I'd hoped. Being reasonably fleet of foot, he did stumble around for a moment, but managed to stay on his feet.

I grabbed him and, for a couple of seconds, we performed an undignified *pas de deux* until my knee found its target and rearranged his family jewels. My action dropped him to his knees a moaning mass. Grabbing his arm and bringing it up behind his back, I pushed him flat onto the ground and knelt on him. The approaching thunder of boots on bitumen told me the officers from the patrol car would soon join us.

A young police officer, making like a front row forward, barged his way through the hedge and tripped over the pair of us on the ground. Still a bit dazed, as he stood up, he demanded, "What the hell…?"

"I assume you have a pair of cuffs on you?" I asked, as I indicated the arm I had twisted up behind the driver's back.

"Ooh, no; I… Uhmm … my partner should…." Any further comment was interrupted by the sound of someone else coming through the hedge.

The second officer picked his way through the branches and stepped delicately around the assemblage on the ground in front of him. "Aah, Miss Whittington, what are you doing here?"

"It's a long story, Jock. We don't have time for it right now. Maybe Ben will share it with you tomorrow."

"Hmm… Aye, perhaps he might. Is this the bloke from that vehicle?"

"Yep; would you have a pair of cuffs for him?" Jock squatted down beside the driver and set about snapping the cuffs around his skinny wrists.

As he hauled the driver to his feet, Jock commented, "He doesn't appear too happy. Seems to be in a bit of pain..."

"That's possible. His soft dangly bits might be a bit tender for a day or two."

"...Probably disrupt his social life no end," Jock chuckled as he handed the prisoner over to his partner. That's when Ben's voice crackled over Jock's radio.

"Where the hell are you guys? There are two wagons trying to get into the cul-de-sac. You need to shift your vehicle."

"On my way, Sir," Jock responded as he pushed his way back through the hedge.

Using his prisoner as makeshift human shield, the younger officer pushed the driver out through the hedge ahead of him. I attempted to follow them out, but didn't get too far. The reason the young officer and his prisoner stopped the moment they broke through the hedge was the sight of Ben walking towards them.

"Was this the one attempting a getaway in that vehicle?" Ben asked with a flick of his head towards a green sedan parked at the other end of the cul-de-sac.

"Yes, Sir, but he's her collar," the young officer said, jerking his thumb over his shoulder at me behind him.

Ben looked me up and down. I followed his example and discovered I looked a lot less clean and tidy than I did when I arrived here. My battles with the hedge and the driver had left me looking somewhat dishevelled.

"Were any of you injured?" Ben's question was all inclusive, but he was looking at me when he asked it.

"I'm fine, and I think your two patrol officers are okay. But, Jock will probably confirm whether the medical examiner needs to take a look at this bloke in cuffs.

"Aw, don't tell me someone has gone and injured the prisoner. There will be nothing but paperwork and enquiries for the next month."

"I don't think that will be the case. In the first instance, it wasn't one of your officers who injured him. And, secondly,

I doubt he will lay complaint. He won't want to advertise the nature of his injury inflicted by a woman."

For a large, older bloke, Jock was fit. After just having run the full length of the cul-de-sac, he jogged back to move the patrol car blocking access to the street. Moments after I heard him start the vehicle, the wail of sirens shattered the silence. Ben signalled to the two paddy wagons to park on the lawn in front of the house. As directed, the two drivers bounded out and flung open the rear doors of both wagons. Ben indicated the driver of the green car, still held firmly by the young officer, should go into the back of one of the wagons.

As the young officer bundled his prisoner into the wagon, Jock arrived in the patrol car. He dragged a bloke in handcuffs out of the back of the vehicle, marched him around to the rear of the second wagon, and shoved him inside.

"Who's this then, Jock, and where did he come from?" Ben asked.

"Well now, soon after we arrived on the scene, this here bloke came along in another vehicle, and was most put out when we wouldn't allow him access to the cul-de-sac. It seems he had business at this house too, and became upset when we prevented him from getting on with it."

Other officers began frog-marching the cuffed occupants of the house out to the wagons. Five more were added to the two already in the vans. Their operation at the house complete, Jock and his partner drove away, and the other officers traipsed back through the hedge to their vehicles parked somewhere on the nature reserve. Ben and I were left standing alone on the front lawn of the house.

"Are you heading off now too?" I asked Ben.

"Not just yet… Emily's forensic guys will be here in a few minutes, along with a couple of detectives, to scour the crime scene throughout the night."

"A couple of detectives…? How did you manage that?"

"They only arrived late this afternoon. I wasn't sure they were coming at all until they arrived. Sam Keller is on loan from Pete Messell at Ralston until we wrap up this case, and the other young guy flew up from Brisbane. He is on loan until we appoint our replacements."

Emily's forensic team arrived while we were talking. Ben spoke to them for a couple of minutes before returning to where I waited. "Have you eaten tonight?" he asked as he sauntered up to me. "And, where is your vehicle?"

"I'm parked on the street just beyond the entrance to the cul-de-sac. No, I haven't eaten tonight and, now you've mentioned food, I'm feeling famished."

"We need to hold a debriefing session tonight. Go home. I'll pick up food on the way through and meet you there in about half an hour."

The thought of Ben's 'debriefing session' did not fill me with enthusiasm. To my mind, it translated as another late night spent being quizzed by Ben about everything I did during every minute of tonight. Nevertheless, it would be good to do it tonight and have it over and done with. It also would give me the opportunity to float past him a few of the things bothering me. And, I was desperate to know what was happening in that house when they burst in.

A few more questions about tonight occurred to me as I trudged along the cul-de-sac on my way to my car. I fished my digital recorder out of my bag and recorded those questions before heading home. There's no doubt I'll have more to add to the list by the time I'm home, in my office, and ready to transcribe the recording.

Chapter 23

"First things first," I reminded myself as I unlocked my front door. In keeping with that approach, I went straight to my office, dumped my bag, and started my computer on transcribing the list of questions from my digital recorder. Once the machine was doing its thing, I went to clean and tidy myself up a bit before the impending long session with Ben.

He arrived soon after – by way of the drive-through service facility – with a bucket of chicken, large box of fries, and tubs of coleslaw and gravy. "It was food that required the least amount of fuss and bother to acquire," he told me as he dumped the bag containing our dinner on the table.

While he went off to wash up, I rushed to add the necessary crockery, cutlery and other tools to the waiting feast. While more of a necessity from time to time when I'm working, tonight the aroma of the chicken and chips almost had me salivating in anticipation. Needless to say, as soon as Ben emerged from the bathroom, we were straight down to the serious business of eating. We made a considerable impression on the quantity of food on offer, but quite a bit of it went into the fridge as left-overs for another time. Then, with coffee and TimTams in hand, we were off to the lounge room to begin a post-mortem on tonight's activities. Ben led off.

"You said you were working tonight, but didn't say what case you were working. How did you come to be at the cul-de-sac at just the right time? Before you begin, I don't believe that's where you started work tonight."

"No, it didn't. Just before seven o'clock, I started surveillance at the rear of the office supplies building. About half an hour later, I witnessed the arrival of a small green sedan. Its driver collected a package, before leaving the site a few minutes later.

I guessed he would visit the 'central location' at some point tonight, so I set myself up to observe what happened if he did."

"What made you target the office supplies building for your surveillance activities?"

"Two things I suppose: Colleen Jenkins unwittingly suggested something might be going on there, and that my client, Trent Martin, was digging into it. When I put two and two together, I thought it might've caused Trent Martin's assault in that alleyway. Yes, it was a longshot. It might have had nothing to do with the mess Stella is mixed up in, but instinct told me it was part of the same operation."

"Yes, but I can't see even a vague connection between something 'fishy' happening in the office supplies place and Stella – other than her husband, Trent, worked for the office supplies firm."

"The office supplies place wasn't on Stella's list to visit. We agreed she wasn't sent there because people might recognise her. But, she wasn't the only courier working for the mob. They also had Rosie, until her demise. They needed to replace her if their operation was to continue unhindered. Perhaps the office supplies place was on Rosie's list, and now was being serviced by her replacement. There was always the chance there were more than just the two couriers. We knew Stella and Rosie operated on the same nights. Maybe other operatives, if there were any, worked on other nights."

"It would spread the workload across the week for the blokes toiling away at the central location. And, it would be easier, with only two working on each night, to schedule deliveries and collections so as to avoid contact between the couriers."

"…Unless something unforeseen happened, such as Rosie's flat tyre."

"So, what was the rationale behind your being in position to witness a courier in action tonight? We had nothing to suggest any couriers would be working tonight, and nothing to indicate anyone would visit the office supplies place."

"You're right. We didn't, but I planned to stake out the building for a few nights in a row until I convinced myself my assumptions about the place were unfounded. Simply put, I got lucky. On my first night of surveillance, I confirmed all my suspicions and assumptions, but it leads to a long list of questions. First: was the little green car's driver Rosie's replacement, or was he a different operative entirely?"

"We won't know the answer to that – if at all – until tomorrow morning at the earliest. It's possible he might refuse to tell us anything. It may well come down to how terrified he is of the mob running him, and whether he is prepared to risk potential reprisals for speaking to the police. What else is on this long list of questions you mentioned?"

"If we stay focused on the driver for the moment, why did he spend so long at the house? My impression from Stella's comments was that they simply dropped off the packages and went home, or collected the packages and delivered them. They didn't hang about at the house. Yet tonight, the car was already there when I arrived at the cul-de-sac, and it hadn't left when you and your blokes arrived. That's a long time to drop off a few packages."

"Well, that leads me to something I was going to tell you sometime this evening … And it's something that might prove an ace in our hand when we question the driver."

I thought better of speaking, and raised my eyebrows instead. If Ben can pre-empt all my questions in this way, it might not be such a long, gruelling debrief after all. Without further prompting, Ben continued.

"Evidence suggests the driver spent so long at the house tonight because he couldn't leave. As you will appreciate, there was a lot of shouting and noisy activity happening inside the house after we stormed the front door. Once things were under control and we looked around, we found a small locked room – an empty storeroom really – in the rear of the house. The bloke who made a break for it out the front door drew our attention to that area of the house when he bolted from back there. In the midst of the melee, one of my officers, who was unable to do anything about it at the time, saw a bloke make a run for it from somewhere back there. When things quietened down, he went to investigate."

"Yes, but the bloke who bolted out the front door wasn't the driver of the vehicle."

"No, he wasn't, but we think he was on guard duty outside the locked storeroom. When we broke into the storeroom, we found the small window there smashed from the inside … presumably by someone no longer in the locked room. No one heard glass breaking, but it's not surprising given the amount of other noise happening. It seems likely – and presumably fingerprints will confirm it –the person held there, and who escaped through the smashed window, was the driver of the little green sedan."

"…Who tried to make a run for it in his vehicle before he discovered his exit was blocked. If your interpretation in relation to the room is correct, it tends to suggest the driver had transgressed in some way and was destined for an unpleasant reprisal. I understand your comment about holding a powerful card. If the bloke had any idea how short his future looked, he might be inclined to trade information for protection."

"Perhaps… but, in the first instance, we're hoping he'll be scared enough by tonight's incidents to loosen his tongue without further enticement. Of course, we would protect him anyway, at least until we wrap up the mob involved – but we won't enlighten him on that one if we can avoid it."

"It will be interesting to know what he has to say. He was operating on a different night from those of Stella and Rosie. Does it suggest he is not Rosie's replacement? Or, is he Rosie's replacement, but they changed his nights because of the contact between Rosie and Stella?"

"I notice we are playing your favourite game again. The one where you keep finding more questions than I have answers. Come on, roll out the rest of your questions. I won't even pretend to know the answers, but they might help inform the questions I'll be asking those blokes we rounded up tonight."

"Okay… Well, first, here is a bonus to keep you happy. Think back on Colleen Jenkins' interview with me: about suggestions Trent Martin no longer had a job with the office supplies firm, and her comments about the reshuffle of old Mr Brannigan's office, which put an inexperienced clerk in charge of work previously done by Trent Martin. Only one person appeared to be working late there tonight, and that person handed over the package to the driver of that green sedan: Brannigan."

"So, you think Brannigan's involvement in the mob's operation might be what Trent Martin was onto… and why he currently occupies a hospital bed?"

"Yeah, I do. It all seems to fit together: the partial phone conversation Colleen heard; a new unskilled clerk being put in charge of an important accounting function; Colleen Jenkins, an unskilled salesperson, being relegated to the sales staff, only because she couldn't be sacked under the prevailing industrial relations climate in that workplace. If anything, it's too tidy, and it's the one factor making me a little uneasy."

"I agree. It does seem a bit too easy. Nevertheless, I'm inclined to agree with you on this one. It would be helpful to shake loose a list of the venues on his route when we interview the driver tomorrow."

"Here is my next question, and it's one you have avoided answering so far: what was going on in the house when you arrived? I mean, from what you saw at the house, was it obvious what the mob's operation was about?"

"Credit cards…"

"What…? What about credit cards?"

"From what I saw tonight, I think there is a substantial credit card skimming operation being run by an apparently ruthless mob. But, it appears to be more sophisticated than your run-of-the-mill skimming operation. Our most urgent task, apart from interrogating all those we rounded up tonight, is to establish which businesses around town are involved. And then, who at each of those business is directly involved."

"Hmm … If we think about the office supplies firm's involvement, we now know Brannigan was a key player, but someone else working there had to be involved as well."

"It's possible I suppose, but explain your reasoning."

"Brannigan spent all day isolated in his cosy office with his secretary and a young clerk. He wasn't out at the front of the store on the checkouts. He didn't have opportunity to skim customers' credit cards. So, at least one other person had to be involved. Unless… Unless…"

"Unless what…?"

"Hang about while I unscramble a thought that's trying to develop… Oh yeah, it could be a possibility. What if there isn't someone on the checkouts involved? What if the skimming only occurs when a customer quotes their card number in some way … as they do when they buy something online?"

"Are you suggesting Brannigan has access to such information and is using it to his advantage?"

"Something along those lines; I don't know about the mechanisms involved, and don't know if it's even a possibility, but, it's the sort of instance of something 'being not quite right,' which might attract Trent Martin's attention.

We know there are at least two couriers operating: the one in the green car, and the other one, who tried to enter the cul-de-sac while the police blocked access. I guess one of those could be Rosie's replacement, and the other could be replacing Stella who, since they attacked her, hasn't worked for them. But, there could be others. Our problem is not knowing how big the operation is, and how much of Millhaven's business community is involved."

"Although I can't say why, I didn't expect an office supplies place to be involved, but it is busy and has a high turnover. That made it desirable for the mob to get their claws into it, while other small businesses probably aren't worth the effort," Ben reasoned.

"Customers of small corner stores tend to spend only a few dollars each visit on things like milk, a loaf of bread, the daily newspaper, a packet of cigarettes ... all small purchases, which they might pay for with cash rather than a card."

"Do you have handy Stella's list of places she visited?" Ben asked.

I retrieved my copy from my case file in the office. On my way back to the lounge room, I did a quick scan of the list. Every entry was one of Millhaven's larger enterprises. Back in my chair, I continued studying the list for a few moments before sharing my thoughts with Ben.

"In spite of my limited knowledge of the operations of some of the businesses on Stella's list, they all are places I believe to have high sales figures; lots of customers buying lots of stuff on a regular basis. I know there are long wait lists for a reservation at both of the restaurants she named. More importantly, she hasn't listed any small businesses."

I slapped the list into Ben's outstretched hand. He mumbled to himself and physically 'ticked off' with his finger each entry as he worked his way down the list. Then, while still holding the printout, he sat staring off into the distance for what felt like an eternity. It was a relief when, after blinking himself back to the here and now, he handed back the list.

"Interesting isn't it, when you think about it? I wonder who the compromised person is at each of those places."

"Compromised…? How do you mean?"

"I was thinking, as with Stella and probably the other couriers as well, maybe the mob had some sort of hold over each of them; something compromising to use to keep them in line. What if a similar situation existed with a key person at each of those listed businesses?"

"Ah, yes. I hadn't considered it in that way. My thinking was along the lines of each of those key people –Brannigan for example – receiving a pay-off for his or her part in the operation, but maybe it was coercion."

"Nah, I couldn't see the likes of Brannigan profiting from the operation, not unless he was a member of the mob running the show. Although, I think there is another possibility. What if, in the case of the office supplies firm, Brannigan is being paid a backhander, but the person doing the skimming was a member of the sales staff, over whom the mob had some hold?"

"Oh, ye-es, that works for me. I can see such a scenario being a possibility … at least with the office supplies place, even if nowhere else."

Our discussion went into limbo while I made fresh coffee and Ben scribbled reminders in his notebook. I was happy for it to remain on hold for a while. The flock of ideas swirling around in my mind were all jockeying for prime position. They were starting to fall into place when Ben interrupted the process by reopening our conversation.

"You said you had a long list of questions. Which ones haven't we addressed?"

"Ah yes, I did have a list of questions before we started, but our discussions added a few more to it. I think I want to discuss those first." Ben nodded and gave me a 'gimme' gesture to start rolling them out. "I'll start with the easy one first. Is it worth staking-out the other businesses on Stella's list tomorrow night, or should we wait to see what comes out of your interrogation of the mob you rounded up tonight?"

"The question is not as easy as you think. I might have to play it by ear, at least until I speak to the driver of the green car, and maybe some of the others as well. After that, I will have a better idea of whether to consider further surveillance."

His approach made sense. With any luck, we might learn enough from the interrogation process to render further surveillance activities unnecessary. The next question I wanted to ask, also might impact.

"Ben, is it likely word of the raid on the house tonight, and the rounding up of those employed there, will reach the couriers tomorrow, and result in none of them working tomorrow night – regardless of whether it was a scheduled night or not?"

"While I have no way of knowing, I don't doubt the couriers will be tipped off about what happened. The most likely outcome is they will all go to ground and collections and deliveries will be on hold for a while. It won't be helpful from our point of view. If the couriers are not working, and the interrogation process doesn't produce relevant information, it will be difficult to identify the couriers. I will add it to the list of 'must have' information to gather from those we rounded up."

"Do you think the main man – the boss – was one of those rounded up tonight?"

"It's possible. I have no way of knowing but, my thinking is, the mob's kingpin was unlikely to be hands-on. I picture him as someone maintaining a position of arm's-length from the operation to ensure a deniable position if things went bad. Again, it's difficult to come up with a definitive answer, when we don't know the scope of the operation. From all we've seen, I believe this is not a small venture, but one of considerable scope. In fact, I am not convinced whatever this mob is up to, is confined to Millhaven."

The next few minutes were taken up with bouncing 'what if' scenarios off one another. While it provided plenty of mental gymnastics, it didn't achieve much. When it was apparent the exercise had run its course, I returned to my list of questions.

"When I called to suggest you might be interested in the activities happening at the central location, you said you were busy. I assumed you were working another case. Was whatever you were doing relevant to this credit card racket we're investigating?"

"No, nothing to do with this investigation… Well, not that I'm aware of. Now your question has me wondering. Does it have some similar aspects which suggest it might be linked? Anything is possible I suppose but… Nah, it's a long shot, and not worth considering at this stage."

"Okay, but what possibilities are there – since you admitted it had some similarities?"

"A call came in from a resident of an apartment in Wellington Towers. The woman claimed there was a serious disturbance happening in the apartment above hers and, after she heard what she thought was a scream, she became concerned. The uniforms on patrol in her area were sent to investigate. They found the apartment in question open, its door damaged, and the interior trashed. When they called it in, I sent my poor overworked one and only detective to investigate. After a bit of a poke about, he called to suggest I might want to take a look. A fair sort of struggle occurred in the living area of the apartment, and quite a bit of blood was spilled. We found no injured or dead body that might've donated the blood."

"Uhmm… A dead body would be a common factor, but the location is a bit removed from the favoured derelict building in the slum area. So, what's happening with that investigation since you left it to deal with the raid on the 'central location' of the mob's operation?"

"I left my trusty detective to take care of a few things before securing the scene and posting a guard outside. Before you ask, I'm not going to check on what's happening there before I turn in tonight. Tomorrow will be soon enough to get involved in this one. Besides, my detective needs to feel I have confidence in him. He won't, if I keep checking on him and looking over his shoulder."

"Did you have any success identifying who owned the apartment – or the occupant, if they were only a tenant?"

"We did get a name, and it appears the person living there owns the apartment. The woman only moved in a few months ago after buying the place. The name didn't raise any flags, so I've asked the duty officer to look into it if he has a quiet moment tonight."

"Ben, I have to ask this. It's intrigued me ever since you and your cavalry arrived at the house tonight. Where did all your troops come from? Did you pull every Millhaven copper out of the bed at short notice? I didn't know you had so many to call on."

"That's because we don't have so many – normally. Everything just fell into place today. It was sheer good luck. While I dithered around for a while because I wasn't sure about it, in the end I let Brisbane know I was concerned about some compromising information to hand about a serving officer. As a result, two temporary detectives arrived in Millhaven on an afternoon flight, one purloined from one of the Brisbane precincts. The other is going to cause me grief for some time to come I imagine. Pete Messell was instructed to send one of his detectives to assist, and the instruction came with the strong recommendation it should be Sam Keller."

"So, Sam is back in town. She should be a great help with both your investigations. But what about all the uniformed officers involved in the raid? From where did they all materialise?"

"It was the other bit of good news. I've been keeping Brisbane informed of progress on the Martin investigation. Because of their growing concern about the nature and magnitude of the operation here, they sent up a contingent of blokes from their emergency response squad. They arrived on one of the morning's flights and spent most of the day settling into their accommodation and familiarising themselves on what's happened so far. They all were at the house under Sam Keller's watchful eye when we left."

A phone call came through to Ben's phone and brought our discussions to an abrupt end. He took the call out on the deck, but decided it would be warmer in my office instead. He seemed in a hurry when he returned to the lounge room. "That was Emily asking if I needed her forensic team to work through the night or only until midnight. I told her only until midnight would be fine, but I needed someone to collect fingerprints and samples from my other crime scene. I don't have any spare officers, and she doesn't have anyone either. So, she offered to do the job herself. I'm meeting her at the apartment in Wellington Towers."

Moments later, he was gone and I was heading for a shower and bed … and, hopefully, a few hours of sleep.

Chapter 24

Last night, sleep took longer to arrive than I anticipated. I was suffering information overload after my 'debriefing' sessions with Ben. My mind eventually wound its way to Sam Keller's reappearance in Millhaven and how her skills and ability as a detective were again assisting in local investigations.

I first met Sam Keller a few years ago when I was working a case in Ralston. She was in uniform then, and she and another Ralston officer, were assigned to me as a protection detail when I wrapped up my case and returned to Millhaven. It was while she was asleep on the sofa in my lounge room, someone broke in and Sam was critically wounded in the subsequent attack. While she was in hospital recovering from her injuries, she was awarded a citation for bravery, and made detective. After about eighteen months, she became Ralston's leading detective. We've become friends, and she has been 'on loan' to assist Ben with investigations on a couple of occasions. Over the years, I have sought her assistance with a couple of my investigations. It will be good to catch up with her again and rebuild some bridges after her last stint here didn't go so well.

In spite of being tired, the night's information dump kept my mind busy too long. I've no idea what time I fell asleep but, judging by how doughy I feel this morning, it was early ... early this morning, that is, rather than late last night. Having decided to ease into the day, rather than rush to be in my city office by the usual time, I dawdled over breakfast and then took my coffee out onto the deck.

"Where are we at with our Martin investigations?" I asked the chatty Willie Wagtail who came to keep me company. There seemed to be so much going on, but it felt as if we weren't making progress. It felt a bit like treading water while everything was going on around us. Adding to it all, my gut was telling me the incident in the Wellington Towers apartment was connected to our Martin investigations.

Ben's comments made it clear he did not agree with my gut, and dismissed the incident in the apartment block as just another crime to investigate. If only I could work out why I think they're linked… The little voice in my head is telling me, if I work that out, the rest of the story will start to unravel, and will allow us to wrap up the whole operation. Perhaps if I don't argue with him too much, my gabby Willie Wagtail companion and I might be able to work it out between us.

My coffee mug was empty and Willie had found other more interesting things to occupy him. A quick glance at my watch told me I had been sitting staring into space for at least an hour – with nothing to show for it. …Or have I? "Another cup of coffee might fix it," I told the universe as I struggled to bring an idea lurking in the back of my mind to the forefront.

After a few sips of fresh coffee, I had confirmed the thought I was trying to connect with was related to the incident in Wellington Towers, and not any of the other stuff we had done in relation to the Martin investigations. "Okay, so what do I know about last night's incident in the Towers? What did Ben tell me?" The problem with asking the universe questions is, it never answers.

It wasn't until my mug was empty that the fog cocooning my brain started to dissipate. Connections between last night's incident and Stella Martin were coming together, but I needed more information. Emily… She and her forensic team worked until late last night. Would she be at work yet this morning? It was worth giving her a call. If I know anything about Emily, she either didn't go home until after she finished analysing all the samples she collected, or she would be in her lab at the crack of dawn this morning to provide Ben with results as early as possible.

As I listened to her number dialling, I tried to work out what I was going to ask her. All I knew after this morning's bout of 'navel gazing' was that I lacked a vital piece of evidence; a vital clue. A clue that might be a linchpin in solving something much bigger than last night's incident in Wellington Towers. I was about to hang up when a breathless Emily answered.

"Sorry, Sonny; I was in the middle of something and couldn't leave it to answer the phone. Are you calling about last night's stuff?"

"Ye-es, but don't ask me what I want to know. The best answer is 'everything'. I'm sorry. I probably shouldn't have called so early this morning. You won't have finished processing everything yet."

"Well, it rather depends on which crime scene you are interested in. If you are asking about the house in the cul-de-sac, I admit there are a lot of samples from there still to analyse. My team didn't leave there till after midnight, and I don't expect them in the lab for at least another hour. Although I have started processing material from that site, there's not much information available yet. But, if you're interested in the Wellington Towers crime scene, you're wrong. I've finished analysing everything from there. If that's what you are interested in, why don't you slip over to my office now to see what I have? If you are coming, don't take too long about it. I haven't given any results to Ben yet, and I will need to talk to him soon."

The good thing about going into my city office later than usual, is avoiding the early morning traffic. Instead of going to my office first, I went straight to Emily's building. Having found a parking spot almost right in front, I raced up the stairs and banged on the door. No one let me in, so I called Emily's number. Moments later she unlocked the door and led me through to her private lab. She spoke to me over her shoulder as we hurried along the corridor.

"As you know, we were stretched a bit thin last night, and I ended up processing the Wellington Towers site myself. I'm unaware how much you know about it, but…"

"I was the one who called Ben and his troops to the house in the cul-de-sac, and later, while we were conducting a review of the night's activities, Ben briefed me on the Wellington Towers incident. He was at my place when he spoke to you, and then left to meet you at that crime scene."

"Great; it saves me giving you background details. Anyway, after Ben took me up to the apartment, he left me there and went to check on his blokes. All I had to do was dust for fingerprints and collect blood samples from the carpet. It doesn't sound like much to do, but it took well over two hours. There were fingerprints everywhere, and I found a couple of other instances of blood to sample."

"It seems none of us had much sleep last night. I gathered from your comments earlier, you have analysed some – or all – of the samples you collected last night."

"All of the ones I collected… Yes, but not much from the house in the cul-de-sac. Most of those results won't be available until sometime later today. My concern now is how to tell Ben about the results of some of the samples from that apartment. I know he'll question their veracity, and probably my ability, but I have double-checked them. I think I'm going wreck his day for him. I couldn't believe some of the results. I checked them again – and then a third time, before I believed them."

"Emily, what have you found? You said you had something I might want to see, but all you've done so far is speak in riddles. What… have… you… found, and why is it likely to wreck Ben's day?"

"Uhmm… Sorry; I think I'm still in shock. I lifted plenty of fingerprints from the apartment in Wellington Towers and, as you might expect, one set of prints predominated. Suffice to say, those prints belonged to the apartment's occupant. I ran all of the prints I collected through the database. There were several hits, but the one that shocked me was a match for the occupant's prints. Her prints are there as a requirement of her work. She is a…

"She's a copper…! And, I'll bet I can give you her name: Shayna Kent. How am I doing so far?"

"How did you know? It couldn't just be a wild guess."

"That's a long story for another time. Your news might not shock Ben as much as you think. He won't be happy about what you've discovered, but, it won't come as a surprise. This confirms…" All of a sudden, a thought elbowing its way in from left field stopped me in my tracks. I paused to let it settle and clarify.

"What is it, Sonny? What's happened? I know that look. You've had an idea."

"Maybe… You didn't happen to find a second match for those prints you're talking about, did you?"

"What…? No, I didn't find a second match. You know as well as I do fingerprints are unique to an individual. Why would you think they might match to someone else as well?"

"It's just a thought, Emily. But, did you check if there was another match for the occupant's prints?" I saw her starting to shake her head dismissively in exasperation, but I needed an answer. "I know you don't understand, none of this makes sense to you, but is it possible for you to run another check on the occupant's prints for me – please?"

After throwing her hands in the air and heaving a sigh of resignation, Emily beckoned me to follow her as she went across to a computer sitting on a desk on the other side of the room. I stood fidgeting as she booted the computer to life and went through the process of logging on.

"For goodness sake, Sonny, pull up a chair and make yourself comfortable. This could take a while. Now, shall we see what the database tells us?"

I watched her fingers clatter across the keyboard. An image flashed up to occupy half the screen. More keyboard gymnastics, and then Emily sat back in her chair with her arms crossed across her chest as she waited. My eyes were glued to the other half – the blank half – of the screen. The little voice in my head was chanting 'come on, come on'. I tried ignoring it, but it echoed my own emotions.

At last, the other half of the screen was blank no longer. A matching image slid in to fill the space. Emily unfolded her arms and sat forward in her chair. She ran the cursor down to bring up text below the images.

"There you go. See there, Sonny," she said pointing to the text. "There is the name of the owner of those prints."

She was right. I couldn't argue with her. How could my gut instinct be so wide of the mark, I wondered as my eyes roamed all over the screen … And came to rest on the cursor. "Emily, run the cursor down further, please. Let's see if there's anything below the entry you have up on the screen now."

With a hard look in my direction and an audible sniff, she reached for the mouse and slid the cursor down the side of the screen.

"Jesus! You are right. How the hell can this be the case? It is not possible for two people to have the same fingerprints. Well, not biologically possible anyway. How am I going to explain this to Ben?"

Emily was hunched in close to the screen. I couldn't see what more she had discovered, and had no idea what she was talking about. "If I could see what you're on about, I might be able to help with your problem." She sprang away and turned sideways to the screen so I had a clear view of the new text she found.

For a moment I couldn't speak. Then, after a false start, I managed to get the words out. "Relax, Emily, this isn't a problem – and it's no great mystery. The database isn't telling you those prints belong to two different people. What it is confirming for me – and for Ben when you tell him – is those prints belong to one person who has gone by two different names during her lifetime." I saw surprise followed by confusion flash across Emily's face. "For some part of her early life, the owner of those prints was Lenore Collins. Then, at some point in her adult life, the redheaded Lenore became the blonde police constable, Shayna Kent."

"You said the database had confirmed the identification for you. Do you mean you and Ben already were aware of the woman's double identity?"

"Let's just say we believed it, but had no evidence to prove it, other than a doctored image, which seemed to support the assumption. I have to go. I have work to do, and you have to break the good news to Ben."

"Good news…! Sonny, what are you going to do? I have a distinct feeling whatever you plan to do is risky and you shouldn't be doing it alone."

I was already on my way out, but I stopped to reassure her I did not contemplate anything risky or dangerous in any way. My parting words before I let the door swing closed behind me encouraged her to call Ben straight away. Then, I was out the front door and galloping down the steps to my car.

The little voice in my head told me not to be stupid, and to visit my office before proceeding with the plan I was developing. It reminded me to collect a couple of vital bits of gear first. Common sense prevailed. Collecting the necessary equipment only delayed me a few minutes, before I was back in my car and battling city heart traffic on my way out of the busiest part of town.

Then, I was at the major intersection's lights. Fewer than half a dozen vehicles occupied the street ahead of me. I focused on not being heavy-footed on the accelerator as I struggled to remain within the legal speed limit. No vehicles hampered my clear run along the street. I knew I didn't have a plan... and, I had about three minutes in which to come up with one.

Still with no clear plan in mind, I made a snap decision to turn right off High Street onto a side street. It earned me a loud and long blast from the vehicle following me when my manoeuvre surprised the driver. If nothing else, I'm getting to know this area well, I told myself as I cruised along to the end of the street, and then onto the dirt track around to the next street. As I hit bitumen again, I sought divine guidance. "Christ, what do I do now? What do I do with my car?"

With no response forthcoming from anywhere, I pulled over behind a hedge that, now rampant, spilled out of its original yard and onto the carriageway, claiming most of the footpath in its progress. This hedge and I became friends during a much earlier case when I used it as cover. Sixty or seventy metres up ahead on the opposite side of the street, the two-storey derelict building looked even more forlorn in daylight. The very nature of the area suggests nobody here works, or even desires a job. In spite of that, the street seemed deserted.

As I scanned the street for any signs of life, I murmured, "No one about and the whole place is as quiet as a morgue." … And then mentally rebuked myself for the unhappy choice of simile.

Even then, I remained unsure about why I was there and what I hoped to achieve. All I knew was I needed to look inside the derelict building. As I approached the mango tree where I hid in its deep shadow on a previous night, I heard a car door slam, followed almost immediately by another door being closed. I galloped to the mango tree and squeezed myself in between its rough trunk and the fence behind it.

While in the process of making myself as comfortable as possible behind the mango tree, I heard two more car doors slam, followed by the throaty roar of a powerful engine coming to life. I didn't pass out, so I assume I must've kept breathing, but it felt as though I held my breath for several minutes. Regardless, my breathing didn't return to normal until a large, dark blue van emerged from behind the derelict building and headed down the street.

Easing out from behind the mango tree, I kept watch until the van reached the end of the street and turned onto High Street. As soon as it disappeared from sight, I galloped back to my car. Now I faced a dilemma. Do I follow the van, or should I check out the back room of the derelict building. As I scrambled into the driver's seat, my phone played its tune: Ben. In that moment, I thought we might be able to cover all bases. Ben's opening line was all the persuasion I needed to make a decision.

"Where are you? And, don't tell me you're in your office, because I know you're not. Where did you go after you looked at the fingerprint results?"

"Shut up and listen. After I left Emily, I went back to my office to pick up a couple of things before coming to the slum end of town to check out the derelict building. A dark blue van just drove out from the building and is heading towards town." I recited the registration number, and suggested he might like to find out what the van's destination might be. "There were two people in the van. They either loaded something into the vehicle, or unloaded something from it, just before they left. I heard them slam four doors. Two of them could have been the rear doors."

I heard Ben mumbling to himself and there was a long pause in conversation before he spoke again. "I see the van. I'm going to stick with it. What are you doing?"

"I'm going to have a quick look at that derelict building. Which way is the vehicle heading; to the north side, or South?"

"We are heading south. Surely they're not heading for the house in the cul-de-sac? Word about what happened there last night must have spread by now."

"Yeah, I agree it's unlikely that's where they're going. Keep me informed, please."

By the time our call ended, I was parked behind the derelict building and about to take a look inside its back room. The weight in each of my hip pockets was reassuring. I took the small torch out of my left pocket, switched it on, and stepped smartly around the door and into the room. At first glance, nothing seemed to have changed since the last time I was there.

A quick look around the room answered one of my questions: no bodies lying around. The blokes in that blue van hadn't unloaded anything – such as a body for instance. In which case, had they loaded something into the vehicle? The thought inspired me to take a closer look at the room. It didn't take long to answer that question too. A patch of dried blood on the floor in one corner told its own tale.

With no need to linger in the room, I bolted to my car and called Ben again. It took only moments to tell him what I'd found. I couldn't tell him anymore anyway, because he ended the call. Moments later my phone chirped loudly in the heavy silence of the place. Ben was back again.

"A couple of uniforms will be there to secure the site in a few minutes. Show them what you found. When they arrive, tell them I've arranged for Emily to collect forensic samples. Anything else you need to tell me?"

"Not really; I don't think I've sent you off on a wild goose chase. By the way, where are you, and do you have any idea where you're heading yet?"

"Yeah, I have a pretty fair idea now. We are in the rural area behind the suburb with the cul-de-sac where the central location is. The van turned off onto a rural property where major construction work is happening. A silver SUV was already there, and a few men seem to be hanging around one of the construction sites. I've parked along the road away from it. I'll try going in closer on foot to see what's going on."

Damn! By my reckoning, Ben was going into battle against at least six of the other team. Not good odds to my way of thinking. Regardless, I had to stay where I was until the uniforms arrived. I had no doubt by then, it would be too late for me to be of use to Ben. I flicked through my contacts to Sam Keller's entry.

"Sonny, what can I do for you this morning?"

"Sam, do you know how to get to Wiltshire Road?"

"Sort of… Why?"

"Ben is out there alone, and he is going in against at least six others. He told me to wait at another crime scene for the uniforms to arrive." I heard her ask someone called Ray if he knew the Wiltshire Road area. Then, she was speaking to me again.

"Give me a couple of minutes…" I shuffled from foot to foot as I waited. "Right, I'm back again. All the details, and quickly please, Sonny."

The sketchy details of the scenario Ben was walking into seemed inadequate to be of much use when I regurgitated them for Sam. I was yelling into my phone in the hope she could hear me well enough over the wail of a siren.

"You do whatever he told you to do. Ray knows the Wiltshire Road area well and thinks he knows which property it might be. Four of us are on our way there now. Ray used to be a pursuit driver, so we are doing a bit of low flying at the moment. We will be there soon, and have plenty of hardware on board. Talk to you later."

As the call ended, I heard a vehicle bumping its way around to the rear of the building. I raced to the piles of junk bordering the edge of the cleared area behind the derelict building, and threw myself in behind a rusty rainwater tank now lying on its side. A patrol vehicle eased its way into the clearing and parked beside my car. I watched the two officers check out the back yard before entering the building. Are they some of the 'good guys', or are they Shayna Kent's supporters? I couldn't be sure.

My hand located the Glock in my pocket. I worked the slider, and then asked myself be BIG question: now what? At that point, one of the uniforms rushed out to my car. His mate followed him out, and they checked out my car. I heard one of the say *what do you think,* tension obvious in his voice as he wildly scanned the cleared area. The other officer replied: *I'm calling it in. Something must have happened to her … and nothing good ever happens at this place.*

It was my cue to reveal myself. I set the safety on the Glock, shoved it back in my pocket, and scrambled out from behind the tank. "Sorry guys, I didn't mean to cause you undue concern. I just needed to be sure you were playing for the right team." Although I sounded cheery enough, I wasn't completely convinced. My hand remained firmly on the butt of the Glock in my pocket.

That's when Emily arrived to collect her forensic samples. She greeted the two officers by name and, as they swapped pleasantries, I heard Emily say she was surprised they were back on the job so early after last night's marathon event. Now convinced, I led the trio inside. A few moments later, having left them going about their respective duties, I was driving away from the derelict house. "Right … now for Wiltshire Road," I said as I turned onto High Street and left the slum area behind me.

Chapter 25

Rather than choose the direct route to Wiltshire Road, I applied 'local knowledge' of the city precinct and utilised lesser roads. On those mainly residential 'backstreets', traffic is light or non-existent, and travel is unimpeded by traffic lights. While just about maintaining legal speed limits, I soon was in the outer suburbs. As I turned onto Wiltshire Road, I slid my window down. Within moments, I was able to home in on my destination.

Almost at the same time as I heard gunfire, I saw Ben's vehicle parked beside the road. Easing off on the accelerator, I almost idled up to park behind it. I slipped out of my car and started off on foot towards the sound of shots. On my way past Ben's vehicle, I stopped, opened the front passenger side door, and reached in under the seat. Thank you, Ben. His spare weapon was strapped under the seat. I reefed it free of its tapes and looked at it.

"Geez, it's a canon – and weighs a ton," I whispered. I was holding a .44 Magnum handgun. It was fully loaded, so I slipped it into my other pocket … and felt my pants sag down in response to the added weight. While I prefer my Glock, if the gunfire coming from up ahead is anything to go by, the more powerful Magnum rounds might be ideal to bring to the party.

A property lay between where I parked and where the action was taking place. I walked onto the first property and headed for the boundary fence separating it from the gunfight. The strip along the fence line hadn't been mowed in ages, and now sported a good crop of long grass, shrubby plants and other weeds. It provided excellent cover as I moved along the boundary for a better look at what was happening nextdoor.

The neighbours appeared to be in the midst of a major construction phase. The shell of a new dwelling was almost completed, and a start had been made on a second building. It would be a massive shed when it was completed. An area surrounding the new buildings was cluttered with stacks of all manner of construction materials, and various pieces of large equipment. The driveway onto the property ran beside the fence I was hiding behind.

Three passenger vehicles stood amongst the clutter. A sedan was parked on the driveway just a short distance onto the property. I assumed this was the one Sam Keller and her colleagues were in. Beside the new shed, and parked partly on the driveway, was a large silver SUV. Further along the driveway, and almost in front of the new residence, the dark blue van I saw earlier this morning was parked as if ready for a quick getaway. People seemed to be taking cover behind almost every suitable object.

Timber and steel stacked just prior to the site of the new shed appeared to be providing cover for Sam and her colleagues. Of concern to me was Ben's choice of cover. He appeared pinned down beside the silver SUV. All the guys from the 'other team' were lined up behind whatever was available along the length of the new shed's site. Although unoccupied, and some distance further along the driveway, the dark blue van's motor had been left running. It sat there idling and ready to go as soon as someone jumped in behind the wheel ... and that presented a potential major problem.

With the driveway so narrow, and the silver SUV occupying part of the width at that point, it left little space for a vehicle to pass between the SUV and the fence. Ben, taking cover beside the SUV, was stranded in the available space between the vehicle and the fence.

As I assessed the situation, movement further along the driveway entered my peripheral vision. The gap between the dark blue van and a pile of bricks was no more than two metres. A crouched body came out from behind the stack of bricks and scuttled across the short distance before diving in through the passenger's door of the blue van. The little voice in my head was barely audible above the clanging of warning bells. It chanted 'this is not good' on a continuous loop.

It would only take the person a few moments to scramble across into the driver's seat before the blue van would be rocketing down the driveway on its way off the property… Ben was directly in its path. If he remained where he was, he would be run down by the van as it made its escape. If Ben took evasive action or moved out of the way to allow the van to pass, he would be exposed and liable to be shot. My assessment of the situation took less than a moment. No time to think about it. I had to move.

In an awkward half crouch, I raced along the boundary towards the blue van. I hadn't gone too far when I heard the engine revving in preparation for a risk-all 'drop the clutch and charge' along the driveway. I stopped behind a patch of multiple clumps of long grass. By the time I was peering through the grass at the van, the Magnum was in my hand. Deep breath, hold it; take aim: an automatic procedure that takes no time. Nevertheless, by the time I was ready to fire, the blue van was hurtling towards Ben.

More automatic responses… I fired two quick shots into the front of the vehicle, and hoped at least one of them hit the radiator. A pleasing fountain of steam erupted from under the van's bonnet. Even more pleasing was the loud crunching sound of metal grinding on metal. God knows what I'd hit, but it couldn't have been more effective if I'd intended it. The van's engine died. Inertia carried it on a few more metres before it shuddered to a standstill. The driver bailed out and received a slug in his leg for his trouble. Ben always was a good shot.

I raced back along the boundary to be opposite where Ben continued to take cover behind the SUV. At that point, as a result of termites having consumed a couple of the posts, the fence was not more than a couple of strands of barbed wire hanging close to the ground. A dead branch from a nearby gum tree lay in the grass. Only about a metre long, it would do nicely. I dragged it back and threw it over the barbed wire to provide a safe bridge over the fence to Ben.

"How is your ammunition holding out?" I asked as I joined Ben behind the SUV.

"What the hell are you doing here? Get away from here. Go Home, Sonny. I don't want you anywhere near this."

"Too bad; I'm here now. So, do you have many slugs left?"

"Nah, no more than one or two... And, I've nothing to show for the ones I've fired."

"Here, take this," I handed him the Magnum. "I've only fired those two shots, so you still have a few to play with."

"Thanks. Now, get out of here, Sonny. That's an order, not a request."

We both froze. The crack of a rifle shot was followed by a scream. "One down and only five more to go," Ben quipped.

"Correction: only four more to go. Your shot caught the van driver in the thigh. He managed to drag himself around behind the pile of sand, but he is out of action. He hasn't moved since, and doesn't seem interested in participating in the fun any longer. And, I think he left his weapon in the van. He didn't have it with him when he dragged himself to safety."

Ben was determined I should leave the area, and I realised my presence was interrupting his concentration. If I didn't leave, I could contribute to an outcome I didn't want to contemplate. At the next lull in activity, I bolted back over the fence and headed for my car. My vehicle was as far as I was prepared to go. Rather than wait in the vehicle, I sat on grass with my back up against the offside rear wheel, and gave my mind *carte blanche* to explore every aspect of the Martin investigations. If nothing else, it might help take my mind off Ben's current situation.

My contemplation of all things Mr and Mrs Martin was rudely interrupted by the sound of boots pounding along the road towards me. I slid sideways and lay prone on the grass to peer out at the road from under my car. While the boots sounded quite near, I couldn't see them. The good thing about a large

*S*UV is it has big wheels and, therefore, high clearance. Without rushing, I carefully rolled under the car to lie on the grass under the driver's side.

From my new position, I had a clear view along the road, and of those boots coming in my direction. Their wearer looked wild-eyed and terrified. He continued along the road until he was level with Ben's vehicle, when he paused for a moment – probably to consider his options. He must have considered it worth wasting a few moments checking whether Ben's car was locked. I knew it wasn't … after all, I'd opened the passenger's door to retrieve Ben's spare weapon from under the seat.

Another quick roll and I was out from under my car and up on my knees … just as the runner reached for the door of Ben's vehicle. The unfit and now exhausted runner didn't offer any resistance when I asked him to go face-down on the grass. My Glock pointing at him might have had some influence. The little voice in my head came to life again, and asked, 'now what?'

It was a good question, and one to which there was only one answer: I would have to stay and keep him covered until someone came to take him off my hands. I had no cuffs. There was a packet of zip ties in the back of my car, but retrieving them would provide my prisoner with an opportunity to escape. Oh well, there wasn't anywhere else I needed to be…

While contemplating my current situation, I realised the affray on the neighbouring property had gone quiet. Was the shootout over, or was this no more than a brief lull in proceedings? I strained my ears for any sound which might provide an insight into what was happening. There was nothing. The sound of someone using a grinder on metal came from further along the road behind me and, in the distance, a tractor was working. The smell of newly mown grass drifted across on the light breeze. But, no sounds of any consequence came from the battle ground.

Just as I was wondering why none of the local residents had shown any interest in the firefight happening in their neighbourhood, the discordant sound of approaching sirens shattered the peace. Maybe a bit late, but it appeared the cavalry was about to arrive. My prisoner tensed as if preparing to spring up and take-to-the-toe again. A wave of my Glock persuaded him otherwise. I was standing over him when the first police wagon drew up beside me.

"Put the weapon down," an officer in a bullet-proof vest yelled at me as he dived out of the wagon.

"Not bloody likely until you have this bloke in cuffs," I yelled back, "and you can lower *your* weapon. I don't think your superintendent will thank you for shooting me while I was preventing his vehicle from being stolen by an escapee from the shootout further along the road."

The young officer hesitated, and looked at his driver for inspiration about what to do next. Then, a second wagon pulled up behind the first one. The hulking form of Jock McIntosh displayed surprising agility as he sprang out of the second wagon.

"Sonny, are you OK?" I nodded. "Where are Ben and the others?" Before I could answer, he swung around to the young officer from the first van, still standing there pointing his weapon at me. "Put that away!" Jock barked at the officer. "What's wrong with you, Lad? Get the prisoner cuffed and in the wagon."

I risked a quiet contribution to the 'conversation'. "I think he is confused about which of us is the prisoner."

Jock snorted, strode over and dragged my prisoner to his feet. Then, propelling the man at the young officer, he growled, "This one, Lad; now deal with him." After a couple of moments supervising the officer's management of the prisoner, Jock came back to me. "Where is Ben?"

"The second property from here… Jock, I'm worried. It's deathly quiet there now. I'm not game to think why, or about what might have happened. When I left, there was no way that bloke could have escaped the scene – but he did."

"Not to worry, My Girl, we'll soon find out what's happening along there. You sit tight here."

With my prisoner now occupying the rear of the first police wagon, their small cavalcade continued along the road to where Ben and the others were. I decided to follow them along the grassy verge beside the road. No plan involved; I just wanted to see what happened at the site, and why it now was so quiet. Replicating my original approach, I marched onto the next property and made for the fence line. I could hear people moving about nextdoor, but no one spoke until the two police wagons drove in.

Then, Ben was shouting orders. I could hear people scurrying about. A few profanities were heard. By the time I was peering through the weeds and grass along the property's boundary, people were being loaded into the wagons. Ben had a word with Sam and pointed towards the pile of sand. It was where the bloke he shot in the leg managed to crawl to before appearing to collapse.

Sam nodded and then strode over to where the action was taking place around the two police wagons. Ben, as though deep in thought, stood and watched for a couple of moments before turning on his heel and striding towards the blue van. The driver's door remained open. Ben leaned in and checked the interior of the cab before continuing around to the van's rear doors.

He swung the doors fully open and then stepped back. I watched him reach for his phone. It was a brief call. He put the phone back in his pocket, closed the van's doors, and walked over to and around behind the pile of sand. It was no more than a brief detour on his way back to the wagons. After leaving the pile of sand, his phone was at his ear again.

Everything seemed to happen fast after that. The wagons were closed up. All the uniformed officers, except Jock, climbed back into the vehicles. The next few minutes were spent watching the wagons executing difficult turns in the narrow space to align them for their departure. With the two wagons on their way back to town, Sam and her three companions strolled back to their vehicle, climbed aboard and followed the wagons off the property. Only Jock and Ben remained, standing hands on hips, in deep conversation on the driveway.

I was about to scramble over the fence to join them when I caught sight of another vehicle picking its way up to the entrance to the driveway. Ben beckoned the vehicle to come in. As it crawled along the driveway, another black vehicle turned in off the road. Ben and Jock hurried to the rear of the blue van. As he did so, Ben beckoned the two new vehicles to follow him.

A gurney from the first vehicle was wheeled to the rear of the blue van. Ben directed the gurney from the second vehicle over to the pile of sand. When the gurneys returned to their respective vehicles, they carried lumpy-looking body bags. Then, their job complete, the two coroner's vehicles headed back to town. With only Ben and Jock remaining on site, I deemed it safe enough for me to join them without incurring Ben's wrath.

It wasn't quite how it panned out, but I came out of the encounter pretty much unscathed. I think Jock's account of how I saved Ben's vehicle from being stolen might have helped. As we stood talking, a small bus drove in. The forensic team had arrived. While Ben went over to talk to their team leader, Jock and I watched the rest of the team unload their equipment and don their protective gear. Then it was time for us to leave, and the three of us walked back to where Ben and I had parked our cars.

As he opened his door, Ben called after me, "Are you going to be in your office today?"

"Yeah, I'll be there for the rest of the day."

"Okay; if I don't catch up with you this afternoon, I'll talk to you tonight."

I was strapping myself in as Ben made a tight U-turn and headed back to town. Ben's question about whether I would be in my office gave me pause for thought. There were this morning's notes to add to my case file, but what else did I have to do today? The only answer was 'not much'. While my Martin case had kept me busy, I was developing concerns about my other two potential new cases.

An optimistic outlook would suggest the Martin investigations might be wrapped up in the next day or two. As things stood, then I would have no cases to work on. While such a situation always caused me some concern, today, the concern level was low. A few days away at my beach place would be wonderful. Nevertheless, I wouldn't allow myself to think about it. Whenever I started thinking about getting away for a few days, a new case came along to ruin it.

After collecting lunch and a newspaper on my way up to my office, I relished the notion of a lazy hour or so before working on bringing my case notes up to date. Others had different ideas. The blinking red message light was bright in the gloom of my office. Professional practice indicated I should deal with the messages as soon as I turned on the lights and opened the drapes. My leisurely hour would have to wait – but I could brew coffee while I dealt with the messages.

As the machine made its usual noises and filled the place with the aroma of fresh coffee, I listened to the messages. Neither of them required a reply. Both simply advised my two potential new cases were going to kick off next week, and the callers would get back to me with details closer to the time. So much for a few days away…

With my newspaper under my arm and carrying my lunch and a coffee, I headed for one of my ancient lounge chairs. Sitting back with my feet up on the coffee table, I planned a relaxed hour or so. Life can be cruel. After only a couple of bites of lunch, Ben bounded into my office.

"So this is what self-employment looks like… Are you able to spare a few minutes for a chat?"

Cheeky sod; my inclination was to say no but, if he had taken the time out of his busy job to come to my office, he must have something worthwhile discussing. I smiled and said, "Coffee? You're welcome to the other half of my sandwich if you are hungry."

"Yes, I could go a decent coffee. And, I haven't had lunch yet, so thanks for the sandwich."

While his coffee was happening, I retrieved an emergency supply of chocolate biscuits from the fridge. By the time I returned to the lounge chairs with his coffee, he had eaten the half a sandwich I had offered. His eyes lit up at the sight of the biscuits. "Now you're talking. I was hoping for something to go with the coffee."

"Ben, did you have something specific to talk about, or is this just a general catch-up after this morning's events?"

"A bit of both really; the main issue I wanted to talk about was the dark blue van. I'm not even going to ask you why you were anywhere near the derelict building this morning, but perhaps it was just as well you were. Your call about the van came just as Emily completed her report on the fingerprints found at the apartment in Wellington Towers. By the way, I meant to thank you for alerting Sam to my situation out on Wiltshire Road. As you know, I followed the van out to the rural area, and encountered a situation I considered suspicious. The rest of the story you already are aware of, so I won't waste time on it now."

"Okay, as you say, I have a fair idea of what happened after you arrived. Perhaps we don't need to discuss it now, but I would like to go through it with you later. Now, is there something specific you wanted to tell me about?"

"Yeah … When you called, you suggested something was either loaded into or unloaded from the van. After the police wagons carted off all the bad guys this morning, I checked the van. The bloke I shot in the leg seemed quite keen to escape and take the van with him. When I opened the rear doors of the van, I discovered why. I found a body wrapped in an old quilt. The quilt matched the pillowcases I saw in the Wellington Towers apartment."

"…And, Emily had just told you the apparent resident's fingerprints matched those on the national database for police constable Shayna Kent. So, am I right in assuming you were not surprised by what was wrapped in the quilt?"

"No, not as surprised as I might have been. It was Shayna's

body in that van. They had not treated her kindly but, judging by the state of the apartment, she put up a good fight."

"Somehow, I suspected as much, particularly after I checked out the back room of the derelict building this morning. Finding her body has thrown all my assumptions about the mob and their operation out the window. Based on little hard evidence, I figured Shayna – or Lenny, if you prefer – was a key player in the mob. Her demise suggests she wasn't such an important player after all, or perhaps she had transgressed – broken the rules – in some way. What's your take on the situation?"

"Much the same as yours… I believed she was involved, but I couldn't get my head around to what extent – or, maybe, I didn't want to accept the possibility one of my officers could be anything other than inadvertently involved."

"So, the question now is: was she just one of the mob's hierarchy, or was she involved because of some hold they had over her … Perhaps something that happened a long time ago?"

"…Such as some incident which led to her changing her identity? Is that what you're suggesting?"

Ben reads me so well. I suppose it comes from having worked together over so many years, but I would like to surprise him occasionally. "Do you have different ideas to contribute to this discussion?" He shook his head. "So, I suppose the next move is to investigate the defining incident which led to Lenny becoming Shayna."

"I have initiated a few things in relation to that. It might take a while for results to trickle in. That's about all I came to tell you but, first thing tomorrow, I think we need to break the bad news about Lenny to Stella. I need to go back to my office now, but we'll talk about all this again tonight. I assume you're not working tonight. Oh, and you might consider inviting Emily to join us for dinner if she has time."

Chapter 26

Emily said she doubted she would make it in time for dinner, but would come as soon as she could escape from work; probably closer to eight o'clock. The pumpkin and blue cheese risotto I made for dinner produced more than enough to accommodate Emily should she need sustenance when she arrived.

Ben and I were just finishing our meal when she arrived earlier than expected. I asked her about dinner. "Yes thanks. I will have a bowl of whatever that is, if there is some left." As I dished it out, she added, "If you guys are finished eating, may I take my bowl through to the lounge room so I can join in the conversation while I eat?"

As Ben and I carried our coffees through to the lounge room, Emily, with her bowl of risotto and a glass of white wine, followed. In the first instance, Ben seemed reluctant to discuss anything of significance. We faffed about flitting from one inconsequential topic to another for about fifteen minutes before Emily brought some focus to the conversation.

"You guys had a busy night followed by a busy day. It's frustrating when you only know half the story, only the part I come to know from the work in my lab. So, come on, bring me up-to-date on the whole story, please." Both Emily and I turned to Ben expectantly, and he responded.

"Well, I can report a significant part of the story fell into place late this afternoon. As you both are aware, this morning we found the body of Police Constable, Shayna Kent, a.k.a. Lenore Collins. I had initiated enquiries into Shayna's background, as well as Lenny's earlier history. While I believed them to be one and the same person – and, Sonny, shared my opinion – I couldn't find the missing link. Even my interstate enquiries turned up nothing. After finding her body this morning, I called in a favour."

I chuckled. "So, how is your brother, Neil, and how are his Federal Police officers behaving these days?" I was surprised Ben held off contacting his brother who is the head of the Federal Police until after we found Shayna's body. "I'm surprised you didn't contact him sooner, when you couldn't match up the two ends of the puzzle."

"It was a bit of a difficult situation. Because of the indications a police officer was involved in criminal activities, the powers-that-be in this state – my bosses – insisted on the utmost discretion and caution in my investigation. It's why I couldn't go to Neil officially, but had to make it a private request; a favour brother to brother."

Emily slammed her now empty bowl down on her side table in a show of frustration. "How long is it going to take the pair of you to get around to sharing the real information? I've had a busy time lately and I'm a bit short on patience. Please, may we hear sometime soon about what Neil was able to discover?"

Ben raised his eyebrows in surprise, and then cleared his throat before launching into his story. "It appears Lenny already had established a relationship with a young lad before she left High School. The lad was a couple of years older than Lenny, rode a motorbike, and hung around the pool hall and other similar salubrious joints with a group of his motorbike-riding mates. If he was employed, nobody seems to know what he did, but it appears he and his mates already had started on a life of crime. There is suggestion they were a group of motorcycle gang wannabes who were being groomed for a future as full members of a club."

"That fits with something Stella said about Lenny and her girlfriends hanging out with a group of local lads who rode motorbikes," I said. I tried to recall more detail from my various discussions with Stella, but nothing else about the 'boyfriends' came to mind. "So, what happened after Lenny left high school? Did her relationship with her bikie continue?"

"Yep, it appears so. Instead of finding a job when she left school, Lenny seems to have hung around with the boyfriend and his mates. The trouble was, the boyfriend was skating on thin ice with the local law for various minor crimes in the area. The pair of them opted to leave town before the inevitable happened and the boyfriend would be out of circulation for a while. After going interstate, the boyfriend soon joined up with another mob and became involved in more high level criminal activities."

"But, what happened to Lenny while all this was going on?" Emily asked. "Was she a bystander – just someone to come home to at the end of the day – or was she involved?"

Ben thought for a moment before answering. "Although there is no hard evidence to prove exactly how it happened, there is suggestion Lenny was coerced, in much the same way as Stella was, to become an operative for the boyfriend and his mob. While the details are a bit blurry, it seems Lenny always wanted to become a cop. Although she never did anything about it of her own volition, the boyfriend and his gang saw a potential tame cop as a valuable asset, and whatever hold they had over her was applied to force her to join the police."

Emily threw her hands in the air and demanded, "How did they think they were going to do that? She is hanging around with a group of criminals, and they think she can just sign up to join the police. I'm sure anyone applying to join would be vetted to within an inch of their life before they were accepted into the Academy."

I watched Ben nodding as Emily spoke. When she finished, Ben took a few moments to marshal his thoughts before speaking. "The gang might not have been fine upstanding citizens, but they weren't stupid. While they wanted a tame cop, they didn't want one with obvious connections to them. So, Lenny had to undergo a major makeover. She needed to change her appearance, open new bank accounts, and change her lifestyle so as to appear not connected in any way to the gang."

"Yeah, I can see how all that was necessary. They needed to create a whole new identity for Lenny. But distancing herself from the gang meant distancing herself from the boyfriend. I imagine that wasn't easy." If I knew what sort of hold they had over Lenny, I might find it easier to understand why she went through with the whole new identity thing, and I shared my thinking with the others.

"The word is, the boyfriend might have had a new 'interest' on the side at the time, and Lenny's suspicions resulted in a few heated arguments. So, it worked for the gang to sever her close ties with them, while maintaining a working relationship. Anyway, the process of converting Lenny Collins into Shayna Kent was successful and, with a whole array of forged documents, Shayna entered the police Academy. Soon after, her long-standing boyfriend – by then no longer her boyfriend – was killed when a job the gang pulled went wrong. It helped sever any lingering emotional or personal ties between Shayna and the gang, but the hold over her continued."

Although I was fascinated by the story up to that point, I couldn't reconcile the small-time interstate gang of young bikies with what I saw as a high level operation here in Millhaven. When Emily and Ben decided they needed a coffee refill and went to make it, it gave me a chance to sit quietly and review all Ben had told us so far.

By the time they returned, I still saw the two mobs involved as operating on two different levels. Maybe I was giving the local operation more status than it deserved. As soon as the others regained their seats, I voiced those thoughts and asked Ben for his opinion.

"You're right about there being two different levels of operations. My brother tells me the Feds were keeping an eye on a fairly major operation happening across states. They also were keeping a casual eye on another small-time gang operating in New South Wales. Sometime during the last twelve months, the small gang was taken over – more like gobbled up – by the larger organisation the Feds were watching. It appears Shayna was part of the takeover exercise.

Not long after, the Feds mounted a major operation against the mob, which suffered major losses as a result. Long story short, the remnants of the mob seemed to disappear after the action against them, until a few months ago when whispers began circulating about them operating in Queensland. My discussions with Neil have confirmed some of those rumours."

Emily was shaking her head in disbelief. "What's the problem, Emily," I asked. "What's bothering you?"

"Okay … The mob has a fairly big operation happening in Millhaven, and either Shayna was sent here as their inside 'man', or Shayna was transferred to Millhaven, and the mob followed to set up their operation here. If she was so important, and possibly a key player in the operation, why did she end up dead? What turned sour for her? What did she do wrong to necessitate eliminating her? Won't her death adversely impact on the gang's future operations?"

Ben studied the toe of his boot for a few moments before dealing with Emily's question. "Possibly… But there is another possibility you're overlooking. Why would Shayna be the only cop under the mob's control?"

"Are you saying you have another bent copper in your precinct?" Emily's eyebrows climbed up her forehead as she asked the question … and mine copied them. Ben answered with a nod.

My mind went into overdrive the moment he suggested the possibility. "Christ, Ben, one of your officers is guarding Trent Martin in hospital, and you have officers posted at the penthouse apartment to protect Stella."

"Relax everybody. The Feds have a fair idea of who it is. One of the blokes who was part of yesterday's new arrivals is a Fed plant. He has a two-fold mission: infiltrate the mob running the local operations; and discredit any cop they already have in their stable. I believe his mission already is underway."

"That seems like a tall order, Ben," Emily mused. "Regardless of how skilled he is, it's bound to take him ages to achieve anything."

"No, it probably won't. A good deal of 'gardening' was done before he came here. The Feds know how to play the game too. They are exerting a strong hold over someone close to the mob who, for the sake of his own good, is feeding scripted information to key players here."

Ben indicated there was no more to tell for the moment. He did say he hoped the new 'plant' might be able to shed some light on why Shayna was killed. I took advantage of the situation to move the topic a bit sideways.

"Are you still planning to tell Stella about Lenny/Shayna tomorrow, Ben?" he nodded. "Do you need me there?" This time, enthusiastic nodded confirmation from Ben. Damn, I was hoping he would handle it on his own. I have something else I needed to do.

As there was nothing more to add to our discussions, and all of us had little sleep last night, everyone seemed in favour of an early night. Ben and Emily left a few minutes later, and I wasn't long out of bed after they left.

****

Our meeting with Stella was hard going, but not as hard as I had imagined. I think there was a dash of vindictive pleasure in her reaction to the woman's having received 'just come-uppance'. What intrigued me was Stella's continued lack of interested in anything to do with her husband. Never once had she asked after him.

The hospital allowed me a few minutes with Trent earlier in the morning before Ben and I broke the news about Lenny to Stella. Over the next few days, I spoke to him several times. They were brief visits but, in short instalments, I told him as much as he needed to know about the credit card skimming operation and how Stella had been dragged into it.

I also told him about Brannigan's role. People who were the key person at each business – like Brannigan –involved in the operation were paid a 'commission' for their efforts. Quite a few business enterprises around town now were missing senior staff members after they were identified as operatives and rounded-up … and that included the office supplies place where Trent worked.

He told me how he regained consciousness to find a termination letter waiting for him. I assured him it was Brannigan's doing because Trent's poking about was getting too close for comfort … and Trent's job remained there waiting for him when he was ready to return.

"Thanks for telling me that. It's good to know, but I won't be returning to my former position. In fact, I won't remain in Millhaven. I'll be returning to work in my family's business in Brisbane. Oh, just so you know, Colleen Jenkins will be coming with me. You see, I knew Stella wasn't having an affair, but she was terrified by whatever she was involved in. I needed to have it sorted and her settled. Once that happened, I could tell her about my plans … and Colleen."

Over Sunday lunch the following weekend, Ben added the final episode to the story. "I thought you might like to know my Martin investigation is wrapped up. The Feds' forensic guys started digging around a bit a week ago. It wasn't a high priority for them until we busted the central location in the cul-de-sac. They were interested in Shayna prior to that, but then they became real interested in her. Our 'insider' reported the police investigation spooked the mob into conducting an audit of their own, and discovered the police seemed to have a particular interest in Shayna."

"So the mob decided they should take a closer look at Shayna too," I suggested.

"Yep, and they found a nice secondary operation running in parallel with their own. The Feds found a strange bank account and, before the mob found out about it, traced it back to Shayna. Shayna's little sideline had been raking it in for her for some time. From evidence found in the Wellington Towers apartment and in another address she used under a different alias, it's thought likely she was planning another complete 'make-over' in the near future in preparation for heading overseas."

"We still have to process some of the evidence collected," Emily said. "How did this credit card scheme work?"

Ben ran a hand across his face and shook his head. "It was so simple. Sophisticated technology used helped make it that way. Let's take the office supplies place as an example. Brannigan was the key man there, but one of the sales staff who worked on the checkouts was the actual operative. They ran a customer's credit card through a special little machine to make a copy of everything on the card. Then a memory stick containing all the collected information was given to Brannigan – who paid a small percentage of his 'compensation' to the staff member."

"All the players must have received enough to make it worthwhile," Emily suggested.

Ben just shrugged and didn't answer. Something still niggled me. "Are you telling me Brannigan was only a go-between and was never physically involved in the actual skimming?" In my mind Brannigan was more involved than Ben made out.

"No, that's not what I'm saying. Brannigan had an active role, but his opportunities were limited to careful selection of the online orders he dealt with. The information he gathered from orders placed by regular business enterprises was used against dummy orders by those businesses."

"Okay, so he was involved, but in a different way. I understand the memory sticks containing the cards' information gathered at the checkout were couriered by operatives like Stella to the central location, but what happened after that? What were they doing in that house?"

"Oh, that was the next stage of the sophisticated operation. The workers there took the information on the sticks and turned it into almost perfect plastic replicas of the original cards. Then, some of the 'new' cards went back to the businesses where they were skimmed in the first place, and the rest were sent out of town. Great care was taken to ensure those 'new' cards were used only in a way consistent with their rightful owner's normal usage."

Emily bounced upright in her chair. "Well, if there is one thing we can take away from all this, it is that we always must check out credit card receipts against our credit card statements. I'll plead guilty about not being too fastidious about doing so every month … but I will be after all this."

"Ben, I'm hearing that the police have removed all the beast's tentacles, but has its head been cut off? Have you rounded up those who ran the operation?"

"It's safe to say 'yes', but don't look for anything in the newspapers for a while yet. There still is a lot of mopping up of minor players happening. Nevertheless, effectively, the operation has been neutralised, and is dead and buried."

"I can't help feeling sorry for Stella," I said. "That fateful reunion with Lenny devastated her life… I was going to add 'and her marriage', but it seems that was doomed prior the reunion anyway. Still, she will find it hard to pick up the pieces and move on after all that happened."

"Have you heard anything of her since the case was wrapped up?" Emily asked.

"Yeah, she called, and we had, what was for me, an uncomfortable conversation. She kept thanking me for being a friend when she needed one most, and for taking the time to help bring the mob to justice. She also told me her husband had left her and taken off with someone from his workplace. After all she already had been through, the end of her marriage was almost the final straw for her. And, it was hard for me to pretend I knew nothing about any of the stuff to do with her marriage break-up. It seems she retains the house, and still has her job. She intends staying in Millhaven while she works at putting her life back together."

Later that afternoon, after Ben and Emily left, I added my last notes to my Martin case file, and typed up my report for Trent Martin. Given the amount of time I was involved with both mine and Ben's cases, Trent probably still had paid me a bit more than I would have charged him – but he did insist I keep it. I'll make one more offer of an itemised account – and a small refund – tomorrow when I email my report.

Tomorrow night I start work on one of my new cases and, on Tuesday, I start surveillance work for the other new case. I will get to spend a few days at my beach place … but it appears that won't be any time in the near future.

The End

Other Books by the Author

An Ancient Solution
A Public Service
Missing!
Connections
A Different Obsession
Shattered Illusions
After The Ball
Unholy Secrets

About the Author

Neive Denis is the creator of the series featuring the Private Investigator, Sonoma (Sonny) Whittington. Neive Denis is the pen name of a writer who was lured from her usual genre to focus on the mystery and excitement that are a part of Sonoma Whittington's world. Neive came into being specifically for this series and, for the moment at least, intends remaining faithful to only stories from Sonny's case files.

This series tells of the intrigue and scrapes – some on occasion life threatening – that are part of the life of Sonoma Whittington, an Australian Private Investigator based in a Central Queensland coastal city. However, Sonny doesn't confine her escapades to Australia, and that provides Neive with an opportunity to weave some of her other areas of interest into Sonny's hair-raising adventures.

See more about Neive Denis and her work at

www.eaglemountbooks.com.au/neive-denis

or contact her at

admin@eaglemountbooks.com.au